I0726353

THE HOUSEWIFE ASSASSIN'S TERRORIST TV GUIDE

JOSIE BROWN

A BOOK BY

SIGNAL
PRESS

Praise for Josie Brown's Novels

"This is a super sexy and fun read that you shouldn't miss! A kick ass woman that can literally kick ass as well as cook and clean. Donna gives a whole new meaning to "taking out the trash."
—Mary Jacobs, *Book Hounds Reviews*

"*The Housewife Assassin's Handbook* by Josie Brown is a fun, sexy and intriguing mystery. Donna Stone is a great heroine—housewives can lead all sorts of double lives, but as an assassin? Who would have seen that one coming? It's a fast-paced read, the gadgets are awesome, and I could just picture Donna fighting off Russian gangsters and skinheads all the while having a pie at home cooling on the windowsill. As a housewife myself, this book was a fantastic escape that had me dreaming "if only" the whole way through. The book doesn't take itself too seriously, which makes for the perfect combination of mystery and humour."
—*Curled Up with a Good Book and a Cup of Tea*

"*The Housewife Assassin's Handbook* is a hilarious, laugh-out-loud read. Donna is a fantastic character–practical, witty, and kick-ass tough. There's plenty of action–both in and out of the bedroom… I especially love the housekeeping tips at the start of each chapter– each with its own deadly twist! This book is perfect for relaxing in the bath with after a long day. I can't wait to read the next in the series. Highly Recommended!"
—*CrimeThrillerGirl.com*

"This was an addictive read–gritty but funny at the same time. I ended up reading it in just one evening and couldn't go to sleep until I knew what the outcome would be! It was action-packed and humorous from the start, and that continued throughout, I was pleased to discover that this is the first of a series and look forward to getting my hands on Book Two so I can see where life takes Donna and her family next!"

—*Me, My Books, and I*

"The two halves of Donna's life make sense. As you follow her story, there's no point where you think of her as "Assassin Donna" vs. "Mummy Donna', her attitude to life is even throughout. I really like how well this is done. And as for Jack. I'll have one of those, please?"

—*The Northern Witch's Book Blog*

Novels in The Housewife Assassin Series

The Housewife Assassin's Handbook (Book 1)

The Housewife Assassin's Guide to Gracious Killing (Book 2)

The Housewife Assassin's Killer Christmas Tips (Book 3)

The Housewife Assassin's Relationship Survival Guide (Book 4)

The Housewife Assassin's Vacation to Die For (Book 5)

The Housewife Assassin's Recipes for Disaster (Book 6)

The Housewife Assassin's Hollywood Scream Play (Book 7)

The Housewife Assassin's Killer App (Book 8)

The Housewife Assassin's Hostage Hosting Tips (Book 9)

The Housewife Assassin's Garden of Deadly Delights (Book 10)

The Housewife Assassin's Tips for Weddings, Weapons, and Warfare (Book 11)

The Housewife Assassin's Husband Hunting Hints (Book 12)

The Housewife Assassin's Ghost Protocol (Book 13)

The Housewife Assassin's Terrorist TV Guide (Book 14)

The Housewife Assassin's Deadly Dossier (Book 15: The Series Prequel)

The Housewife Assassin's Greatest Hits (Book 16)

The Housewife Assassin's Fourth Estate Sale (Book 17)

The Housewife Assassin's Horrorscope (Book 18)

The Outer Limits

Do not attempt to adjust the picture. There is nothing wrong with your television set.

Not yet, anyway.

We are controlling transmission. If we wish to make it louder, we will bring up the volume. If we wish to make it softer, we will tune it to a whisper.

We will control the horizontal. We will control the vertical. We can roll the image—make it flutter. We can change the focus to a soft blur, or sharpen it to crystal clarity. For the next three hundred pages, you are to sit quietly. We will control all that you see and hear.

None of this will kill anyone.

Well, not yet.

You see, you are about to participate in a great adventure! You are about to experience the awe and mystery that reaches from the inner mind to the Outer Limits—

Of fear and suspense.

Do not worry, dear readers! Rest assured, for your comfort and safety, your guides on this new viewing experience are Donna and Jack—

Okay, yeah, maybe you should be worried.

CHAOXIANG "CHUCKY" CHAN JONESES OVER THREE THINGS: WHITE-blonde blue-eyed kewpie doll pole dancers, Vancouver Canucks games (to which he has front row seats), and his $360,000 red Lamborghini Huracán.

Sadly, his car is in the shop getting some much-needed bodywork. It seems that its low-slung chassis ran over a fallen lamppost in the middle of the road. Chucky is the reason the lamppost was there in the first place. Cars seem to go bump in the night when you drink and drive while a stripper performs unmentionable acts.

Luckily, Chucky was wearing his seatbelt. However, the stripper's bucket seat contortions left her with even more bodywork than the car's. At least Chucky picked up her medical bills. She'll always have a rod in her back, but the doctor assured her she'll have a better nose than the one that got smashed when she was propelled through the windshield.

I've correctly guessed that Chucky would haunt Vancouver, Canada's largest Lamborghini showroom in search of a replacement vehicle. And because my latest mission dictates that I be his replacement girlfriend, I got there a few minutes after him. To make it easy for him to see me in the role, today I wear a platinum blonde wig styled in a gamine cut. My contact lenses—really video feeds monitored by Ryan Clancy, my boss at the black-ops organization that employs me, Acme Corporation—are vivid blue. It's also why I'm wearing a black push-up bra under my low-cut sheer white silk blouse, and a tight white mini-skirt with six-inch heels.

If you saw me, I wouldn't blame you in the least if you thought my attire left nothing to the imagination. Bingo! That's the point. To assure that Chucky gets it too, I sink into the passenger seat of a sleek black $1.9 million-dollar Lamborghini Centenarios roadster with my legs parted just wide enough that his imagination goes wild and his fifth appendage hardens. This is a predictable reaction since, as we circled each other in the showroom, he stared at my ass long enough to notice that there was no visible panty line.

I reward his smirk with a crooked index finger that invites him to join me.

My interest in Chucky has less to do with his bank account than that of his father's: Huang Fu Chan just so happens to be China's Minister of Natural Resources. During his administration, graft has boomed to new heights, thanks to too many collapsing mine shafts, and too few honest owners.

That is, until now. Chucky doesn't know it yet, but Daddy Dearest disappeared about six hours ago. Acme's guess is that he's now the guest of the MSS—China's espionage agency, the Ministry of State Security—and is being interrogated in some black site located deep in the Tian Shan Mountains. The lives of miners and the reputations of China's current administration may be gone, but Huang Fu's ill-gotten gains are an acceptable substitute.

Vancouver is bulging with *fuerdai*—superrich second generation trust-funders who, like Chucky, have no qualms spending their parents' hard-stolen money on hot wheels and fast women, in that order.

Or is it the other way around? Not that it matters. In either case, today's his lucky day.

When it comes to staying in his father's good graces, Chucky's sole responsibility is to hold onto the safety deposit box key that contains a list of the banks where Daddy has salted his cash stash. Chucky wears it on one of the silver chains around his neck, but not for long if I have my way.

Of course, at the same time, I won't let him have his way with me.

After stealing the key, I'll snatch the list from the safety deposit box so that Acme's COMINT liaison, Emma Honeycutt, and our tech ops leader, Arnie Locklear, can hack the accounts. The CIA will then trade Huang Fu's funds for a couple of Chinese-Americans who are being held as political prisoners.

After exchanging lascivious leers with me, Chucky saunters over to the car, leans in, and asks, "Want to go for a test drive?"

"Are you the salesman?" I purr. "Don't count on me for your commission. In the club where I work, the tips aren't that big."

His chest puffs up. "I don't sell 'em, I buy 'em." To prove his point, he snaps his fingers at one of his two bodyguards. "Yo, Tong, grab the keys to this ride from the showroom manager."

The goon shuffles off. A second later he returns with the key fob and tosses it to Chucky, who hops into the driver's seat. Revving the engine, he asks, "Where to?"

I tweak his nipple under his skintight T-shirt. "Let's hit the open road—say, up the coast? I know of a little cabin in the woods off the 99, right over Brunswick Beach."

Chucky takes the requisite two-point-six seconds to prove the roadster can hit sixty miles-per-hour from zero.

We're off.

WE HAVE A SHADOW: CHUCKY'S GOON SQUAD.

They have one too: my mission leader and main squeeze, Jack Craig. He follows in a nondescript black Lexus—a ubiquitous vehicle in well-heeled West Vancouver, and certainly not as ostentatious as the Lamborghini.

In case Jack loses us on the open road, Abu Nagashahi, another Acme operative, is several miles in front of us, in a white paneled van. Thankfully, the sluggish mid-day traffic over Lion's Gate Bridge affords both cars excellent visual surveillance.

The whole time, Chucky won't shut up. He rambles on and on about his assets and holdings, as if I'm a banker who can grant him a mortgage. No, it's more like he's got something to prove to a woman who isn't acting at all impressed.

The babbling is to be expected. At every red light, he takes a hit of the cocaine in the vial dangling from the longest silver chain around his neck. It's next to the one that holds the coveted safety deposit box key. Now and then I'm rewarded with a glimpse of it. I ache to jerk it off his neck and then shove him out the door into oncoming traffic, solving our problem in a quick and dirty way. But, no, I must follow Acme's much more discrete plan for Chucky.

Traffic loosens up when we hit Highway 99 on the West Vancouver side of the bridge. Suddenly Chucky is doing his best to break the sound barrier—or at least achieve the speed claimed in the Lamborghini's spec sheet: two-hundred-and-seventeen miles-per-hour.

Ten or so miles zip by us. In a flash, we're as far north as Horseshoe Bay, where 99 becomes the appropriately named Sea-to-Sky Highway because of the way it clings to the cliff that winds its way around Howe Sound.

Can Jack keep up? I look in the side-view mirror to reassure myself that he can. Yes, he's there, about a hundred yards behind us. Unfortunately, so are Tong and his buddy.

Suddenly, Chucky realizes I'm not paying attention to his boasts. Worse yet, I'm slapping away his groping hands. His eyes narrow as he blurts out, "Hey, um…how 'bout giving me some head?"

I snort. "What…are you kidding? So that I end up with a broken nose, like your last girlfriend?"

He looks over sharply, completely ignoring the fact that we're weaving to and fro on hairpin curves. "Who told you that?"

I shrug. "Dude, it's all over town. Sorry, but if I'm going to distract you, it's going to be someplace we can both enjoy it"—I nod at the car with his bodyguards, now right on our heels—"but not with your cheering squad tagging along. What's with the chaperones?"

"Haven't you heard a word I've said, bee-hatch?" He takes his eyes off the road to lean in close. "I'm a very important guy! They come along to protect me." He puts his hand between my thighs.

"Look, sweet cheeks, if you make me happy, I'll make you happy—"

He grabs me by my neck and shoves my head into his lap.

He figures out quickly that it was poor judgment on his part when I bite him—hard—on his thigh.

Chucky's howl is cut off by the sound of glass breaking. A barrage of bullets shatters the rear window.

I duck onto the floor of the passenger seat.

Instinctively, Chucky looks behind us. As bullets hit his head, it explodes, sending skull fragments and brain matter in all directions.

When his body jerks in my direction, I see that his right eye is dangling from his optic nerve. His seatbelt holds him in place, but his foot has stiffened onto the accelerator.

I scream, "What the hell?"

Jack yells into my earbud, "Chucky's bodyguards are shooting at the car!"

"Driver down!" I shout back.

The car is now racing along out of control. To take the wheel, I lean over his body and jerk it out of its counter-clockwise trajectory—

And off the road we go.

The car skids down the embankment, skimming the tops of the evergreens that cling to the cliff before crashing onto blacktop once more.

It's not easy steering a car from the passenger side, but I do the best I can, zigzagging down this side road. Still, we are going at a breakneck speed.

"Donna," Jack shouts, "You're headed for the ferry!"

He's right. HORSESHOE BAY is emblazoned on the banner above it. *The Queen of Capilano*, hauling both passengers and cars to Bowen Island, has started to inch away from its dock.

I'm just about to nudge Chucky's foot onto the brake for a

modulated stop when a bullet pings the roof of the car. Somehow Chucky's bodyguards have followed me down the hill.

Instead of trying to stop, I've got no choice but to shove his leg harder onto the accelerator in the hope of making it onto the boat. As the car picks up speed, it has lift-off—

Flying off the dock, over the water—

Only to land firmly on the stern of the boat. I shove Chucky's leg onto the brake just in time: it skids to a stop beside some other cars.

As Chucky's head snaps forward and back, the nerve holding his eyeball breaks—

And the eye rolls onto my lap.

I smack it to the floor. *Yuck!*

Passengers on the upper deck clap heartily at my feat of derring-do. Not the ferry's purser. He scowls as he clambers down the stairs toward me.

I leap out of the car before he has a chance to look inside of it. "No one gets a free ride," he glowers.

I shrug as I pull out a wallet tucked deep in my décolletage. From it, I pluck a credit card and hand it to the guy. His eyes, now the size of saucers, are glued to my breasts. I guess he thinks I'll pull a rabbit out from there, or maybe a string of colored hankies. Well, at least it keeps him from rubbernecking the car and the dead body inside of it.

After handing me a receipt, he walks away, shaking his head.

I stare back at the shoreline, scanning it until I see Chucky's bodyguards. They've abandoned their car. They're running toward the smaller docks dotting the shore in the hope of securing a motorboat to follow the ferry.

Jack has done the same.

"I thought they were here to protect him. Why did they kill him?" I wonder out loud.

"For the key to the safety deposit box. While following you, his bodyguards heard from MSS about Huang Fu Chan's new status as a political prisoner," Ryan explains through my earbud. "They were offered a bounty to take it from Chucky. The fact that he's collateral damage—or for that matter, you—doesn't mean anything to them."

"Where is this ferry headed?" I ask.

"Snug Cove, an inlet on Bowen Island," Jack answers. "It's a twenty-minute ride. And from the looks of things, you'll be met with a not-so-welcoming committee. I'll try to head them off. In the meantime, grab the cargo and lock up the Lamborghini so that no one is any wiser regarding Chucky."

Jack is breathing heavy, which tells me he's moving fast to find a boat before Tong and his buddy leave the dock—

But he's too late. "Chucky's goons just punched out a man, and are making off with his Bayliner Cabin Cruiser," Jack reports.

Yep, here they come.

I watch as Jack, thinking fast, waves down a Sea Ray Bowrider coming into port. It has three bikini-clad women. Whatever he says to them has them giggling and tossing him the keys. *Hmmm….*

Still, Chucky's assassins have a head start.

As they speed toward the ferry, I open the driver side of the Lamborghini and yank the key and its chain from around Chucky's neck. The key is cold when it slips between my cleavage.

"Grab the fallen eyeball," Ryan shouts.

Ewwww. "Why, pray tell?" I ask.

"Just do it!" he commands. "And then take your cell phone and get as close as possible to text me a straight-on photo of the other eye. To get into his bank vault, we'll need both for the eye scan."

I groan, but grab the loose eye. Then I yank my iPhone out of my skirt pocket. Straddling Chucky, I put it up against Chucky's other eye, and mutter, "Say cheese," before I text it to Ryan.

Next, I shove Chucky onto the passenger seat so that I can finally take the wheel. Since this was the last vehicle onto the ferry, it will also be the first one off—

And not a moment too soon. Chucky's goons are trailing the ferry by a mere fifty feet.

No better time than now to give them what they want: Chucky.

I run to a nearby utility closet and grab a crowbar. It's just the right length to prop against the accelerator. I lodge the other end against the steering column, and then I start the ignition.

The Lamborghini's engine purrs to life. I shift the gear to reverse—

And off it goes.

Zero to sixty in two-point-six seconds has it in mid-air. Another two seconds puts it on a downward trajectory.

By second number six, it has landed on top of Tong's Cabin Cruiser.

The explosion sends a spout of water sky high.

The passengers are too busy ogling the collision to notice little old me as I make my way toward the front of the ferry.

As Jack zips by in the Sea Ray, I smile and wave.

By the time I file off the ferry, he's already docked. Better yet, he's secured a prime outdoor table at Doc Morgan's Pub.

"I ordered your favorite: snow crab legs and a cabernet," Jack adds.

"I can't wait to hear what you told those women to get their boat," I mutter as I tear open a crab leg.

"Only that my one true love was on that ferry, and I had to stop her from making the biggest mistake of her life: marrying the wrong man." He shrugs. "It was half true, anyway."

"You've got that right." I kiss him through a mouthful of crab.

"Eat fast," Ryan warns us. "You've got to head back to West Van and hit the bank before it closes."

No rest for the weary.

It takes a half-hour to devour the crab.

It's good to be alive.

RYAN WAS RIGHT. CHUCKY'S EYES WERE WORTH SCANNING.

To get through the vault's security system, I wear contact lenses. One reflects the retina scanned off the popped eyeball. The other lens, which duplicates the retina of Chucky's left eye, was created from picture previously texted to Ryan.

The security system's approval is signaled with a pleasant ping. The alternative would have been the shrill bleat of a siren, so I stroll into the vault.

The key opens Chucky's safety deposit box with no problem.

The list holding the names of a dozen or so offshore banks, account numbers, and passwords is inside. I take it, replacing it with another created by Acme. Should someone else come looking for the list, this will lead him or her on a wild goose chase. At the same time, it releases a Trojan virus that allows Acme to trace the perpetrator.

I quash the urge to toss Chucky's eye in the box with the fake list. Instead, I'll give it to Ryan for the mission file. Granted, it would have made an interesting souvenir from this mission, but the Lamborghini would have been a nicer one.

2

Family Ties

"The meaning of life? That's simple. Try to be happy, try not to
hurt other people, and hope to fall in love."
—Mallory Keaton

*You may not always agree with your family, but you will always
love them.*

*Sure, sometimes one of them might make you so angry that you plot
ways to make his or her life miserable; nothing too serious. Heavens,
you'd never maim or disfigure—*

Okay, maybe. Depending on the slight.

*But, remember: if a family member is callous enough to offend, or
insists on doubling down with more vitriol, and then is too stupid to
apologize before you go all Hannibal Lecter on his ass, do yourself a favor
and skip the next family reunion. Your auntie may love you dearly, but
she's not above supplementing her Bingo money with the reward that
comes with your arrest.*

It's always great to be home again.

On this Labor Day afternoon, the residents of Hilldale are out in full force. In every third driveway, gangly arms flail amid grunts and swears during some pick-up basketball game. Because Jack and I have the windows down in the car, our noses are tickled by the smell of seared meat wafting from backyard grills. Greetings shouted between neighbors are answered with waves and chuckles. With snide asides and rolled eyes, gossip is volleyed across picket fences.

Just as Jack and I pull into the driveway, the paperboy rides by on his bike. With a backward toss if not a backward glance, our copy of the *Hilldale Signal* slaps against the veranda's steps.

Aunt Phyllis is awakened from her nap on the porch swing. She raises her sunhat, exposing one eye: all she needs to take note of the culprit, who earns a middle-finger salute from her. By the time she sees us, the other four fingers join it in a welcoming wave.

Considering the mound of dishes I left in the sink before leaving for Vancouver, I'm surprised we didn't get the same greeting as the paperboy.

Jack leaps out of the car first to pull our bags from the trunk and then to open my door—yes, he is a gentleman. I snatch the paper as I step onto the porch. I bend down to give Aunt Phyllis a hug. "Did you miss us?"

She laughs heartily. "I haven't had time. Between running my craps game and refereeing Trisha's fight club, it's been a bit hectic around here."

Jack's kiss on her cheek comes with a chuckle. "You've got a great sense of humor."

"You think I'm kidding?" Aunt Phyllis wags a finger at him. "Silly boy! Wait until you see her shiner! On the plus side, the house always wins, so dinner is on me."

"You're going to get off easy," I tell her. "We're too tired for anything but take-out."

I'm about to walk off with the *Hilldale Signal* when Aunt Phyllis grabs my wrist. "Not so fast, young lady! I've been waiting for that paper all afternoon!"

I hold it just out of reach. "Let me guess. It now carries a Santa Anita handicappers' column?"

"Yes…but not just that," Aunt Phyllis insists. "The buzz all over town is that they're shooting a movie in Hilldale, and that they're looking for extras. Maybe they'll need a sexy cougar to spice up the plot line."

"Oh, joy," Jack mutters under his breath.

"Oh, brother," I counter.

We've had the dubious honor of being consultants on a movie —one that turned out to be based on our lives. When my ex-husband, Carl, used his new position as the United States Director of Intelligence to frame us as domestic terrorists, we'd hoped that its around-the-world on-location film shoots would prove to be our get-out-of-jail-free cards. It was—but only because Carl had us watched, which came in handy when we led him to the few people he needed to exterminate before they blew his cover as the head of the Quorum, a covert-ops organization that finances international terrorism.

Eventually, we killed Carl.

Recently, we captured Eric Weber: the Quorum's leader, and the operative who turned Carl into a triple agent. Unfortunately, the Quorum's tentacles are long and run deep within the halls of government—not only those of enemy states, but our allies' as well.

And, yes, within the United States government.

So you see, our job is far from done. All too often it feels as if we are chasing ghosts. But cast a bright enough light on the wraiths creating the anarchy, and you expose them for what they are: shadow puppets.

Despite being in a maximum-security prison, Eric is somehow still pulling all the strings.

Sometime soon, I'll figure out how he does that.

Aunt Phyllis sucks in her cheeks and bats her eyes. "What do you think? Am I ready for my close-up?"

Jack chucks her under the chin. "In my mind, you'll always be a star."

My aunt blows him a kiss. "Donna is a lucky lady. If she hadn't married you, I'd have snapped you up myself."

I hand her the paper. "If they sign you up, we can say we know someone who *is* someone."

"I'll give it a go, but you're the beauty of the family. Albeit, these days Mary is giving you a run for your money."

As if on cue, the front door opens. My eldest daughter comes bounding out, her younger brother and sister on her heels. A second later, Jack and I are cocooned in a group hug. "We thought you'd never come home," Trisha scolds us.

Jack laughs. "We were gone, what, three days, tops!"

"And we called to check in every night," I remind her. We do so on every trip, via a secure cell phone with a masked global position system that spoofs our location.

"Did you bring us anything?" Jeff asks.

Jack gives me a mischievous grin.

Oh, no—Chucky's eyeball.

As he reaches into his valise, I grab his hand in mine. He winces when I dig my nail into his palm and groans, "Nope, sorry —but I'll bring you something really cool next time."

I release my death grip.

As Jack rubs the pain from his palm, he glances at the back-page ad of the *Hilldale Signal* tucked under Aunt Phyllis's arm and murmurs, "I hadn't realized there are so many houses for sale in Hilldale. And from the look of this ad, Penelope Bing's husband, Peter, handles the majority of the town's listings."

"He's the number one realtor in town," I remind him. I point to the slogan in Peter's ad:

With Me, You'll Get Bigger AND Better!

"Is he talking about a house?" Jack asks. "Or is he boasting about his—"

I punch his arm. "Why must men's minds always end in the gutter?" I pick up the paper. "Lucky guy! He's also got the listing for Hilldale Summit. Apparently it had its grand opening last week."

The newest section of our planned community boasts another thirty tricked out McMansions. To up the ante, each one a mini-Versailles on three acres of emerald-hued fescue behind its very own walls of stone and stucco. These new estates range in price from two-to-four million dollars. So, yes, the commissions are gravy on top of what Peter already makes. I'm sure Penelope is ecstatic—not just for what it adds to their bank account, but because it's keeping him too busy for his extracurricular activities. Peter's dalliances are an open secret in Hilldale.

Suddenly, I notice the headline on the front page. "Aunt Phyllis, you're wrong about some movie being filmed here. From what the newspaper says, it's a television show."

Aunt Phyllis is much too proud to wear glasses. Instead, she raises the paper a few more inches away from her face to get the words in focus. "*Hot Housewives of Hilldale?*" she frowns. "Well, that takes me out of the running—unless I can bag one of the neighborhood bachelors between now and the date of the cattle call."

Mary looks over my aunt's shoulder. "Oh, my God! Interviews start tomorrow! Listen to this!" She grabs the paper and reads: "'Do you feel you and your family are ready to be famous? If so, call this number to set your appointment for a chance of being one of the six lucky ladies who will star on the reality television series, *Hot Housewives of Hilldale.* Beyond the fame of being a TV star, you could parlay this memorable experience into many financial opportunities, including corporate sponsorships, paid appearances, and a book contract that showcases your best talents.'"

"Mommy, do you have any talents?" Trisha asks innocently.

"Of course she does." Jack's glance at me comes with sly grin. "In fact, I can think of two, off the top of my head. Then again, one of them could land her a life sentence in the big house."

I shut him up with a scowl. "Sorry, folks. The Craig family is better off far from the glare of television cameras." Not to mention municipal webcams and U.S. satellite surveillance. Time to veer this conversation onto safer ground. I look around. "Where is Evan?"

The seventeen-year-old son of Robert Martin—the man who was my very first crush—now lives with us. His mother, Catherine, was my very first enemy—almost mortal, as it turns out. I survived her attempt to stab me to death. On the other hand, the hit she put on Robert took his life.

The extermination was carried out by my ex, Carl. Small world, isn't it?

"He's lifeguarding at the Hilldale Country Club. I'm on my way there now—to meet Babs and Wendy." Mary blushes as she speaks.

When Jeff puckers up and makes kissing sounds, she gives him a dirty look.

Evan and Mary's mutual admiration society of two has been duly noted by the entire family.

"We wouldn't mind a dip. If you wait a few minutes, you can ride over with us," Jack promises.

"Sure, but you'll move fast, right?" Jeff asks. He holds up his cell phone, encased in a clear plastic bag. "With all the homes popping up, there are a couple of new girls hanging by the pool these days. Morton has a crush on one of them. Cheever promised him a fiver if he can hold his breath for three minutes under water. I told him I'd video-record him before he suffocates."

Mary snorts as she laughs. "Why don't you wait until after Evan's shift? That way, he won't have to give him mouth-to-mouth resuscitation."

"Why? Are you afraid you'll get Morton's cooties when you

kiss Evan?" This time, when Jeff mocks her with kissing lips, she elbows his gut.

Grunting with pain, he adds, "Hey, that hurts!"

In Mary's sudden move, the thin nude-hued string straps of her swimsuit are revealed. They look all too familiar. Apparently, she's wearing something from my Acme slut gear collection: clothing (or, what Jack calls, "costumes") that I keep in the back of my closet. In this case, it's a tan string bikini. The front of its barely-there thong bottom could pass for a pirate's eye patch. The life of a sparrow is not for the modest among us.

I pluck one of the top's straps. "You went through my closet?"

Mary turns white, but then shrugs defensively. "I didn't think you'd mind. Besides, all of my swimsuits are too small on me!"

I tap the strap. "Really? Smaller than this one?"

She winces because she knows I have her there. "I mean they're too *young* for me."

"Well, this one is too 'mature' for you."

"But—but Wendy's mom lets her wear a thong—"

"No buts." Not if it's Mary's. "Sorry, not happening."

"But—there's no time! The pool closes early today since school starts tomorrow!" Hoping for a reprieve, she looks over at Jack.

He thumbs in my direction. "What she said."

Frustrated, Mary stomps inside.

I sigh. Some things never change—least of all Mary's attempts to push boundaries where Evan's attentions are concerned.

We're just about to go into the house when Jack and my phones buzz simultaneously. We stare at each other first and then at them. Like me, Jack know what it means: we won't be hanging at the pool with the kids. We are needed at Acme headquarters.

Jeff and Trisha give exasperated sighs. "Does this mean you won't be going to the pool with us?"

I turn to Aunt Phyllis. "Would you mind going with them?"

"Not at all—but I don't have a swimsuit here at Villa Craig." Phyllis snaps her fingers. "Hey, now that Mary is out of that sexy little number, maybe you'll lend it to me. Certainly, it should get a few bachelors looking my way."

I'll say.

I'm not the only one who thinks so. Trisha's eyes grow big, and Jack is snorting so hard that he nearly doubles over.

Like I said, it's always great to be home. And, one way or another, I will always make it back to my dear, sweet family.

3

Alias

"There's something that happens when you discover the truth about someone. I know a little about this. The truth changes everything."
—Sydney Bristol

A good spy can be anybody.

She is an old friend. At the same time, she is a stranger.

Her seductive pout promises you that she'll be the best lover you ever had. But her dead-on aim assures she'll be the last person you see before you die.

How do you know you can trust her? You don't. You can, however, prepare yourself for the worst-case scenario:

The day she learns what you really think of her.

You'll do this with a one-way ticket to a place she'll never find you.

When you figure out where that is, don't bother to write.

"CATCH." I TOSS CHUCKY'S EYE, BAGGED AND TAGGED, TO RYAN.

His reflexes are good enough that he catches it with one hand. "Job well done," he concedes. "In fact, it's already bearing fruit."

Like the well-heeled lady I am, I ease myself into one the conference room chairs next to Ryan while Jack flops down into another across from our COMINT liaison, Emma Honeycutt.

Emma welcomes me with a wave, all the while swiping away furiously on the screen of her iPad. Two chairs away, her husband, Arnie Locklear, pounds away on his MacBook, still oblivious to our arrival.

On the other hand, Abu Nagashahi, our mission team's cutout and cleaner, is picking out the blue M&Ms from the bag in front of him. He offers them to me. "I'm a traditionalist," he explains.

I smile. Still, I shake my head. "I'm on a diet."

Disbelief weighs his head heavier to the right. "You're slim enough. Heck, I've seen you crawl out of spaces no more than two feet wide!"

I point to the M&Ms. "That skill set comes with a price."

Ryan glances at his watch and then sighs. "Where the hell is Dominic?" he growls.

Emma rolls her eyes. "He texted he'd be a few minutes late. He's getting fitted for a tux."

Jack snorts. "With all the tuxes he gets fitted for, you'd think he moonlights as a maître d'."

"If you saw his tailor, you'd know why he owns so many of them," Arnie murmured. His hands made an hourglass shape.

This is not lost on Emma. As he ducks behind his screen again, he adds, "He claims he likes how she blushes every time she measures his inseam."

I turn to Jack. "You've been in a locker room with him. Is he really so awfully small?"

Jack is laughing so hard that he almost falls out of his chair.

"Speak of the devil," I murmur.

Beyond the conference room's glass walls, every female Acme

handler is peeking above her cubicle to get a better look at who has just walked in: Dominic Fleming.

In fact, he is wearing a new tuxedo.

He saunters through the room as if it's New York Fashion Week before taking the chair closest to mine.

I crook my finger toward him.

Preening, he leans in close to hear what I have to say.

I snuggle up to his ear and whisper, "Your fly is open."

Mortified, Dominic turns white. He stands up quickly and turns around, glancing downward—

For a moment. When he turns around, it's to glare at me.

I giggle. "Gotcha!"

"I say, that's hitting below the belt, old girl," he grumbles.

"At least this time he has a reason for a new penguin suit," Ryan replies. "He needs it for our latest assignment, thanks to your good work, Mrs. and Mr. Craig. The CIA's exchange of Huang Fu Chan's bank assets netted our client some interesting U.S. domestic terrorism intel involving ISIS, which was somehow intercepted by the MSS."

"Since when do the Chinese care if a few of our citizens get blown off the face of the Earth?" I ask.

Ryan shrugs. "They don't. But besides demonstrating a little quid pro quo, the Chinese have invested more than one hundred and fifteen billion dollars in the Middle East. Not to mention loaning another fifty-five million to countries in the region."

Emma's lips purse into a frown. "Which is why the Chinese have finally joined the rest of the U.N. Security Council's international coalition in fighting Middle Eastern terrorists. It took them long enough, right? Especially after that baloney about not wanting to quote-unquote interfere with the region's internal conflict. Ha!"

Arnie rolls his eyes. "Yeah, until the Chinese run into the same issue on their soil."

"And they have," Ryan informs us. "ISIS has been rallying

Chinese Muslims in China's Xinjiang Uighur Autonomous Region to take up arms against their oppressors and create an independent Islamic state in Xinjiang. It's yet one more reason that the MSS is more than happy to let us take it down, on our soil to boot."

"The enemy of my enemy is my friend," Jack replies.

Ryan nods. "Exactly."

"Terrorism makes for strange bedfellows." I shake my head in awe. "Still, how do we know MSS's intel isn't bogus?"

"The tip has been verified by a CIA SocMINT team tracking online chatter. ISIS is intent on exposing the United States' vulnerability to domestic terrorism by ensuring an attack on American soil —sometime this month, in fact."

"How?" Abu asks.

"For some time, ISIS has been looking for a platform to highjack —in this case, television," Ryan explains.

"How do they figure?" Jack asks.

"Its Middle-Eastern terrorist strikes are too distant—and recently, too frequent—to cause much shock and awe on the American psyche," he explains. "We're tethered to our phones' apps, our video games—and yes, TV reality shows. So, why not hijack one? The terrorists can hold the celebrities hostage. Worse yet, kill them off in front of their adoring fans."

"Granted, some of those people are so vapid that you want to strangle them," Emma murmurs. "But kill them on air? Talk about an extreme cancellation clause!"

"Has the intel revealed which show has been targeted?" Abu asks.

Ryan's pause leaves us in suspense. Finally, he takes a deep breath: "It's called *Hot Housewives of Hilldale*."

Cold dread runs through me. "Come again?"

"It's to be the latest reality series in an already successful franchise. And it's being produced by our old friend, Addison Montague. *Variety* announced it about a year ago."

Jack murmurs, "I guess I should add a few entertainment trade magazines to my must-read list."

"Addison is producing it? Talk about a small world," I exclaim. "I thought his company made only feature films."

"Like most successful producers, Addison's media empire straddles both film and television," Ryan replies. "His *Hot House-wives* shows are big moneymakers, and top the ratings in their time slots. Knowing this, President Chiffray himself asked Addison to set the next show in Hilldale. With it shooting so close to POTUS, it's certain to be catnip to ISIS. We anticipate a cell or two will try to infiltrate the show as contestants."

"To participate, they'd have had to buy or rent in Hilldale within the last year," Abu points out.

"Which certainly narrows our pool of suspects," Arnie agrees. "And to be on the show, be it a man or woman, the terrorist will also need a spouse."

"I'm sure he's already secured one," Ryan replies. "It may be a woman who is sympathetic to his cause. Given the timeframe of the show's announcement, the terrorist would have been stateside long enough to have at least one child. Another possible telltale sign is a childless marriage."

"In other words, any marriage that took place within the last year will be suspect," Emma counters. "But that doesn't necessarily mean his wife will be of Middle Eastern descent."

"Hundreds of people show up at these cattle calls. How will the terrorists fool the casting directors into putting them on?" Jack asks.

"There may be a bribe involved. Or maybe the chosen ones' backstories will be just too good for the showrunners to pass up," I muse.

Emma sighs. "In any event, we'll have to throw a large net if we're to catch the suspects."

"Alright, people, pay attention for your assignments," Ryan growls. "Mr. Montague has been kind enough to make room on his production staff for some of you." Ryan's eyes move to Abu. "You'll be manning one of the cameras. Arnie, besides monitoring all the audio and video feeds from Acme, you'll be acting as the mission cut-out, as well as shadowing any and all prime suspects."

Arnie and Abu nod to him.

"Emma, you'll take the role of Addison's production assistant. In that capacity, you'll act as the handler to some of the families. This also allows you to observe them up close and personal. You'll also supervise the COMINT background checks on the six families chosen to participate."

Emma salutes Ryan. I can tell by her Mona Lisa smile that she already loves this assignment.

"And Dominic has been hired as the host of the show," Ryan adds.

"As such, a new tuxedo was in order," Dominic declares loudly. He believes this, even if the rest of us don't.

"Addison will make sure that the other families chosen are at the top of our suspect list." Ryan turns in my direction. "Which brings me to your assignments, Mr. and Mrs. Craig. You're applying to be one of the lucky families chosen to compete in *Hot Housewives of Hilldale*."

"What?" Jack's exclamation is louder than mine.

"Not to worry, Jack, my man. With your handsome mug, you and the little missus are a shoo-in." Addison Montague's gruff growl comes from the direction of the conference room door.

Yep, there's the man himself. Tall and toupee'ed, his shirt is open nearly to his navel, revealing the three gold chains of various lengths resting against his massive manscaped pecs.

Addison crushes Jack in a bear hug. Then it's my turn. He's too smart to try the same with me. Instead, he bows over my hand, gracing it with a gallant kiss. But when he rises, he can't help but lick his lips at the one woman lucky enough to escape his casting couch.

If only every wannabe actress knew my little trick of breaking necks with a single twist.

"In any regard, the Craigs will be ideal competitors." Addison rewards me with a thumbs-up.

"Wait…we're competing for something?" I frown. "I thought you said it's a reality show!"

"It is…sort of." Addison leans in as if he's in network pitch mode. "You see, this part of Orange County isn't home to a whole hell of a lot of celebrities—"

"By that, do you mean has-been actors?" Jack retorts scornfully.

"Yeah, exactly!" Addison holds up his hands toward Jack as if he's his prize pupil. "To give viewers what they want—you know, a few people to cheer for, and maybe a couple to hate—these mediocre families need some sort of competition."

I feel my lips pursing in exasperation. "Like *Survivor*? You mean, you're letting the competitors vote on who stays and who leaves? But that won't work! What if the Last Family Standing is that of the terrorist? Or worse, what if he uses his early exit as an excuse to accelerate his mission before we're on to him?"

"Not to worry, Craigs," Addison assures us. "No way would we let the families vote on each other! Otherwise, you guys would be the first out the door."

Jack scowls. "What makes you say that?"

Addison holds up his hands. "Hey, pal, don't shoot the messenger. I can't help it if the little lady here isn't exactly Miss Congeniality." He nods in my direction.

He's right. Still, I'd never trade my exceptional baking skills and honesty for my neighbors' mediocre culinary talents and sugar coated backstabbing.

My stabs are real. And deadly.

Another reason why I shouldn't be on camera. "Let me get this straight: we're supposed to be living with cameras in our faces for twelve weeks? If that's the case, there's no way we'll be able to take down the terrorists without blowing our covers!"

"Problem solved." Addison smiles supremely. "I've already convinced the network that the only way to compete with all the binge-watching of viewers on the premium cable networks is to run this show over seven consecutive nights. If the ratings go through the roof—and my showrunners will make sure of that—the network will win this upcoming fall sweeps period. And it may set a new pace for unscripted reality shows."

"With all the editing to be done, is it logistically possible?" Emma asks.

Addison shrugs. "Sure. We have four to six cameras on during group gatherings, and each home will have cameras in every room. The first hour of the show will be pre-recorded. Our editors will work around the clock to pluck the juiciest footage of the previous twenty-four hours. However, the show's second hour will be live."

"So, that's the draw for ISIS," Jack murmurs.

Ryan nods. He isn't smiling. It'll be a tense seven days for all of us.

"My only regret is that Jeff has to be in front of the cameras too." Addison sighs. "Best assistant I ever had! The way he poked holes in scripts? Why, that kid is like an Aaron Sorkin mini-me!" He shrugs. "That's okay. We must put country before commerce, right?"

Jack grins. "Spoken like a true patriot."

"Hey, I mean it," Addison insists. "I've been accused of a lot of things, but supporting terrorism ain't one of them."

"Not to mention, it could kill your ratings—no pun intended—*and* your stock price," I mutter.

"Yeah, I thought of that, too!" Addison laughs. "To keep things interesting, after each day's assigned task, viewers will vote by texting to a number designated for each family. The family that earns the most votes by the seventh show wins! And I'm not just talking about fifteen piddly minutes of fame, either." Addison leans in for his big close. "There's a very lucrative reason to be the last clan standing. The winners gets a cash prize that is the equivalent of one year of a thirty-year mortgage, based on an up-to-date sales assessment after taxes."

Now you're talking. Okay, yeah, I'm in.

Jack's mouth abruptly closes. I guess he's on board too.

"Let's get back to the business at hand," Ryan growls. "Only Addison will know your real identities. However, he may not always be on the set. An executive producer also acts as the showrunner who's in charge of the crew, and has total control of the final on-air product."

The screen changes to a picture of a woman: a svelte and toned brunette in her mid-thirties. Her Marc Jacobs couture dress fits her slim body as if it is welded onto it. Her sleek hair is sliced at a severe angle that accentuates her high cheekbones.

Her lips don't smile. They smirk.

"This is Brin Patterson," Ryan explains. "What can you tell us about her, Addison?"

"For one thing, she's a ballbuster." By the way Addison winces, I presume he means that both metaphorically and physically. "I'd like to say that her bark is worse than her bite, but I'm not here to lie to you."

My guess is that he knows this, first hand. In fact, if I examine his neck for puncture marks I would not be surprised to find wounds that match her perfect little teeth.

"Just do as she asks and you'll, er...survive," he warns.

Ah, I get it. Despite what Addison won't tell Brin, she owns him.

On the screen, Brin's face is replaced by another woman who is also in her mid-thirties. "This is Lucy Trumbull. She's Brin's second in command," Addison explains. "Brin calls the shots, but Lucy's opinion carries a lot of weight because she's the queen of talent manipulation."

I take a moment to scrutinize Lucy. From the looks of her— short and slight, with coiling auburn hair; scruffy jeans, no make-up, and eyes that avoid the camera—she is the antithesis of her immediate superior.

She looks sad. I wonder why?

I turn to Addison. "Is there any possibility that our suspect is part of the crew?"

He shakes his head. "My crew is made up of seasoned pros who belong to trade unions. Granted, the show is new, but most of them have worked together on other Montague reality shows. For the most part, they can vouch for each other"—He nods toward Abu and Emma—"just like I'm vouching for your two operatives there."

"In other words, if ISIS infiltrates the set, most likely, it'll be as a contestant," Jack deduces.

Addison nods.

"Family interviews start tomorrow," Ryan reminds us. "Once we get a handle on who's left standing—besides Donna and Jack, that is—we can pull together dossiers on them." He rubs his eyes in anticipation of whatever fresh hell that may wreak. "Here's hoping we discover the terrorist's identity before the show gets on the air."

No arguments there.

However, the moment the bad guy is taken into custody, I'll beg Ryan to allow the Craigs to hang in the show as long as we can. It would be nice to have someone else write out our mortgage payments for the next twelve months.

"WHAT? THE PRODUCERS OF *HOT HOUSEWIVES OF HILLDALE* ARE coming here...to interview us?" Mary is wary—even more so because we've waited until everyone is home and gathered around the dinner table to break the news to them. She eyes me suspiciously. "Why the flip-flop? You were the one who said it was stupid to audition."

"I...don't know. I mean...maybe it'll be, you know—interesting." Is my smile too wide? My guess is yes. From the frightened look on Trisha's face, I reason I must seem like a deranged clown.

The way Mary frowns, I can tell she's not buying what I'm saying.

Evan shrugs. "If we get chosen, it may not look so great on my college applications. And, besides, I need to focus on my grades so that they don't slip." He gives an apology with a shake of his head. "Of course, if it's something you and Jack want to do, I completely understand, Donna. I'm sure I can hole up with one of the guys on the lacrosse team until the filming is over."

Mary's distress shows itself in the way her eyes grow wide with concern at his possible defection. "Well, then it's settled. We're not doing it," she exclaims adamantly.

Jack lays his hand on Evan's shoulder. "Look, Evan, no one says we'll even be selected. And even if we are, we'll lay down some ground rules. For example, we'd tell the producers that our children can be in front of the cameras only after their homework is completed."

As Evan wavers, his shoulders relax. "Well...I guess it would be kind of fun. From what I overheard at the pool this afternoon, every girl in town is crazy over the idea of being on television."

"Which means, they'll go crazy over you too, if we get chosen," Jeff points out.

Mary's scowl deepens.

Trisha brightens. "Will I get to wear make-up?"

"No," I declare adamantly.

"Oh." Her pout mirrors her older sister's. "Well, how about some new dresses?"

"In fact, they do put you in new clothes," Jack informs her.

Mary seems to relax at that tidbit of good news. "Well...I guess it can't hurt to talk to the producers."

I can barely keep from pumping my fist in the air. The last

thing we need is to have the kids pull a mutiny and kill our chance at the mission before it even starts.

"Glad you kids came to your senses," Aunt Phyllis declares. "No time to waste. We have to decide which characters we're playing!"

Jack looks at her as if she's crazy. "What do you mean by that? They're looking for normal, everyday families."

She snorts. "Like heck they are! Haven't you watched any of those shows? They want drama—and lots of it!" She scrutinizes me. "For example, they'll want one of the wives to be devious... Nah, you can't do devious."

It's my turn to scowl. "Oh, yeah? Says who?"

Before I can tell her how I've made my life a masterpiece of devious, Jack claps his hands over my mouth. "That's okay. Donna will settle for the Perfect Mom trope."

Trisha's frown shows her confusion. "What's a trope?"

"It's a character or plot cliché," Jeff explains.

"Oh." His little sister thinks for a moment. Then: "Is Cheever's family going to apply?"

Jeff rolls his eyes. "You better believe it! He says his mom is pulling out all the stops, whatever that means."

"It means she's going to make a fool of herself," I mutter.

Trisha nods. "So, she wants to be the crazy neighbor lady trope."

"Or the neighborhood bitch trope," Aunt Phyllis mutters.

I give her a warning look.

Jack sighs. "If so, she's got that particular trope hands down."

He's close enough for me to nudge him into silence.

"Or the cougar trope," Evan murmurs. "You should have seen what she was wearing at the pool today!"

"Yeah, no kidding." Jeff laughed. "When Morton called it a Band-Aid, Cheever almost drowned him."

"How many times did she ask you to rub sunscreen on her back, Evan? I seemed to have lost count," Mary teased.

"Wow, if she can be all those tropes at once, why would they want anyone else in the show?" Trisha wonders out loud.

Point well taken. And it would certainly make our lives easier.

But, alas, this isn't really about her. It's about some guy on a suicide mission.

I rise to remove the dinner plates and get the dessert. Mary helps and follows me into the kitchen. She waits until she hears the others laughing over some other possible clichés that Penelope might embody before placing her hand on me. Looking me in the eye, she says, "Remember our pact: only the truth."

"Of course," I reply warily.

"Mr. Clancy wants you to apply to the show, doesn't he?"

She watches me quietly as I think how to answer her. "You know that your father and I aren't allowed to talk about our work," I remind her.

"Gotcha. Okay, don't tell me." She smiles. "Wow! We're going to be on TV!" Her eyes sparkle excitedly. "I wonder what trope I should be?"

"The teenager who is the goody-two-shoes," I warn her. "Otherwise, you'll be the teenager who gets grounded and stays in her room for all seven episodes it's on the air."

"Okay, Mom, I can take a hint. I'm the one who'll be so boring that I won't get picked up for Season Two."

If there is a Season Two, it's because we've accomplished our mission.

"YOU'RE AWFULLY QUIET," JACK SAYS. HE LOOKS UP FROM THE MISSION file he's reading on his iPad. It contains dossiers on Addison and the rest of the production staff. The goal is to look for any discrepancies that might mark them as accomplices to the terrorists' plan of destruction.

I should be doing the same, but I'm sure it's obvious to him that

I'm not, since my iPad has gone into sleep mode. I lay it on my nightstand. "Listen, since we're already a shoo-in for the show, when the producers come to interview us tomorrow let's not denigrate ourselves in front of our children."

"I'll shake on that." He holds out his hand. But as our hands meet, he pulls me close to him on the bed. "Long after this assignment is over, we don't want any crazy antics to haunt us."

We then seal our commitment with a kiss.

Not that we'll stop there.

Here's hoping we all get cut. It's much better than getting blown up.

4

Married...with Children

"Honey, could you come out in the backyard with me? I have the
urge to bury something!"
—Al Bundy

*Marriage is a very special commitment between two people. Raising
children together is also a unique and challenging commitment between
two parents.*

*Parents, here are three tips for keeping both while avoiding
commitment to a psychiatric ward:*

- *Tip #1: Never fight in front of the kids. Yes, you heard me. All
  guns, knives, bombs, drones, and other WMDs — Weapons of
  Marital Destruction — cannot come out until after the kiddies
  are in bed.*
- *Tip #2: Always show a united front when your children ask
  pointed questions, or show defiance. It pays to have already
  prepared a go-to phrase that will nix any doubt to the
  contrary. Try this one: "Only if your mother says it's okay."
  Fathers, if that doesn't fall trippingly off your lips, remember:
  practice makes perfect!*

- *Tip #3: Never make promises to your children that you can't keep. Doing so means you'll both end up paying for it, one way or another.*

If one of you has a habit of ignoring all of this advice, expect to pay dearly for it: if not with your life, then with big bucks to your wife—during the inevitable divorce.

TRISHA DOESN'T PAUSE FROM HER TAP DANCING—THREE BUFFALOS, A flank step, a brush, and three more buffalos—even as she lifts her nose into the air. "The house smells yummy!"

I slap down my computer screen. I'm watching Brin Patterson, the executive producer and showrunner of *Hot Housewives of Hilldale*, eviscerate one of the town's mean mommies, Tiffy Swift, with just one sentence: "So, is it true, as your neighbors say, that your husband once had an affair with your stepsister?"

I pray Trisha didn't hear it too—or for that matter, Tiffy's response (that is, once she quit shaking from her anger), which is a series of cuss words that would make a sailor blush.

"I'm baking an orange chiffon cake," I say brightly and loudly. I glance over to the oven timer. "But there's still a few more minutes to go."

And just in time for our visitors: the show's producers. I will be serving it with coffee, which they seem to want constantly, and drink so much that they might as well take it intravenously.

They've spent the past three days visiting the homes of the show's eager applicants. I know this because one of Arnie's jobs on the camera crew is to tape the prospective talent interviews so that Addison, along with Brin Patterson and Lucy Trumbull, can replay them all tonight. They'll then argue over which families make the final cut. Six lucky families will get the word sometime tomorrow that they'll be starring in the newest show in Addison's reality franchise.

Arnie has tapped into the camera feed. All footage will also be uploaded to Acme's secure cloud for further analysis. Once our suspects are chosen to appear on the show, background dossiers will be created on each of the principals.

In her role as a production assistant, Emma plays gopher to the producers, bringing them the numerous cups of Starbucks they need to get them through their day. That's okay. The audio feed she wears—not for us, but as part of the production crew—picks up all of their utterances beyond their caffeine requests, including every snide comment about prospective contestants.

As the old saying goes: if walls could talk…

They will, in a few days, throughout Hilldale. As soon as we know whom the contestants are, the producers will have cameras in every room of their homes, except for the bathrooms.

And Acme will tap into the feed. Hopefully, it will be enough for us to catch the terrorist before he or she has time to act.

"What exactly are the producers looking for?" Jack asked Arnie yesterday after he and Emma slipped out from work.

"The short answer is women who are the biggest drama queens in Hilldale," Arnie muttered. "And the crazier, the better! In fact, the task of the production assistants—Emma included—is to gather as much gossip as possible, on everyone. That way, the producers know which wives to pit against each other. If Brin has her way, the feud between the Hatfields and McCoys will look like a Kardashian pillow fight compared to what will happen on this show."

Suddenly, I'm dreading this assignment. I can only imagine the rumors about me that must be flying out of the Collagen-plumped lips of my neighbors.

The producers are leasing one of the empty houses for sale in Hilldale Summit to use as their studio, offices, and a place to sleep if filming runs long into the night. It was Peter Bing's suggestion—or more than likely Penelope's, in the hope that it would endear Brin and Lucy to her. They are renting it for a rock-bottom price. Somehow Peter convinced the builder that being able to say it was "Ground Zero for a *Housewives* franchise" will enhance its selling price.

Ground zero is apt—hopefully, not for a lethal reason.

Ah, time to enhance the cake with my special award-winning ingredient: a cup of Triple Sec. I pop open the oven, splash it on generously, then leave the oven door open a crack so that the alcohol can burn off as opposed to flame up.

"Why is Daddy mowing the lawn with his shirt off?" Trisha asks.

The real reason is that he has pecs to die for. Seeing Jack as man candy will certainly make us an obvious pick for the show.

Not that Trisha needs to know that. Instead, I say, "He must have just gotten too hot."

My youngest nods emphatically. Trisha points out the dining room window. "Mrs. Bing must be hot too because she took off both her shirt and her pants."

What the hell…

As I run toward the window to see if Penelope's unveiling has caused Jack to run over his toes with the mower, I pass Trisha, who casually adds, "I'll be in the playhouse. Call me when the cake is ready."

I get to the living room in time to see Penelope drop onto her chaise lounge and roll over onto her back. She unlaces her bikini to avoid a tan line. Oops, no, it's to flash Jack. Go figure.

I can see why Trisha thought she was stripping down to a fare-the-well: her bikini bottom is no more than a G-string. I can't imagine what her excuse is for untying its sides. After all, she's wearing a thong.

Ah! Now I know why: to call Jack over and ask that he spread sunscreen on her back. To his credit, he pretends he can't hear her yelling over the lawn mower.

I'm so busy watching that I've tuned out the rest of the world. Jeff is shouting, "Mom! Someone's at the front door!"

Aunt Phyllis is still upstairs primping, so I guess I'll have to answer it. Maybe that's a better idea anyway. If first impressions count for anything, she may scare them off.

As I make my way to the foyer, I run my fingers through my hair and then smooth the pleats in the skirt of my dress. After adjusting my lips into a pleasant smile, I open the door.

But, I've barely got the word "Welcome—" out of my mouth when Trisha runs in, screaming, "Mom! The oven is on fire!"

"Um…excuse me!" I'm rushing back into the kitchen when I hear Brin chortle through the audio feed, "Oh, brother! And this is the one everyone says can bake?"

"The tip-off that she is a lousy cook is that she isn't a heifer like the last mom," Lucy replies.

As they giggle, Brin retorts, "Well she must be good at something. Otherwise, how could she hold onto to that hunky husband of hers, what with all the sluts in this 'hood?"

I've got to admit she's got a good point there.

One of my lesser known "talents" is that I'm a good shot. If Brin knew this, would it scare her off? From what she just said, my guess is no. Anything that creates drama for the show is fine by her.

She doesn't know it now, but she may get more than she bargained for.

"HOW LONG WILL IT TAKE FOR YOUR HUSBAND TO GET OUT OF THE shower?" Lucy cranes her neck toward the staircase to our second story like a toddler looking up the chimney flue on Christmas, waiting for Santa's arrival.

I've got news for her. Any gifts Jack has to bestow are all mine.

Otherwise, everything is going wonderfully—

I think.

"Jack will be down by the time the coffee has brewed," I assure her. "As I was saying, Trisha here is a Daisy Scout! I volunteered with the cookie sales drive, and we raised the most in Cali—"

"Yeah, okay, wonderful, very noble," Lucy interrupts.

Well, at least she's not yawning, like Brin. Frankly, I'm surprised Brin isn't snoring. Granted, I have been babbling on about my children's exemplary grades, and I've been the soul of discretion regarding my neighbors' true peccadilloes.

I am a saint.

Alas, my children might as well be statues. Mary, Evan, and Jeff, stiff-backed and unsmiling, sit on the settee opposite our guests. Sadly, they couldn't escape like Trisha and Aunt Phyllis, who I sent to set up my antique coffee service.

I felt this was a wise move since great-aunt's get-up sent Trisha into a fit of giggles. Not that I can blame her for losing it. Aunt Phyllis has made good on her threat to position herself as the neighborhood cougar. To that extent, her more-salt-than-pepper coif is now dyed jet black. Her eyeliner is thicker than Cleopatra's. Her breasts, trussed in a bullet bra that thrusts them forward like twin zeppelins flying side by side are barely contained in the shortest, ugliest pink polka-dotted wrap-dress in history.

After making her entrance, she squeezed onto the couch next to Addison. But her attempt to sit on his lap was stymied when he quickly scurried into one of the wingback chairs.

"We've got a couple of questions for the children if you don't mind," Lucy's look makes it clear she wants me to shut up.

I shrug. "Sure…okay."

The kids' reaction is to bolt straight up in their seats. You'd have thought Lucy had indicated that waterboarding would be used as an interrogation tactic.

She turns first to Jeff. "I see you're entering the ninth grade. Who do you hang with?"

"Morton and…well, Cheever," he answers with a wince.

Brin flips open the iPad in her hand. "And you're such a great athlete."

Jeff relaxes into the settee with a smug smile. "Yeah, well, I'm our team's star pitcher, and I also play basketball."

Brin smiles encouragingly. "I was a middle child, like you. Do you like it?"

"Yeah, I guess," he relays warily. "I mean…well, I think it also helps to be the only boy—at least, I was until Evan moved in with us."

The spotlight then shifts to Evan. He keeps his face as blank as possible while answering Lucy's softball questions regarding his stellar grades and Lacrosse victories.

But then suddenly she asks, "What was it like to move all the way across the country to live with a family you barely knew before your parents died?"

At this point, Evan's face loses some color. "I'm…just grateful that the Craigs were kind enough to open their home and their hearts to me. Donna was an old friend of my family—"

Brin leans in, better to corner unsuspecting prey. "You mean she already had a relationship with your mother, Senator Catherine Martin, and your father, Robert, the billionaire tech entrepreneur?"

"Yes." Evan's stare dares her to ask him anything else.

Noting his discomfort, Mary puts her hand over his, but only for a second. The moment she sees Lucy smirk, she quickly pulls it away.

Brin sees her gesture too. Suddenly, she turns to my daughter. "Mary, sweetie…wow! And you're entering your junior year! Lots of fun, eh? So, do you have a boyfriend?"

Mary blushes, then says, quite adamantly, "*No.*"

By the sly smile on Brin's face, she caught the fact that Evan looked away.

I'm prepared to leap into the fray with some other tepid Craig family success stories when Brin turns to me. Batting her eyes, she asks oh so sweetly, "I'm sure getting thirsty! Why don't you go check on that coffee?"

What does she think I am, some flunky assistant, like Emma?

Calm down…Remember, you're here to win this.

I grit my teeth and reply. "Then I better go check on what's keeping Aunt Phyllis and Trisha with our refreshments."

"Hey, while you're in there, can you add some honey to my order?" Lucy asks. She dismisses me with a wave.

"Some coconut sugar would be nice, too," Brin adds. "Oh, and some almond milk, if you have it."

Even Addison, who must pretend not to know me, has a request: "Whisky, too."

Why am I not surprised?

I do my best not to stomp out.

It's on the tip of my tongue to remind these interlopers that I'm not some Urth Caffé barista, but then I realize they wanted to get rid of me for a few moments so that they can question the kids without me.

So be it.

I also commend myself for nixing any thought of putting a diuretic in their coffee, but only because I'll be pouring mine from the same pot.

From the looks of things in the kitchen, Trisha hasn't been much help. Instead, my floor is getting scuffed as she shuffles off to Buffalo over and over again, but she stops cold when I come into view. "May I go back in now? Please? Pretty please?"

I have no recourse except to nod my permission. Excited for her chance to impress, Trisha gives me a stronghold hug and heads toward the living room.

But, when Aunt Phyllis starts out after her, I turn her around and march her toward the back door. "Brin wants coconut sugar, and, sadly, I've got none to offer her. So, traipse down to the Hill-dale Safeway and grab some, okay? Thanks!"

"What? No! I've got to get back in there, coach!" she pleads. "I watch enough of these shows to know that I'm a character that the viewers will love at first sight!"

"You have a point, but now is not the time to make it—especially when the showrunner is jonesing to sweeten her coffee," I say firmly.

Aunt Phyllis's Hail Mary is to block the door with the toe of one of my new twelve-hundred-dollar deep violet Louboutin pearly suede point-toe four-inch pumps she borrowed, knowing full well that I can't afford to ruin the most expensive shoes I own. "Didn't you see the chemistry between that Addison guy and me? I tell you, we had a luuuuuv connection!"

"Come back with the coconut sugar, and we'll talk about how you'll make your play," I promise, as I shove her out the door.

By then, hopefully, the producers will be long gone.

If not, I can only imagine what Aunt Phyllis will do.

Is it too much to ask that she follow my children's lead? Thus far, thank goodness, they've been the souls of discretion. What could go wrong?

WHILE I POUR THE HONEY INTO A TINY BOWL AND PLACE IT ON MY antique silver coffee service along with a small pitcher of the almond milk Brin demanded, I eavesdrop via the Acme camera feed in my contact lens as Trisha asks, "Did you know that I tap dance? Do you need a tap dancer on your show?" Without waiting for an answer, she goes into her dance routine.

"Cute, but no—we're not *America's Got Talent*." Brin's clipped words can't stop my little budding Eleanor Powell from her star turn: six Buffalos in a row—

Until Brin adds, "I hear there are some boys in your class that are real meanies. Is that correct?"

Trisha stops mid-shuffle as she thinks. "Not in my class, but Jeff's friend, Cheever is a real ass—"

Jeff slaps his hand over Trisha's mouth. "What Trisha means to say is that Cheever can sometimes be…well, a handful."

"What a mature answer," Lucy commends him. Will her saccharine tone accomplish the goal of making him open up? "Do you always stick up for your friend? I mean, did you let him off the hook when he told your mom that the only reason Jack would marry her was that he got her pregnant?"

Jeff scowls. "You know about that?"

Brin's hard-edged laugh makes me shiver. "His mother happened to mention it. She also said that your mother's reaction was so violent that he peed his pants. Is this correct?"

"Well…yes, okay." Jeff's tone is defensive. "But Mrs. Bing started it!"

"Your mother set the poor woman on fire at least twice," Brin counters. "Could that have anything to do with why she dissed your mom? And was that any reason for your mother to make the poor kid wet himself?"

Addison puts his arm on Jeff's shoulder before my son says something he may regret. He likes the boy enough to look out for him.

"Obviously, you've only heard Mrs. Bing's side of the story," Mary retorts. "The woman has always hated us. Before Jack, she used to…" She stops, realizing that her hurt feelings are catnip to the show's producers. "Just…well, never mind."

"We know she's called your mom a terrorist," Lucy's tone is all good-cop. "You have a right to hold a grudge."

To hell with letting them tear my kids apart without me there to protect them! If they say one more cruel thing, this scalding coffeepot might find itself tipped over one of their heads.

I'm just about to march in there when Jack declares, "Pushing back doesn't mean you're holding a grudge."

His voice has them all turning toward the foyer entry. He has changed into a dry T-shirt and jeans. By the way in which Brin nudges Lucy, she must think he cleans up well. "It means you're not going to let others define you," he continues. "I respect my wife for doing so."

Brin bats her eyes at him. "You've admired her for several years, haven't you—even before you and she formally met, am I right?"

"Why would you think that?" Jack's question comes out in a snarl.

Brin swipes a few pages on her iPad. Glancing down, she replies, "Our reconnaissance shows that you knew her former husband before meeting her—God rest his soul." She pouts to feign sympathy. "Oh! And let's not forget that he took your wife away from you—"

Jack snatches her iPad out of her hands and scans it. "This paper you're reading from is marked Classified. It's from a CIA dossier. Where the hell did you get this?" He scowls accusingly at Addison, who shakes his head slightly, as if to assure Jack that he had nothing to do with it.

"So then, it's got to be true," Lucy points out. "Were you the cuckolded husband looking to court and marry Donna as a way to get back at Carl?"

Jack glares at her for the longest time. Finally, he tosses the iPad back to Lucy.

She catches it with one hand.

But her triumphant smile disappears when Jack says, "Perhaps appearing on your show is not in our family's best interest."

At this declaration, even Addison's mouth drops open.

Brin's eyes narrow. "Hey, look at it this way: because of our research, at least you have a chance of making the show. If we were to go on the malarky your wife was feeding us, you'd have been too boring. Viewers would fall asleep."

No time to wait for Aunt Phyllis. I better get out there before they write us off—and we're told to abort the mission.

I toss a few spoons onto the tray along with six of my best

China cups and saucers. I was going to serve the orange chiffon cake too, but that was before it turned into a flambé.

Ah well, they'll have to do with what's left of our Daisy Scout Cookies. Even if I had an opportunity to sprinkle, say, a few Trim Mints with arsenic, I wouldn't have time to signal Jack and the kids to leave them on the plate. Besides, I doubt the murder of a couple of the show's producers would stop the network from its decision to film *Hot Housewives of Hilldale.* If anything, headlines touting that a prospective contestant killed the showrunners would only make it a bigger ratings hit.

Any way you shake it, I'm in a lose-lose position.

I HAVEN'T EVEN HAD A CHANCE TO POUR THE COFFEE BEFORE BRIN stands up. Ignoring the spread in front her, she glances at her watch instead. "Wow, this is all so lovely, but we're late for our next appointment."

The kids look relieved to hear they're going. Jack's stony demeanor means I'll have to play good cop—and fast. "Gee, that's too bad." Putting out my hand, I add, "Well, good luck in your star search. I'm sure everyone in town will be watching it."

Brin cackles at the obviousness of my statement. "Train wrecks are always worth gawking at, aren't they?" She shrugs. "And in this 'hood, we've got so many to choose from!" She doesn't wait for me to show her the front door. They are all out so quickly that you'd think they'd seen a ghost.

Or something much worse: in this case Aunt Phyllis, chasing their car down the street in my new heels. As she shakes the sack of sugar at them, she yells, "But you didn't give me a chance to show you what I can do!"

I swear, if Aunt Phyllis scuffs my new Loubies, she's going to see exactly what I can do...

"So, what do you think?" Jeff asks. "Are we going to be on the show?"

"I wouldn't count on it," Jack mutters.

Trisha is disappointed enough to declare "Darn it!"

On the other hand, Evan sighs, relieved. Mary's face expresses a myriad of emotions beginning with relief and ending in wistfulness. Not getting her fifteen minutes of fame makes her wonder if she'd ever regret it.

I can assure her she would, but some things you have to find out on your own.

From Ryan's angry shouts coming in over our earbuds, I guess he agrees with my husband, but it doesn't mean he's happy about it.

Jack and I do the same thing at the same time: pull our earbuds out before we hear the obvious, followed by the inevitable:

We screwed up, and we're off the mission.

As if channeling Ryan, Aunt Phyllis wags a finger at Jack. "I don't understand why you even wanted to try out for the damn show if you were going to blow it by being such a rude stick-in-the-mud." She turns in my direction. "As for you, a little cleavage would have gone a long way. Just sayin'."

Jack mutters. "Oh, brother! I could use a nice stiff drink."

"Good. Go find one." She opens the front door. Pointing a thumb at me, she adds, "And take Miss Goody Two-Shoes with you."

She doesn't have to ask us twice.

"I GUESS CALLING BRIN'S BLUFF WAS THE WRONG DECISION." THERE. After three glasses of a good Zin, I've finally found the guts to admit we were wrong.

We're at the Sand Dollar, a place where we always get a great steak and a stiff drink, and at least tonight, no view of the moon rising over the Pacific Ocean's horizon.

Jack shakes his head adamantly. "Not at all. In fact, they'll want us even more. I mean, come on: we're the perfect couple!"

That earns him a kiss. He leans in and pulls me closer. When our lips part, I sigh. "Look, we can tell each other what we want to hear all day long, or we face up to the fact that Ryan isn't happy with how we handled today."

Jack chugs the last of his scotch rocks. "We made a decision. And we stuck to it. If Ryan doesn't like it, he can—"

Anna, our waitress, taps him on the shoulder. "Your designated driver is here."

"What do you mean? We brought a car." He holds up his key fob.

The velocity in which he twirls it on his index finger gives it lift-off.

Anna catches it. Shaking her head, she murmurs, "Right, sailor. But since you don't have your land legs as of yet, I've called an Uber for you." She helps him to his feet. "Time to sleep off whatever misery you two are celebrating"—she nods toward the restaurant's entrance—"unless you want to help me close up this joint."

I shake my head—much too adamantly, if my searing headache is any proof. "Nah. We've got to get home 'cause tomorrow we hear that we aren't going to be on TV."

Anna laughs—from the ringing in my ears, too loudly. "Oh, my God! Don't tell me you guys put in for that Hilldale reality show!"

"Yeah, but, it's not what you think," Jack insists. He then pauses because he's either remembered where we are and what we do or because he is too drunk to remember what he has to say. Sadly, my guess is it's the latter.

"If it's any consolation, everyone in here tonight also applied, and they also let on that somehow they think they screwed it up." Anna rolls her eyes. "I guess the producers are ballbusters. Figures. I've seen their shows. They make fools of everyone."

It's on the tip of my tongue to declare we can do that all by ourselves when we hear a horn tooting.

"Up and at 'em! Your chariot awaits." Anna helps me to my feet.

When I trip out of my heels, Jack bends down to pick them up, only to hit his head on the table before stumbling out after us.

A Lincoln Town Car is parked curbside. *Nice.*

Anna does her best to push me into the back seat. Jack falls in on his own.

"Can you tell the driver your address?" Anna asks gently.

"I've got them covered," the driver says.

He should. He's Abu.

What a surprise…

As tipsy as I am, is it any wonder that I suddenly feel as if I'm the wittiest woman in all of Orange County? Indeed, not. With a flick of a wrist, I proclaim, "Home, James."

He waits until she closes the door before turning to us and shaking his head. "Sorry, your Ladyship, but Ryan needs to see you both, *toute suite.*"

Yikes.

The utterance of our boss's name has a sobering effect on Jack as well. His impish grin flattens under the dual weight of Ryan's response to our going AWOL, and concern of what might have happened in the meantime.

"Oh, and by the way, you can now tip Uber drivers," Abu adds.

Jack is lucid enough to raise a brow at this pronouncement. "Seriously? You mean to tell me that Acme isn't picking this up?"

Abu shakes his head. "Hey, don't shoot the messenger—I mean, the driver. If you two hadn't pulled a disappearing act…"

"Yeah, okay, we get it." Frowning, Jack leans back and closes his eyes.

He stays that way until we get to Acme.

As we get out of the car, I toss a fiver at Abu. "Don't get too used to this cover. In a couple of years, Uber will be using driver-less cars."

Crestfallen, he mutters, "You're kidding, right?"

I shake my head.

Abu slaps his forehead in disgust. "I guess next time I'll be picking you up in the ice cream truck. See you inside as soon as I park this jalopy." He pulls away from the curb so quickly that the tires shriek as he hits the road.

By the time we walk in the front door, Jack and I are sober. Any hangover we get has nothing to do with the amount of alcohol consumed, and everything to do with what Ryan shouts at us for blowing our chance to go undercover.

5

Star Trek

"Mr. Spock, the women on your planet are logical. It's the only
planet in the universe that can make that claim."
—Captain James T. Kirk

*If you assume the life of a star is glamorous, think again. Pity the poor
woman whose quest is perfection!*

*She can never go out of her house—make that, her mansion—unless
her hair is perfectly coiffed, her toilette creates the illusion of a flawless
face, and her attire rivals that of a pop diva.*

*Her physique must be sylph slim and tautly toned and eternally
tweaked—preferably by the same surgeon on call to Mattel for the yearly
redesign of Barbie. Otherwise, the tabloids will muse over her love life,
dig up any childhood strife, and then tout it on the cover with a distorted
photo that makes her look half as sane and twice as fat.*

*The half-smile that never leaves her face is in anticipation of the click
of the paparazzi's cameras or the cell phones of her multitude of stalking
fans. Heaven forfend she should be caught frowning, scratching,
sneezing, eating—or worst of all, fighting with her beloved!*

Finally, when all of the attention becomes too much to bear, she retreats deep within the confines of her gated estate; all the while wishing that the peace she finds there could be wrapped around her, like an invisible cloak, whenever she dares to venture out again.

Hush, hush, sweet starlet! Don't you realize that the first time, "Oh, by God! There she is!..." is replaced with "Weren't you Whatshername?..." You grudgingly understand that stardom can go as quickly as it came.

Be careful what you wish for. Now, smile pretty for the cameras!

EVEN THIS LATE AT NIGHT, ACME IS A BEEHIVE OF ACTIVITY. RYAN'S door is closed, but the moment we arrive, his assistant, Natasha, immediately shows us in. He's got his back to us as he stares at the traffic crawling up the 405.

Arnie and Emma are already there. Their toddler, Nicky slumbers away in the sling strapped across Arnie's chest, his small lips quivering. Emma puts a finger to her mouth to silence us. Is it because she doesn't want us to wake Nicky, or because it might disturb Ryan?

When finally Ryan turns around, I notice he's wearing a Bluetooth. "Yeah, okay," he says to the caller. "Thanks for the update."—His eyes hone in on me in particular. "I'll let them know."

The call must be over because he pulls the device from his ear. "Sit!" Ryan barks. He glowers at us.

Jack's eyes meet mine. We slip into chairs on opposite sides of the room. Yes, we do this on purpose. Call it survival instincts. If Ryan shoots one of us, the other has a better chance of getting away. Someone has to make it home alive to raise the kids. Heaven help them if they're left with Aunt Phyllis.

"I take it we're out?" I ask.

Our boss shrugs. "Seems that way. According to Emma, in

Addison's defense, he put up a hell of a fight to get you on the show. But Brin fought him tooth and nail. So he's asked us to come up with a Plan B."

"Maybe it's for the best," Jack reasons.

"No, it's not. At least, not as far as Acme is concerned. Or POTUS, for that matter." Ryan scowls. "Frankly, Jack, I'm disappointed in you. Lucy was willing to put up with your surliness because she knew that the show's viewers would quote-unquote salivate over you." He rolls his eyes at the thought. "But Brin has you pegged as a troublemaker who won't play ball on camera. I'd expected you to at least try to get on her good side—no matter what it took."

Jack and I both know what he means by that. From the look on Jack's face, he doesn't care for Ryan's implication any more than I do.

"Even if Jack had played up to her, it probably wouldn't have made a difference," I counter. "She's only looking for couples who have strife and drama in their lives."

Granted, we certainly have our fair share—but the public certainly isn't supposed to know about it.

Ryan's head whips around in my direction. "Sadly, you're right, Mrs. Craig. It probably wouldn't have made much of a difference if Jack were more amenable, considering that they found you, in their words, 'more boring than watching paint dry.'"

I'm so angry that I pop out of my seat. "I beg your pardon?"

"You heard me. They were wondering why Jack married you in the first place. Addison did his best to convince them you were—again, his words, not mine—'a fox.'" His shrug is all the proof I need that, personally, he doesn't necessarily agree.

What the—

Hell yeah, I'm a fox!

"So, what now?" I mutter sarcastically. "Do they want Jack to go on as a bachelor?"

"Funny you should ask," Ryan retorts. "In fact, I suggested that exact idea to Addison—"

"You did? Well, screw—"

"And he, in turn, floated it to Brin and Lucy. Sadly, Brin was adamant about axing all of the Craig family." Ryan shrugs. "You'll be relegated to reconnaissance—gleaning what you can from the chosen contestants when you run into them—and window dressing, when needed. Speaking of which, we've got a list of at least four families who have made the cut. Three of them fit our suspect profile. And today, we intercepted chatter that indicates the terrorist was accepted on the show."

Oh, no.

Hell no.

He nods to Emma.

She swipes to a screen on her iPad. The wall-sized monitor comes to life. "Take notes, folks. Here are our suspects…"

"Couple Number One is Patty and James Garrett," Emma explains. "He's a retired USAF pilot. His last tour of duty was spent at Creech AFB, in Nevada."

"In other words, he was assigned to the Unmanned Aerial Vehicle Battlelab," Jack murmurs.

"He'd pilot drones to wherever they're needed?" I ask.

Jack nods.

"As for his wife, Patty," Emma continues, "she's a stay-at-home mom. I guess it's smart for her to do so since they have six children, ranging in age from two to sixteen. They moved into town about four months ago."

The photo on the monitor shows them in a classic modern family portrait. The entire family is decked out in white shirts and jeans. They are gathered in a pastoral outdoor setting. It seems as if the photographer had a hard time getting them to smile.

James wears his beach boy blond hair at military length: a mere quarter-inch to his skull. His angular face, broad shoulders, muscular arms, and slim waist attest to a twenty-plus-year regimen of push-ups and sit-ups. Sadly, the dark lines created by his sullen scowl undermine the perfect picture of youthful vitality.

His wife Patty's dimpled grin belies her struggle to keep her squiggling youngest, Joey, in her plump arms. Despite holding her child in front, she can't hide the fact that her girth seems to be twice that of her husband's.

"Jenna is sixteen," Emma continues, "The oldest boy, Jason, is fifteen."

Neither child is smiling. In fact, Jason isn't even looking at the camera.

"Their brother, Jordan, is thirteen," Emma continues. "Their daughter, Jody, is twelve, Juliette is six, and the youngest, Joey, is only two."

"Patty isn't your typical O.C. yummy mommy. Why do you think the Garrets made the cut?" Jack asks.

"Brin loved the tension between the parents, not to mention the two older kids give James a hard time. Jenna ignores him, whereas Jason is surly. Or, as Lucy thinks, if the showrunners push the right buttons, one of the kids will explode on camera."

Nice folk.

"Jordan is in Jeff's class," I point out. "He's quiet to a fault. And Jenna is in Mary's grade. From what Mary says, she's not very outgoing either."

"If she's that shy, I can imagine that all of this public exposure isn't going to be fun for her," Jack adds.

"And they've agreed to it for all the wrong reasons," Emma responds. "At first, James wasn't too happy that Patty applied to the show without his permission. But he changed his mind when he heard about the cash prize. In fact, he was very flirtatious with Brin. Patty was almost in tears."

I feel my face tightening into a grimace at the thought. "I can only imagine. Patty's body type is the antithesis of Brin's."

Ryan nods at Emma to move on. The monitor now shows Tiffy and Teddy Swift with their son, Logan, a sixth grader. The photo is also a family portrait-style: white shirts, blue jeans, and taken in Hilldale Park. "Donna, I know you're familiar with the Swifts."

"Don't remind me," I growl under my breath.

Tiffy is in Penelope Bing's posse. She may wince while carrying out Penelope's mean-mommy not-so-random acts of cruelty, but she never declines the dishonor of participating in them. I guess she figures that by being the perpetrator, she keeps her son from being the victim. Logan's preference for ballet to his father's favorite sport, football, would make him an easy target for Penelope's bullying son, Cheever.

Speaking of Penelope, is it too much to hope that she didn't make the cut?

Sadly, the next photo proves it is. You guessed it: another white-shirt-and-jeans family portrait of Penelope, her husband, Peter, and their cheeky offspring, Cheever, move to the head of the class.

"Am I seeing things, or is that little troublemaker cross-eyed?" Abu tilts his head as he moves in for a closer look.

"Yep, it's him, not you. I guess this was the best photo of all the ones the photographer must have taken." Ryan sighs, shaking his head. "Tell me, Donna, what are the skeletons in their closet?"

I shrug. "Both Penelope and Peter are into S&M, with and without each other. As for Tiffy, she's bulimic. It doesn't help that her husband leers at other women. Since both of these issues aren't exactly private, it isn't exactly intel, just…the facts of their lives."

Ryan asks, "Could either couple knowingly, or for that matter, unwittingly, be involved with a terrorist?"

I think for a moment. "Unwittingly, perhaps. It's a long shot. Penelope is disdainful of all new neighbors unless they have some celebrity patina. However, if money were an issue for either family, I'm sure they'd at least consider it."

"Reason enough for us to monitor them as well, twenty-four-seven. If so, and we can turn them, we'll be saving them from making the biggest mistake of their lives." Ryan motions for Emma to continue.

Emma announces, "Our next contestants are a doctor and his wife." The picture on the monitor shows a never-before-seen couple, both of whom are blond, and for once, aren't posing for a family portrait. Instead, the photo is a candid shot taken on a porch swing of an expansive veranda. A little tow-headed toddler sits between them. "Ariel and Franklin Powell, MD, and their two-year-old son, Connor, moved to Hilldale just six months ago. In their interview, Ariel rhapsodized about how they were high school sweethearts."

Abu reads from the mission statement: "His CV checks out: undergrad at the University of Southern California. Medical school at UCLA. He did his residency there as well."

"Why would they have applied to the show?"

"You mean, besides the fact that he's still paying off his medical school loans?" Emma replied. "Just think about the visibility a show like this would give a doctor who's new to his community."

"I guess you're right," Ryan conceded. "Well, I hope the contestant slot isn't wasted on the four we've seen thus far. As for the fifth?"

Emma takes this as her cue to put up the next photo. "Roger Pembroke is an author who writes thrillers. He isn't married and doesn't have children, but he lives with his fiancé—a former British model named Sienna Woodruff—in one of the bigger new homes in Hilldale. His celebrity gives him the sort of cachet that is catnip to Brin."

"He writes the *Alpha Force* covert op series, right?" Arnie perks up at the name. "He was formerly CIA, so he still has some connections, which is why some of his plots are scrutinized so carefully."

"Why would this guy stoop so low to do a reality show?" Jack wonders out loud.

"Supposedly, it wasn't his idea, but Sienna's," Emma replies. "She sold it to him as a way to get visibility for his book series. She also sees it as a springboard for her acting career. And since he sees her as his 'muse,' he agreed."

Ryan walks over to the monitor for a closer look. Frowning, he says, "The fact he agreed to the scheme could be proof that he's been compromised. For example, for all we know, he's used his books for steganography—covert messages buried in photos or letters. Let's scan his books for anything that may have been a cipher meant for an enemy state. We'll also dig deeper into his background in order to fully vet him. Right now, he's our number one suspect." Finally, he sighed. "Emma, who's our final suspect?"

"Something tells me this couple will tie them for first place," Emma warns us.

The photo on the monitor switches to a couple in their early-thirties: both blond-haired and blue-eyed. They are dressed casually, in khakis and white shirts—appropriate attire for what they are doing: riding tandem, on a camel over sand dunes under a cloudless azure sky. "Professor Gerald Farnham was recently hired to teach International Law at Hilldale State University," Emma says. "He's spent a good portion of his academic career in Turkey, Egypt, and Saudi Arabia. In fact, he met his wife, Cassandra, in Dubai."

"What do we know about them?" Jack asks.

"They are American," Emma replies. "Both speak several languages. Besides English: French, Russian, German, and Farsi. For years, he taught U.S. contract law at foreign universities. She supervised refugee camps for the UN."

"Any children?" Abu asks.

"Two sons, both adopted. The youngest, Sami, is a high school freshman—Jeff's age. He was adopted by Cassandra from an Iraqi refugee camp—her last posting." Emma's voice tightens. "His legs were blown off by an IED tossed by ISIS insurgents. Despite wearing prosthetics legs, he's wheelchair-bound."

"So sad," I sigh. "And the other son?"

"His name is Adam. Cassandra met him while she was supervising a UN refugee camp in that Chechnya." The picture now on the monitor shows a handsome boy around Evan's age. Despite swarthy skin and dark hair, he has startling blue eyes.

"He was only seven when she adopted him," Emma adds.

"Chechnya is an al Qaeda stronghold," Abu reminds us.

"The Farnhams don't seem like the typical reality TV stars," I murmur.

"They aren't," Ryan concedes. "But since you and Jack were vetoed, I pressured Addison to include them. We're tracking some unusual Internet traffic to their home address."

"Let me guess," Jack replies. "It originates from some known terrorist regions." He turns to Emma. "How did Addison sell Brin on them?"

Emma snorts. "He didn't have to work too hard. They were a great interview: openly hostile with each other, and critical of their unworldly neighbors."

"In other words, they came off as snobs," Jack replies.

Emma laughs. "Bingo! It doesn't hurt that Adam is such a cutie. Granted, Brin thought Sami's affliction would be a downer to viewers, but Addison convinced her that having a family with a disabled child would be a great 'feel-good' angle for the show."

"More to the point, what did the Farnhams give as their reason for wanting to participate?"

"Cassandra explained it: they wanted to draw the viewers' attention to the strife that is taking lives and maiming innocent victims in the Middle East..." Emma stops abruptly. She didn't intend for the answer to sound ominous. And yet, saying it out loud gives her reason to pause.

Finally, Ryan stands up. "Interesting, to say the least. Alright, everyone, get a good night's sleep. We've got a long week ahead of us."

It'll seem like a lifetime.

Here's hoping that when all is said and done, it won't cost any lives, either.

6

Queen for a Day

"Would YOU like to be Queen for a day?"
—Jack Baily, host of the 1945 game show.

Not blue-blooded by birth? Aye, a sacrilege and a shame!

No need to worry! Every Cinderella deserves her Prince Charming. To be important, one must look important! So, to that end:

1. *The fact that you lack the wardrobe shouldn't be a detriment. Solution: check out online couture options, such as Rent the Runway! He'll never know the gorgeous gown that first captures his eye turns into a pumpkin at the stroke of midnight eight days hence. (Or, that you traded it in for another…and another…and another…)*
2. *Willing to admit that you aren't exactly "the fairest of them all?" Pshaw! All it takes is a little sprucing up! Make your must-do list, then check it twice to ensure it includes the following: mani-pedi, massage, facial, lash dye, haircut, and a regal up-do. No doubt the works is far above a scullery maid's pay scale. Solution: Groupon coupons! Half-price deals will*

keep your Shrek side at bay—at least until after your royal wedding.

3. *Where does one find a king (and future husband)? Their hangouts are many! Try skiing the powdery slopes of glamorous Courchevel, France; or island-hopping from the Greek isle of Scorpios; or hobnobbing with the trim and titled at Paris fashion runway shows. Trekking to these posh locales may draw down your bank account (or your banked airline miles), but it will be worth it if you end up rubbing elbows with the next King of Whatever.*

If you want to be queen for more than a day, whatever steps you take in the next twenty-four hours may help you secure a manly monarch for a lifetime—so get off your throne and get out there!

I'M QUEEN OF THE HILL!

Well, almost.

The midpoint of my sunrise jog finds me atop the second-highest of the headlands that separate Hilldale from the Orange County towns hugging the coast.

The tallest headland, even closer to the waterfront, is crowned by Lion's Lair, the grand estate that serves as the "Western White House" for President Lee Chiffray, his first lady, Babette, and their daughter, Janie, who claims our Trisha as her bestie whenever she's in Hilldale.

Since I'm not one of her mother's favorite people, our daughters' relationship drives Babette to distraction. It wasn't always that way. When I was accused by her first husband, the billionaire industrialist Jonah Breck, of being a crazed killer out to get him (he got the first part of that right), she stood by me when an assassin's bullet—from the gun of my ex-husband, Carl—took him down.

Since Lee came into Babette's life, our estrangement came

about via several twists and turns: she is twisted enough to think I'm after her husband, and I believe she's been turned by the Quorum.

In fact, the father of the child growing in her womb is that of her murdered terrorist lover.

I killed him. I had good reason to do so: he was attempting to rape me. Talk about complicated, right?

Lee is quite aware of the strain between Babette and me. Still, this doesn't stop him from pining after me. And it certainly doesn't stop Jack from bristling every time he catches Lee's sad-dog eyes shifting in my direction.

Does Lee's guilt over his feelings make him blind to the possibility that his wife, the First Lady, may also be a Quorum operative?

Is Jack's jealousy the root of his inability to trust Lee?

Is my life a soap opera, or what? Talk about the ultimate surreality show! Ha! Thank goodness Brin doesn't know this stuff.

Jack, who's been eating my dust since we left the house, finally comes into view. He's still feeling the aftermath of his hangover. Not me. Knowing that my family's daily travails and trivialities won't be water cooler fodder for millions of voyeuristic viewers has given me a new lease on life.

Thank you, God.

I look skyward at the two brightest morning stars, Venus and Jupiter. In the receding darkness, they'll be obscured by the rising sun's crepuscular rays. This impermanence is a temporary illusion. The planets will survive long after Earth's human residents have played out their individual reality shows.

And after Jack and I are no longer.

The two planets move in tandem now, but eventually, the time-space continuum will succeed in separating them from Earth's point of view.

That's okay. For now, these orbs are together—and so are we.

The thought of Jack never fails to swell my heart with love.

We've grown together, never more so than when fate has tried to pull us apart.

I honestly believe that souls are eternal, and that the love one shares with another will last through infinity. In that regard, Jack will always be with me.

My exuberance at this thought is demonstrated with a jump for joy—

Landing me on top of a rattler.

My ear-piercing scream energizes Jack. He bounds up the hill in long, quick strides.

As the snake scurries off in one direction, I tumble down the hill in another—

Landing in scrub brush.

Jack gets to me before I can limp out on my own. Noting how I wobble on a now very sore ankle, he sweeps me up into his strong arms, holding me tightly to his broad chest.

It's a type of chivalry that will never go out of style.

Still, I'm somewhat embarrassed. "Seriously, you don't have to carry me all the way down the hill."

"Are you kidding? I'm always looking for a great excuse to hold you." He nuzzles my forehead before kissing me, deeply and sweetly.

Finally, our lips part. I blush as I laugh. Looking down at the countless number of homes surrounding the base of the hill, I murmur, "Thank goodness most of our neighbors will still be sleeping. They'd be shocked at such a public display of affection."

"What say we give the early birds a real show? It's been a while since we made love in the great outdoors." Jack's brow raises in anticipation of my response.

"I'll tell you what: if you run a bath for me, I'll let you scrub my back...and all that implies."

I've never seen a man run so fast down a hill.

～

We enter a house silent except for Aunt Phyllis's snores.

Jack sets me down on the bed in our master suite. After undressing me and icing my ankle, he warns, "Stay put. I'll get you when the tub is filled."

I reward him with a throaty chuckle. "Promises, promises."

When he scoops me up again, it's to witness his handiwork: a tub filled with bubbles.

Tea candles flank the ledge surrounding it. He lowers me into the water, and then strips down. When he drops into the water, a tsunami rolls over the side of the tub.

"Now we'll both fall and break our necks," I warn him.

"Not if we're careful," he argues. "And I'm always careful. You know that."

I shrug. "Not a word I'd use to describe you. Exacting, perhaps."

"Exactly." He grins mischievously as he takes a sponge off the tub's ledge. Then, lifting my leg with the tender ankle, he scrubs my foot, very gently.

I giggle at his touch.

"Bend your knee," he commands me.

"Why?"

"Don't argue. Just do it," Jack growls.

"Yes, sir." I salute him playfully before doing his bidding.

Soon, he's doing mine. It starts as he moves the sponge further up—over my calf, then my knee, then my thigh.

But then the sponge drops into the water, but Jack's hand stays in place, kneading my thigh with his broad palm, inching ever higher with his long fingers—

I gasp in anticipation.

He does not disappoint.

A finger and thumb probe first, strumming me as if I'm a finely tuned guitar. If Jack wants me to sing for my supper, I cannot oblige. I refuse to wake up the whole household. However, my moans are soft but fervent.

Tit for tat. I take him in hand.

I'm not at all surprised to find him already stiff. I know he's ready to burst because he flips me over so that I'm on my knees, places my palms onto the slate ledge that surrounds the tub, and then kneels behind me.

When he enters me, another wave sloshes over the side and onto the floor, but I don't care. What water is left in the tub ebbs and flows with our lovemaking: gently at first, then more violently.

My orgasm is the eye of our shared tempest, absorbing our raw lust. All too soon, this surge is too great for me to hold onto and I find myself drowning in the streams of our conjoined emotions: desire, surprise, wonder, pain, pleasure, ecstasy, joy—

And love.

Always love.

By the time Jack collapses onto my back, spent, I'm surprised that there is any water left in the tub at all.

A few minutes later he whispers in my ear, "I think we put out all the candles."

"Not to worry," I tell him.

The flame that counts most still burns brightly.

As I push him onto his back, he hits his head on the waterspout.

"Ouch! Don't kill me!" he grumbles.

"Yeah, okay, I promise." When I cross my heart, I notice the cold has stiffened my nipples.

Jack notices too. I stop his leer by pushing him down again—

Oops, can't have him drown! I mean, I can't go back on my promise, right? So I release the stopper.

As what's left of the water circles the drain, he says, "By the time we get out of here, our skin will be wrinkled."

It's a small price to pay for love.

~

SOMEONE IS BANGING ON THE BATHROOM DOOR.

"Who is it?" I shout as I scurry onto my feet. I groan when I realize I've put weight on my bad ankle.

Jack leaps up out of the tub too, before taking my hand and helping me onto the furry bathroom rug.

"Mommy! Come out! Someone is at the front door!" Trisha sounds alarmed.

"I'm…busy! Please wake Aunt Phyllis," I command her.

"But…she's in the bathroom too."

"Um…Okay, we'll be out in two minutes. Go wake up Mary."

Trisha sighs loudly as I hear her stomp off.

Jack slips my terrycloth robe onto my arms, and then tightens it with its sash. No, it must be his robe, because it keeps slipping off my shoulders.

Tit for tat, right? I reciprocate by wrapping a towel around his middle. To show his appreciation, he pulls me in close and kisses me fervently.

Shrinkage? Ha! No problem there.

"We've…got…to…go…" Despite Jack's unwillingness to let me loose, I fumble with the bathroom door—

Only to find our bedroom door has been left open and a camera crew, led by Dominic, has somehow found their way into the room.

Behind them are our horrified children and Aunt Phyllis: still in her bathrobe and sporting a depilatory cream mustache.

"What the—"

Before Jack can finish his sentence, Dominic proclaims, "Congratulations, Donna and Jack Craig! You've been selected as contestants on *Hot Housewives of Hilldale!*"

"But—" I stammer.

"As such, you're invited to a reception tonight at the *Housewives'* mansion, where you'll meet the neighbors who, like you, will represent your beautiful community to the world! And for one of our lucky contestant families, all of their dreams will soon come true!" Dominic points his index finger as if it were a six-shooter. "Perhaps…that lucky family will be yours!"

I take Dominic's finger and twist it all the way back until our associate-slash-host is wincing in pain. "I say, old girl," Dominic whimpers, "I'd like to keep all my appendages right where the good Lord intended them to be—"

If that's the case, he's lucky I haven't grabbed the most sensitive one, which he sports below his waist.

"Okay—CUT!" Brin steps out from behind Abu, who is holding one of the three cameras focused on us: hopefully, not just on the robe slipping off my shoulder, or the tent under Jack's towel. "Ha! Well, what do you know! Your kids weren't immaculate conceptions after all!" Brin guffaws, as she hands Lucy a dollar.

They actually bet on our desire for each other?

Before I can reach over and slap them both silly, Jack grabs me tighter and holds on with all his might. I'm still breathing heavy as he growls, "You know, a simple phone call might have given us a heads-up that you'd be rolling in here with a full camera crew."

She wags her high-gloss talons at Jack. "Oh, no, *mon chéri*! It is much more fun this way. You never know when you might walk in on someone *in flagrante delicto*." She opens her hands wide toward us. "Case in point."

"You aren't seriously including this footage in the show, are you?" Jack steps menacingly toward her.

To Brin's credit, she holds her ground. "Of course I am, Jack, honey," she purrs. "It's ratings gold! Without it…well, let me put it this way: if you want to win this thing, these displays of affection —made public, via the show—will pay off in a big way." Triumphantly, she glares back him.

He smirks…but backs off. Not because of anything she's said, but because we're back in the game.

And Ryan would have our heads on a platter if once again we took ourselves out of the competition.

The stakes are deadly. Only Jack and I can stop what is about to happen.

Brin waves us away as she turns on her four-inch Gucci stiletto heels.

The rest of her crew follows, including, sheepishly, Abu and Emma.

As if ensuring us that we've done the right thing, Aunt Phyllis gives us a thumbs-up. "Way to go to seal the deal!"

I guess I might feel better about it if she lost the gooey mustache.

"Boo-yah! We're in," I crow to Ryan. Jack winces as I high-five him.

"Yeah…um, how did that happen, anyway?" he asks Ryan.

"We had a little luck," Ryan replies. "One of the other contestant families dropped out."

"Who?" I ask.

Ryan frowns. "The Swifts. Logan found his mother passed out on the bathroom floor, so he called an ambulance. It turns out she was dehydrated after one of her bulimic purges."

So sad. Despite her membership in the mean mommies coven, I really do feel badly for her. It can't be easy living in a prison of one's *Vogue*-induced vanity.

Desperation is a damp sheen always visible on my thin-skinned neighbor. When Tiffy first moved into town, I tried to befriend her, to no avail. In the Machiavellian minds of Hilldale housewives, you're either revered or reviled. Noting how I'd fallen into the latter category because of Carl's absentee status, she quickly aligned herself with Penelope Bing and Hayley Coxhead. Now that she's lost the status of being one of the show's Chosen Ones, will she see it as a wake-up call to address her illness, take it as a put-down, or continue on a path that may one day kill her?

For her sake, I pray for the former. Well, at least now she won't be dealing with the insane pressures of playing a role in what you might loosely call, a reality show.

"Don't let this bit of luck make you cocky," Ryan warns us. "According to Emma, the producers think the only reason you were caught with your pants down—I mean, in your bathrobes—is because you were tipped off that they were coming. Brin is still betting that you'll be ejected from the show—unless you keep things spicy when the cameras are rolling."

"Tipped off? Ha! As if!" I shake my head. "Wait...you mean they can reject us if we do something they don't like?"

"Yes, according to the contract you signed along with your application. But don't worry. Besides a morals clause, there was one which stated a minimum viewer approval rating."

"In other words, to stay in the game, we can't put the audience to sleep," Jack retorts wryly. "Not to worry. We'll do whatever it takes to stay in the game."

The ghost of a smile graces Ryan's lips. "You don't have to convince me."

I cringe as I imagine what our kids will think when they see us going all kissy-face on television: la, la, la, too-much-information, too-much-information, too-much-information...

"According to Emma, Brin insists on handling you personally." Ryan's eyes drill into Jack. "You need to win her over and make her think she's controlling you off camera."

Jack shrugs. "Sure, okay."

We both know what that means. I try not to grit my teeth at the thought.

As for Ryan, his glare attests to the fact that he doesn't believe Jack.

"Who's my handler?" *Let it be Emma...*

"Lucy," Ryan replies. "She's sharp, and knows when she's being played, so you'll have to convince her you've let your guard down. Be loose in front of the camera. Become…well, like the other women."

"In other words, a vindictive bitch," Jack explains blithely.

Seriously, does he think he's being helpful? When my eyes narrow, he takes the hint: *Shut. Up.*

But to Ryan, I purr, "Easy, peasy."

I'm totally lying. He and I both know it.

However, too much depends on either of us admitting the truth.

7

Desperate Housewives

"Oh, for God's sake, Bree! You're a woman. Manipulate him.
That's what we do."
—Gabrielle

If you still buy into the traditional concept of a housewife as a married woman who sits on the couch all day in her negligee, carefully choosing one bonbon after another to have with her Starbucks non-fat decaf latte while watching her daily dose of soap operas and talk shows, think again. More than likely, this married (notice I'm not saying "happily") woman has too much on her mind to indulge in any binge fest whatsoever.

After doing dishes and the laundry, cleaning the house, vacuuming the floors, picking up the dry-cleaning, and then schlepping the children to and from school and any other extracurricular activities, she has very little time—if any at all—for herself. So, yes—of course, she's desperate—

Desperate for a few moments to close her eyes.

Craving a hot soak in the same tub she just scrubbed to a fare-thee-well.

Most of all, hopeful for some thank you that recognizes all the little acts of kindness she does for everyone else.

Ideally, from her mister.

So yes, Desperate Housewife's Husband: whisking her away for a much-needed, just-the-two-of-you getaway will do the trick—

And the sooner, the better. Before she hurts herself.

Or worse yet, hurts you.

"I UNDERSTAND WHY YOU WANT TO GO TO THIS COCKTAIL THINGY THE producers are throwing, but why do we have to hang with the other kids in the show too?" Mary grumbles. "Jenna Garrett isn't just shy; she's practically comatose! And her brothers and sisters are weird, too. They're all so quiet! And that Sami dude…I mean, I know he's in a wheelchair, but that isn't what makes him creepy to the other kids. It's almost like he's psychic or something." She shudders at the thought.

I can't say I blame Mary for her reticence. Whereas she has been the butt of some mean girls' jokes, she has never had the good fortune (bad luck?) to be the envy of her peers.

"My guess is that the other kids are just as concerned as you about how they'll come off to their friends, or for that matter the whole world." I smooth Mary's hair before kissing her forehead. "Like Dad and me, just try to make the best of it. As for tonight, all they ask is that you guys hang out in the big media room in the *Housewives* mansion and get to know each other better. That isn't so bad, is it?"

Mary shrugs. "I guess not."

"Just one word of caution: don't rise to the bait of any drama the producers may suggest. If all the kids stay grounded, they'll focus on the adults instead." Lucky me. "Besides, you only need to interact with these families when the cameras are rolling. Otherwise, you're free to hang out with your own friends."

Mary groans. "I may not have any friends by the time this is all over. Wendy is so upset that her mother wouldn't apply to the show that she quit speaking to me! And Babs…well, it's as if she's lost any ability to have an opinion of her own. All she does is copy everything I do or say." She rolls her eyes. "Can you believe she asked me if she could manage my fan club?"

Okay, yes, now I'm laughing. At first, Mary snickers at me, but when I fall onto the sofa, she ends up giggling too.

When I finally get ahold of myself, I gasp, "What do you think, should I ask Aunt Phyllis to run my fan club?"

Mary doubles over—and lands beside me. Still laughing, she retorts, "Are you kidding? She'll have the biggest fan club of us all!"

At this, I can't help but roar even louder.

Aunt Phyllis's head pops through the door. At least, I think it's Aunt Phyllis. This person has her face, but my aunt's long silver mane has been replaced with a jet-black French twist. She's wearing my best pearls with her little black dress. "Hey, keep it down in there! I'm in the middle of an interview with Howard Stern! I'm now his official onsite reporter for *Hot Housewives of Hilldale!*"

Yep, that certainly shuts us up.

Mary and I sigh in unison. Reluctantly, we rise from the sofa. Time to get ready for our close-ups.

"Donna! DONNA! Over here!" Penelope Bing, standing by herself, waves frantically at me from across the spacious terrace of the show's rented mansion, where all ceremonies of the show are to be filmed.

"Do I have to go over too?" Jack grumbles.

"I don't," Aunt Phyllis declares. Without further ado, she grabs a martini off one of the cater-waiters' trays (does she recognize him as Arnie? Apparently not, despite the fact that his fake mustache is slipping) and makes her way to the other women.

I assure Jack, "Feel free to mingle with Peter and the rest of the menfolk."

Who look as if they wish the earth would open up and swallow them whole. Peter is sweating through his Brioni suit. Professor Gerald Farnham's nose is so far up in the air that it's easy to see he could use a good nostril hair trimming.

Roger Pembroke only has eyes for Ariel Powell, whom he stares at with open fascination; whereas the good doctor, Franklin Powell, is scrutinizing every woman's face—and the rest of their bodies, for that matter.

James Garrett also stares at the women: their chests. When our eyes meet, his smirk turns into a leer.

Sadly, this is not lost on his wife, Patty. She glares at me, her lower lip quivering.

Before I walk over to Penelope, I decide it's best that I follow Aunt Phyllis's lead and also introduce myself to the other women. My competitors are clustered in one of the few sections of the terrace that are not crisscrossed with the cables tethered to the cameras being rolled around the slate floor. Arnie has already warned Jack and me that the sound booms perched over our heads are augmented by microphones hidden in the netting hung over-head. This way, every utterance of the contestants can be overheard.

To counter this, if we need to signal one another, we will talk in code: "Happy" being the operative word. For example, if we feel Acme needs to pay attention to a likely suspect, we should mutter, "Ariel seems inordinately happy," or "James doesn't look too happy," depending on the mood they are currently exhibiting. (In James' case, the taciturn smirk seems natural, so this should not surprise anyone else who may be listening.)

Since Acme is tuned into all of the show's audio and camera feeds—even the ones secreted in the nooks and crannies around the *Housewives* mansion and those soon to be covertly hidden in every contestant family's home—there is no need for Jack or me to wear our video feed contact lenses. However, we will always wear our Acme-issued earbuds so that we can hear Ryan's directives, as well as any cross-chatter between our mission team.

Patty hesitates before taking my outstretched hand. When she finally does, I find myself holding her sweaty palm. "Pppleased to meet you," she stutters.

Cassandra's greeting is purred through gritted teeth: "Ah, Donna Stone—I mean, Craig. Your reputation precedes you."

Just what the hell does that mean?

On the other hand, Ariel might look like a real-life Barbie doll, but her smile is warm and genuine. "Nice to meet you! You say you live on Hilldale Avenue? We're right around the corner from you!" Her eyes sweep across the room, taking in the hubbub around us. "Isn't this exciting? I've always wondered what goes on behind the scenes of these reality shows—but I never thought I'd be part of one!"

Sienna, a willowy redhead whose supermodel height puts her at least a head above the rest of us, snorts with laughter. "Well, here's hoping it'll be worth our time, and all the intrusion into our lives. Otherwise, we may all be hunting for new agents." She nods at me. "Speaking of which, who are you signed with?"

Confused, I shrug. "We're not selling our house."

"I meant your *talent* agent." Sienna sighs impatiently. "Surely you have one! You aren't yet signed with anyone? Interesting. I mean, you're just as beautiful as the rest of us..." She glances over at Patty. "Well, most of us."

Patty's face puckers up at the slight.

Before I can say anything, Aunt Phyllis butts in: "The whole Craig family's been approached by the big guns: CAA, WME, ICM, UTA…hey, it's just a matter of who's willing to bring the juice with licensing deals and book contracts."

Whereas this laundry list of alphabet soup means nothing to me, apparently, it's touched a nerve with Sienna, who isn't smiling anymore.

Suddenly, Arnie appears at my side. He carries a tray containing various colorful libations. "Another cocktail, ladies?"

These women don't need convincing to turn in their current unfilled glasses for ones that may help them forget that signing onto the show could be the biggest mistake of their lives.

Arnie's nod to me indicates that he now has what he's come for: their fingerprints along with their husband's, all of which will be run through the INTERPOL database for possible matches.

I snatch a glass of red wine from Arnie's tray. But before I can take a sip, Cassandra nudges me. Nodding toward Penelope, she declares, "Your very aloof friend is practically apoplectic that you're not yet at her side. I hope she doesn't find some way to hold it against you later. I mean, isn't that what these shows are about?"

Not this time. It's about discovering which one of you is married to a terrorist.

And the sooner, the better.

"A pleasure meeting you," I murmur, as I float in Penelope's direction.

I don't have time for my frenemy's bitchery. But if she's got any real reconnaissance on these women and their husbands, I'm all ears.

"Look at those women! Who the hell are they, and how did they get chosen?" Penelope says as she belts back some fizzy drink as if it's water.

"Lucky for us, I guess," I mutter.

Her eyes narrow as she turns her gaze to me. Make that me and my twin, as I'm sure the way she grips me to steady herself she must be seeing double. "Ha! Luck had nothing to do with it! Peter told me that my...er, his list of upstanding citizens was shunted aside like yesterday's graffiti."

"You mean confetti."

"Yeah, okay, whatever." She swats away an imaginary pink elephant, and in the process spills her drink of the same hue.

As she tosses the empty glass onto Arnie's tray, she commands him: "Another one of these Peach Thunderbirks"—she burps—"I mean, birds. ThunderBIRDS."

"It's a Pink Cadillac," he counters.

She scowls at him. He glares back. Finally, she blinks. "Yeah, yeah, whatever." She dismisses him with a wave.

She's slurring her words. I wonder how many of them she's already had. She's adding another reality show trope to an already long laundry list of them: neighborhood drunk in need of an intervention.

Sorry, not now. I need Penelope's tongue as loose as possible. "Come, come, now, Penelope! They can't all be bad."

Her brow lifts so high on her Botoxed forehead that it almost disappears into her fringe. "I didn't say that they're bad. I stated that they're nobodies." She crooks a finger at me. "Peter was their realtor—not just for the purchase of their homes, but the sales of their old hovels. So, of course, he got a peek at the skeletons in their closets—metaphorically speaking." She waves her arm in the other women's direction. "Before moving into Hilldale Summit, the heifer over there, Patty, lived with her hubby and brood on some backwoods pig farm, outside of Modesto. And the meal ticket for that tall drink of battery acid, Sienna, just got his last book contract canceled. He had to sell his place in Malibu at a loss." With her other arm, she waves wildly at Cassandra. "Miss Ol' High and Mighty's egghead hubby is lucky even to have his little community college gig after the riot he incited in his last place of business—somewhere in Dubai." She slurps the icy dregs of her drink.

"What about Ariel and Franklin?"

Penelope shrugs. "He's certainly got the right pedigree. Frankly, I'm surprised they're slumming here in Hilldale. You'd think that with all the fistfuls of dollars UCLA is offering, he'd have settled in Beverly Hills."

"What kind of doctor is he?" I ask.

"Plastic surgeon," she snorts, which is her way of letting me know she thinks I'm the stupidest person in room.

But before she can answer, Dominic proclaims, "Ladies, please gather 'round by the fireplace with your gents! We've got a few announcements to make—and yes, your reactions to them are being recorded, so smile pretty for the cameras—which, from this moment hence, will be your constant companions!"

The contestants don't realize how truthful that statement is.

Jack's bemused smile is paired with an intense stare. I turn to see who has his attention:

Brin, who is giggling at whatever Dr. Franklin Powell is saying to her. Dominic stands there too. His grin grows wider with the good doctor's every utterance.

Here's hoping their little joke isn't at the expense of the rest of us.

I TAKE THE LAST SEAT ON THE END OF ONE OF THE SERPENTINE couches flanking the fireplace. Video monitors hang all around the room, high above our heads.

By the time Jack joins me, there is nowhere to sit but on its overstuffed arm. With a naughty smile, he leans over me and whispers, "Would you prefer to sit in my lap?"

I can't help but laugh. I whisper, "You'll do anything to win this damn thing, won't you?"

"From what I'm hearing, I'll have very stiff competition." He chuckles at his little double entendre.

"Quiet on the set," Lucy hisses. She raises her hand for the camera countdown. "Rolling in three…two…"

Just as she silently mouths the word "one," Dominic walks

between the couches and then turns to face the cameras. "Welcome to *Hot Housewives of Hilldale*, where the question on everyone's lips is, surely, 'are my neighbors naughty…or nice?'"

One camera sweeps to the left of the sofas while the other moves right. Both take in the shit-eating grins plastered on the contestants' faces.

Can they also discern the panic in our eyes?

"We'll let you decide, as you watch how they treat their families, their friends, and their spouses." Dominic takes a step toward the only camera of the four on the set that flashes a red light. "While the next seven days unfold, you'll be rooting for your favorites." He grins mightily. "Each night, you're invited to text the name of your favorite housewife—with a smiley face— to the phone number at the bottom of your television screens! To make things even more fun, if you feel a particular couple isn't giving you the titillation you deserve, text us their names, followed by a frowny face, and a vote will be deleted!" He leers knowingly at the camera. "In any regard, we want to hear from you—and they do too! You see, some very lucky family stands to win a full year's mortgage payments!" In case any viewers have doubts, Dominic nods emphatically. "Now, don't you wish you lived in Hilldale, too?"

He throws out a hand toward the couch. "Allow me to introduce you to the hottest housewives in Hilldale, California!"

"The cameras are now on you, wifeys and hubbies, catching every little frown," Brin shouts over the intercom from the production cave, somewhere deep in the bowels of the mansion. "So, keep those smiles on your faces!"

Through our earbuds, Jack and I hear Brin crow, "Look at them! They're so scared you'd think we were going to show them butt-naked…well, okay, sure some of them. Cameras Three, Four, and Five: as the couples are profiled, be ready to catch some reaction shots…"

Oh. Hell.

Glancing up at the monitors, we are treated to the montage now playing for the viewing audience: the couples, at home and around town, taken from the previously taped audition interviews.

In a moment, the montage freezes on Roger and Sienna, hugging as they watch a sunset from their new hilltop home.

"Even the quiet community of Hilldale has its fair share of suspense," Dominic divulges to the audience. "Or in this case, a suspense novelist. Best-selling author Roger Pembroke and his fiancée, actress Sienna Woodruff, are this exclusive little town's newest residents."

Finally, it cuts to a live close-up of Roger and Sienna. Both are ready for it, with broad smiles and entwined hands. From the monitor, we see that their names are superimposed on their chests.

"Why Roger and Sienna moved here is no mystery," Dominic continues. "Hilldale stokes the imagination, what with its elegant homes, plush lawns—and its many dirty little secrets! But none are as scandalous as Roger and Sienna's."

Hearing this, Roger's smile fades.

Wariness darkens Sienna's eyes, which now shift to Roger just as his move to her. "What the hell does this clown mean by that?" she hisses through clenched teeth.

Roger's lips don't move when he growls back. "Nothing, my dearest. Just play along."

"Our next couple, Professor Gerald Farnham and his wife, Cassandra, have traveled and taught around our war-plagued world. Now, however, they seek peace in this little patch of heaven known as Hilldale, as the professor settles into a new teaching position," Dominic reveals.

One of the live cameras moves in close to the Farnhams. Cassandra's pursed lips can do no better than a tepid grin. On the other hand, her husband moves in as close as possible to her. As he wraps his arm around her waist, she flinches.

"The Farnhams' sons, seventeen-year-old Adam, and fourteen-year-old Sami,—who was handicapped by a terrorist's bomb—

must certainly view their parents as saints for having plucked them out of refugee orphanages." Dominic pauses dramatically. "Still, everyone has a dark side. Will the Farnhams' reveal itself under the scrutiny of their neighbors? Will this friendly little on-air competition be this amazing family's undoing?"

To Cassandra's credit, while the camera lingers, her fury stays clenched tightly in her fists.

"Another couple who will warm your hearts are Patty and James Garrett," Dominic insists.

Hearing her name, Patty freezes like a deer caught in headlights. Her husband's arm goes around her: not to comfort her, but to bolster her before she succeeds in shrinking into the back of the couch.

"This retired military dad and full-time mother are parents to six—yes, count them, six children!" The monitor switches to a pre-recorded video of all the Garrett children in the kitchen of their new home. The oldest girls, Jenna and Jody, dish out food for their siblings, while their mother changes toddler Joey's diaper on the far side of the breakfast banquette.

The oldest boy, Jordan, scowls silently at his coffee mug.

James walks in. The smile on his face seems forced. Still, he propels himself to her side.

But Patty doesn't realize he's there. Just as he bends to kiss her forehead, she rises, and her head slams into his mouth. James pulls back. Angered, he raises his hand.

"Did you see that? He almost exploded!" Brin exclaims jubilantly. "Bring it, big boy! Bring it on!"

In the video, Jordan smirks as he watches their interaction. On the other hand, Jenna's fright causes her to freeze. The milk she's pouring in her sister Juliette's cereal bowl flows onto the table.

The last thing seen before the camera cuts away to Dominic is her father shaking his head angrily at her.

Dominic clicks his tongue sympathetically. "Maybe having four children instead of six in the house leaves a little more time for some passion."

"Or, maybe, instead of six kids, they should have opted for six tuxedos instead," Jack mutters under his breath.

Oh, no—next up is Jack and me. "Prim and proper Donna Stone Craig is envied for her ability to whip up mouthwatering desserts!"

A video of my accepting a blue ribbon during the Hilldale Independence Day Pie Contest morphs into footage of Jack, mowing our lawn without his shirt.

"And her hot hubby, Jack, who is considered the neighborhood DILF." Dominic's last two acid-tinged words don't exactly roll trippingly off his tongue. Suddenly, the screen swipes to this morning's gotcha moment, just as Jack carried me out of the bathroom. His robe has already started its slide off my shoulders. Thank goodness Jack's towel is still tied around his taut waist. Albeit, with what is rising beneath, it was only a matter of time before the producers would have had to move the show to a cable network.

"Slut," Penelope mutters just loud enough for everyone to hear. Arnie's frown indicates that the microphones have picked it up too.

"Love it!" Brin purrs unknowingly in my earbud. "The claws are out! Who's handling Penelope?"

"Um…me," Emma's voice is practically a whisper. "Along with Cassandra and Ariel. Lucy handles Patty, Sienna, and, er, Donna."

"You're Addison's little darling, aren't you? If you want to get out from under him—and knowing him, take me literally, honey—see what you can do to egg her on. Lucy will give you a few pointers, right Lu?"

I don't hear anything, but I presume Lucy is nodding.

"Donna's Aunt Phyllis keeps up with all of Hilldale's comings and goings," Dominic assures the audience as he puts his arm around her.

Aunt Phyllis winks broadly at the camera. "That's right,

Dominic! Make sure the cameras stick with me because I know where all the bodies are buried."

Gulp.

Damn Aunt Phyllis! The last thing I need is for the FBI to start digging up my rosebushes…

Pretend you didn't just read this. *Or else.*

"As for the reigning king and queen of the hill—at least, here in Hilldale"—even Dominic frowns at this weak joke—"look no further than realtor Peter Bing, and his glamorous wife, Penelope."

Penelope's frown flips upside down into a fake smile. Her breasts jut out as she leans into her husband. "Buying your home here—and from whom else, but Hilldale's number one realtor, Peter Bing?—is merely the first step on a journey soon to be filled with fast friends and exciting events! As the town's most active community leader, every civic activity is stamped with Penelope's exacting imprimatur. Be it a school fundraiser or a society gala, not a week goes by in which she isn't cracking the whip over her minions at some function."

I guess that little pun hit too close to home because Peter winces—as do I, when the monitor cuts to the most memorable of the middle school's dances, which took place when terrorists happened to take over the same hotel. Penelope gasps when she sees what is now showing on the monitor: her liquor-soaked gown catching fire just as the hotel's chef lights up a cherries jubilee.

Ah, memories.

Apparently, Penelope remembers it differently. She is scowling so hard at me that I swear I can hear the Botox in her forehead cracking.

Dr. Powell must also be concerned because he lays his palm on her forehead as if to rub out any wrinkles stronger than the Botulinum toxin holding them at bay.

"Will one of Penelope's competitors knock her off her mean-queen throne? If so, our cameras will be there to capture the power play."

Power play? *Give me a break.*

Oops, the logs in the fireplace are dying. But when I rise and poke the embers, Penelope practically jumps out of her skin. Frankly, I don't understand why she's still so skittish. I mean, come on! The last of her third-degree burns is barely visible…

Last but I doubt the least of our group torture, a live shot of the Powells appears on the monitor. As with every previous couple highlighted, their names are superimposed on their chests.

In a voice-over, Dominic proclaims, "Our last couple is someone on everyone's lips—at least, in Hollywood! Hilldale is home to one of Los Angeles's most sought-after plastic surgeons, Franklin Powell, and his most beautiful patient: his wife, Ariel."

Like everyone else, my gaze instinctively shifts from the monitor to Ariel. Ah, so Mother Nature had a little help along the way!

A blush creeps up her neck and her smile wavers, but she keeps her eyes straight ahead. Franklin must have noticed her stress too because he squeezes her hand tight enough that she grimaces.

Dominic drones on: "As the go-to nip-tuck Titan to the stars, Franklin has seen his fair share of body fails. But here in Hilldale, where perfection is the goal of every wife, has his own fallen short of his great expectations?"

Upon hearing this, Ariel purses her surgically plumped lips.

To his credit, Franklin pats her hand reassuringly. But when our eyes meet, he leers at me.

Was he aware that it was caught on camera? My guess is yes.

"Did you see that?" Lucy asks the production crew. "Looks as if the hot doc has a thing for Delicious Donna!"

Hmmm, not such a bad nickname…

Okay, yeah, I'm smiling at this.

"Hey, look—she's flirting back! …Oh, darn it! Hunky Hubby seems oblivious to it," Brin pouts. "As does Franklin's little Barbie doll."

Um—not. Hunky Hubby hears every word you say—

Which is why Jack now turns to glare at him. Love it! He's such a natural at playing the devoted husband…

"Ladies, so that you get to know each other better, we've arranged a girls night out for you!" Dominic's grin widens lasciviously at the thought. "Get ready to be whisked away to the VIP Lounge at the Casa del Mar Hotel, overlooking beautiful Santa Monica Beach. Once there, the bubbly will flow as you let your hair down. Think of it as your opportunity to create a new—well, let's just call it 'sisterhood of the traveling panties.'"

The women stare at him before giggling uncomfortably.

Except for Penelope. She finds his little joke so funny that she cackles hysterically as she slips off the couch. Thank goodness she *is* wearing panties.

Arnie's camera lingers on her while the other cameras catch the horrified expressions of everyone else—including Peter.

"Cut!" Brin finally shouts into the earbuds of her production crew. Laughing raucously, she adds, "Well, what do you know? We've already got our Luscious Lush and we're barely five minutes into the first episode! Hey, you, New Girl: make sure she sobers up before getting into the limo so that she doesn't barf on the way over to the hotel."

"Yeah, okay," Emma mutters.

"Wait!" Lucy's eyes grow big. "Wouldn't barfing on them make the others hate her more?" Lucy points out.

Brin thinks for a moment. "Nah, not worth it. We'll lose the free limo service for the rest of the season. Besides, the Bing bitch gives them so many reasons to hate her anyway."

True that.

"And New Girl, after you sober her up, round up all the heifers and move them into the stretch. Then tell the menfolk and Grandma Moses that they're dismissed for the evening—but that we're holding onto the middle- and high-schoolers. Lots of fun and games still to be had there, I'll bet. Right, Lucy?"

Lucy's response is a hysterical giggle.

Jack squeezes my hand and whispers, "Everything will be all right."

I hope he believes it, because I don't.

My only regret is that Brin won't be in the limo with us. Should one of the doors happen to come unlocked when she leaned (was pushed?) on it, I'd always wonder whether she would have bounced when hitting the pavement at sixty miles an hour.

I'm being herded out with the rest of the women when Ryan whispers in my ear: "A social media account identified with the ISIS chatter has posted a response from an ISP address tied to the *Housewives* mansion."

Jack puts a drink to his lips so that the cameras can't see him before replying: "Almost every one of the husbands has his phone out and is texting or checking for messages."

"The women do, too," I divulge in a murmur.

In other words, the respondent could be any one of the contestants.

"Damn it! The crew as well," Ryan admits. "Arnie is trying to isolate the GPS signal now, but it will be like finding a needle in a haystack, and he may not do it before everyone heads out." He sighs. "Well, at the very least, we know the terrorists are among us."

Yes, but who are they?

For all our sakes, I hope we find them soon.

8

Sex and the City

"Maybe we can be each other's soul mates. And then we can let men be just these great, nice guys to have fun with."
—Charlotte

That city folk live more promiscuous lives is a suburban myth—pshaw! Ladies, here are a few reasons why such a notion is laughable:

- *Reason #1: If there aren't already more women than men in a city, chances are most of the few good men are already married. This is true in seventy-eight out of one-hundred major U.S. cities. If you're lookin' for love, relocate to all the right places: where you'll find wide-open spaces and more men with wide-open hearts.*
- *Reason #2: To paraphrase Forrest Gump, sexy is as sexy does. Love is a many splendored thing even in towns where the highest building is only three stories. As for randiness, low populations don't necessarily translate into small town values. Bottom line: if the Welcome Wagon is a'rockin', don't come a'knockin'.*
- *Reason #3: Even if you do find a handsome bachelor, there has*

got to be a reason he has stayed single all this time. Test: open his refrigerator. If you find body parts, take this as a broad hint that he's not your Prince Charming. (Tip: Don't break up in person. You may never get out alive.)

EVERYTHING WILL BE FINE.

Ha! That's what he said.

For the past half hour, I've repeated it like a mantra in my head as the barbs from my fellow female contestants bounce around the back cabin of the stretch limousine. Between the six of us, we've gone through four bottles of Brut: three shared amongst everyone, while the fourth was slugged back by Penelope as if it were mother's milk to her.

As if reading my mind, Arnie whispers into my ear, "Smile pretty—now and at the Casa del Mar. There are cameras hidden in the eaves at the lounge and also on the waiters, who have been hired to provoke the contestants. Still, while there you'll need to do some reconnaissance. One task is to establish from Ariel a time in which you can plant a Trojan virus on Franklin Powell's home computer. Over the next few days, we'll have to do so on those in all the homes. Your second task tonight is to learn from Patty why James got an early discharge. His file is sealed, but records show it was honorable."

"On it," I murmur.

Despite everyone having had two glasses of champagne already, Cassandra proclaims grandly, "Toast! Here's to six women brave enough to be picked apart by each other in front of all of America!"

She then proceeds to pour from yet another bottle of Brut into our flutes. Her aim is poor enough that the fizzy elixir slops over the top and onto our frocks.

Oh, just dandy.

Suddenly, the limo driver makes a quick stop, causing everyone to slide to the right and spilling the last dregs of bubbly onto our shoes as well. Besides slurring our words, we will now slosh our way into America's hearts and minds.

⌘

"ANOTHER APPLETINI?" ONE OF OUR ALL-MALE WAITERS ASKS Penelope.

By now, you'd think he was clued in to her personal Morse Code: two pats on his ass means yes, she's ready for another drink; whereas one pat and a quick cupping of his dangly parts indicates that she's his for the night.

My guess is that he's pushing the Stoli because he's hoping she'll pass out before he has to earn his tip the hard way.

Even if most of the women in our group weren't already inebriated, the waiters would still make their hearts go pitter-patter. Frankly, I haven't seen this much Grade-A beef outside of a butcher shop; or, better yet, a Chippendales' lounge.

Having been tipped off as to why we're honored with their presence, I've promised my personal pourer a bigger tip if he brings me water instead of vodka. So far, he's earned it.

Penelope isn't the only one of our party who seems to have been tempted. Cassandra perked up at another of our designated boy toys. Perhaps Professor Farnham doesn't make the grade where it counts most. And Patty looked longingly at another of the men, only to blush when catching my sidelong glance.

Suddenly, Patty's waiter hands her a large envelope. Her eyes grow wide, and her hands shake too hard to open the envelope's clasp.

Sienna sighs loudly. "Oh, give it here!" She practically snatches it out of Patty's hand. Opening it, she pulls out a sheet of paper. "Ah! Here we go. Our trials by fire." Her eyes glisten mischievously. "'It's time to play games with your new gal pals!

How about Truth or Dare? Each envelope enclosed here has one of your names on it. Pick the person you feel you can trust most to read it to you. If you fail to answer, you must follow their dare to the letter.'"

Ouch.

Alas, Penelope waves away her personal Mr. Chippendale. Even she knows it's time to get down to the business at hand: making the rest of our lives miserable. "Ooooh, fun! I'll go first."

Sienna slyly smiles as she hands Penelope her envelope. "Choose someone to play with you—unless you'd like me to do the honors."

Penelope snorts loudly. "Sorry, you're not my type."

Sienna looks miffed, but it's Cassandra whose brow raises wickedly. "What a disappointment. Just think of what a tryst between the two of you could do for the ratings."

Penelope's slow burn is visible by the ruddiness of her neck and cheeks. To her credit, for once in her life, she thinks before speaking. Finally, she mutters, "I'll play with…Donna."

Yikes.

"Good luck," Sienna murmurs. Her lack of sincerity is palpable.

I rip open the envelope and first read it to myself.

Oy.

Finally, I take a deep breath and turn to Penelope. "How many men have you had sex with since your marriage to Peter?"

Someone gasps—Ariel, from what I can tell without turning my head in her direction. I'm too mesmerized by the kaleidoscope of emotions playing out on Penelope's face: shock, fear, anger—

Finally, determination. "Too many." She shrugs. "Let's just say I quit counting after it ran into double digits."

Sadly, I believe her. In any event, at the expense of her dignity and her reputation, her answer should keep her in the game.

In ten years' time, when Cheever is an adult and looks back at all of this, what will he think? It should matter to Penelope and Peter. Sadly, I'd guess that the money or the fame matters more.

"Your turn," she says to me. "Truth or Dare, Donna Stone?" She emphasizes my former surname as if I don't deserve the one I took after remarriage. "Have you had an affair with President Lee Chiffray?"

"No." My answer comes not too fast but deadly firm.

The next voice I heard via my Acme earbud is Brin's as she exclaims to her crew: "Ha! Way to bring the drama, Pickled Penelope! That girl is in it to WIN IT! Hey, New Girl!"

Emma's voice comes in, fed from another locale. "Yes?"

"Dig up the details on Stone Cold Donna and POTUS. Where there's smoke, there's got to be fire."

"Will do." Am I the only one who hears the dread in Emma's voice? I hope so. Despite Brin's determination to put me in my place, I plan on being last gal standing—next to my target.

Onward ho. "Who's up next?" I ask brightly.

Cassandra raises her hand. "I'll take the plunge."

Sienna hands her the envelope marked with her name. "And who would you like to 'dare' to speak the truth?"

"Let's see…" As Cassandra's stare moves from Sienna to Ariel and then to Patty, she shakes her head. When it comes to Penelope, she laughs outright.

Finally, she eyes me. "I think I'll stick with the stony Mrs. Craig."

As I take her envelope, I declare, "I promise to warm up." She asked for it: the hot seat.

To that end, her question does not disappoint: "It asks, 'Why did your husband get fired from the University of Dubai?'"

Interesting. Exactly the question I want to know…

If a woman is ashamed, a blush starts at her chest, crawls upward through her neck and as high as her forehead. The face of an outraged woman will change its color to that of a blister. On the other hand, if she is about to lie, the hue of her eyes loses any intensity as it hardens to stony darkness.

Because Cassandra's does the latter, I assume she has steeled herself from the other more telling emotions. Even her laugh is chilly. "My dear, where did you get the silly notion that he was let go? In fact, the dean begged him to stay on, but we felt the boys were at an age that if they were to acclimatize to Gerald's homeland, it was best to move them before they got much older."

"With his academic record, couldn't he have taken a much more prestigious position than one at Hilldale State University?" I insist.

Cassandra's eyes narrow. "Are there two questions on my card?"

"No," I admit. Drat.

"Then I believe the rules allow me to ask my own question, or offer a dare." Her smile is an angry slice of malice. "Let's stay play-mates, Donna, shall we?" She leans in seductively. "What happened to your first husband, Carl?"

"You know about him?" I try to keep the shock out of my voice.

"You're not supposed to answer with another question," she says as she wags a finger in my face. "I heard it from your little friend there, Penelope. She loves to dish on those with wicked pasts." Her smug smile is accompanied by a full-body stretch. "If you're afraid to answer, feel free to take a dare."

"Not at all," I reply nonchalantly. "Carl disappeared. No one knows where. I'd be the last person he'd reach out to since he is now *persona non grata* with our government."

"See? What did I tell you?" Penelope's words slur as she waves a hand in my face. "It pays to have friends—with benefits—in high places. Hers got rid of her ex."

I keep my eyes on Cassandra. I could still take Penelope out with a sidekick that would send her reeling over the terrace rail, but why give Brin yet one more thing to crow about?

Finally, I nod to Sienna. "Who's the next victim?"

Sienna reaches into the folder. Her eyes slide toward Patty. "You're up to bat."

Patty blanches. She hasn't even come to the plate and already she's choking.

Her prayer that the question is a soft ball won't be answered. I totally ignore the ridiculous one on the card (Did you really want six kids, or did your husband make you skip birth control?) and ask the one relevant to Acme: "What was the real reason that your husband left military service?"

"What?" Brin screeches into my ear. "That wasn't the question on the card! Who the hell does she think she is, changing it—"

"Wait!" Emma warns her. "Look at Fatty Patty's reaction!"

She's right. All color has drained from Patty's face. "He was… honorably dis…discharged," she murmurs.

"That wasn't what I asked," I prod her gently but firmly. "What was the real reason he retired?"

"Because…because he wants to spend time with…our children…while they are still young." Her tone is insistent, but her eyes plead with me to let the issue drop.

"Hmmm. Well, maybe there's some drama there after all," Brin grudgingly admits.

I have to grant her wish. There is nothing else I can do without looking like a bully. And besides, now is not the time to get a straight answer from her.

Brin must think otherwise because she declares, "She's lying! I can smell it."

I doubt this, but yes, Patty has released her fear in a pungent sweat.

The others sniff the air before scooting away from us. I too hope to get away from the poor woman's all too obvious anxiety, but it's not to be. Patty's eyes darken. Her voice is a guttural growl: "Your turn, Donna."

Here we go again.

"Will you be chasing after our husbands?"

What? Is she kidding?

From the look on her face, the answer is no. She knows James is attracted to me and honestly wants to know if I reciprocate his desire. I stifle the urge to laugh if only to keep from embarrassing her even more.

"I have no interest in anyone other than my husband. Despite what you've heard otherwise." I nod in Penelope's direction.

The fact that Penelope leers like a jack-o-lantern justifies my suspicion that she's the source of Patty's misinformation.

"Isn't this fun?" Sienna murmurs as she pulls another envelope from the file. Seeing the name on it, she opens it herself with a sad smile. "My, my! I guess you'll see how well I can hide my dirty knickers."

"We can't trust you to read the question." Penelope snatches it out of her hand. It takes her a while to adjust her eyes. When she does, she grumbles, "Why is it in Chinese?"

I sigh as I pluck it out of her hand. It takes me a second to see that she's reading it upside down. I flip it, then read: "Why won't Roger marry you?"

Sienna is the last person in our little entourage that I'd ever expect to blush. "He has proposed. In fact, we're to get married—on a future episode of the show."

"Unfair! Unfair!" Penelope hops up out of her seat. "That means the show will turn into a showcase for you—"

"And all of you will be my bridesmaids," Sienna adds coolly.

"Huh? ...Oh!" Penelope drops back into her chair. "Well, then..."

Sienna rolls her eyes before turning to me. "Since you're already used to it, what say I try to stump you to take a dare?"

I shrug. "Sure, what the heck? Go for it."

"If your ex-husband were to reach out to you, would you report it to the NSA?"

"Of course." No hesitation there. Ha! Even if he weren't already dead, I'd be the first to call anyone and everyone who has ever wanted to lock him up and throw away the key, or better yet, hang him from the highest tree.

I make a hell of a hangman's knot.

Still, I wonder: why would she ask such a thing?

Even as I think this, she pulls yet another envelope from the folder. "Ariel, are you ready to give your ounce of flesh?"

Ariel's Cheshire cat smile fades as she nods. "Why break protocol?" She takes the envelope only to hand it to me.

"Get her to tell you about her daily routine," Arnie reminds me.

I nod slightly, but when I read her real question, I pause.

Interesting.

Okay, I'm game. I read it as is: "Do you know your husband's secrets?"

The blood drains from Ariel's face—proof enough that her response was worth breaking protocol. Livid, she retorts, "He...we keep no secrets from each other! We've known each other too long —since high school. He worked hard through med school; he works just as hard for his practice, and he's an ardent supporter of our family."

"Look, don't shoot the messenger," I remind her gently. "I just asked what is written here." To prove my point, I hand it to her.

She glares down at it. After collecting herself, she nods calmly. "Alright. Sorry I snapped at you. It's just that...well, you'll soon learn—all of you will find out that he's a saint!" She shakes her head angrily. "I should have never agreed to be on this show!"

"Hear, hear," Cassandra mutters.

"That little miss goody two-shoes better not start a mutiny!" Brin shouts in my ear. "She knows we're doing Doctor McDreamy a big favor by having him as a contestant."

Oh, yeah? I wonder what that would be? I guess we'll soon find out.

"We've got to find out when Ariel will next be out of the house," Arnie insists.

"Yep, okay," I promise with a whisper.

"And…the very last envelope is for Donna." Sienna holds it up gleefully.

"Really? I don't think so. At this point, you ladies know more about me than my obstetrician." I stand up. "Feel free to hang in here. I'll catch a cab home."

"I'm going with you," Ariel, Patty, Sienna, and Cassandra say in unison.

Penelope burps loudly. "Party poopers." Her eyes flutter as she flops to the floor.

Mr. Chippendale sighs as he flings her over his shoulder and follows us out the door toward our limousine.

As the others climb in, I pull Ariel to one side. "Look, I hope you aren't still mad at me for having asked the producers' stupid, prying question. Seriously, I like you, and I'd hate for this difficult experience—or any others we have on the show—to stand in the way of us exploring the possibility of friendship."

Her lips stay pursed as she hears me out. When I'm finished, she tears up. "I'd…I'd like that as well. This wasn't how I'd hoped to meet my neighbors and make new friends. And it certainly wasn't what I thought it would be like to be on this show!"

I chuckle. "You and me both. Hey, since we're not due on the set until tomorrow afternoon, why don't we grab a coffee in the morning?"

She smiles as she nods. "Okay…Oh, wait! I can't, sorry. The Hilldale mommy-and-me group is meeting at the country club. We swim with our tots and pre-schoolers."

"No problem," I assure her. "We'll make it the next day instead. My kids will be in school, but feel free to bring your little guy with you."

"I'd appreciate it, since Franklin now only works in the mornings, to accommodate the show." She holds out her hand. "I hope this is the start of a beautiful friendship."

Yes, I take it.

And yes, I feel guilty for doing so. Here's hoping I'm not caught while breaking and entering into her home.

It's been a long day. I can't wait to get home and hug my kids.

I GET HOME TO FIND THAT MY CHILDREN ARE VOMITING IN STEREO.

Thankfully, it's just two of my kids: Mary and Jeff. Trisha is sound asleep.

I relieve Evan, who has been monitoring Jeff's travails as he hovers over the hall bathroom toilet.

Mary is doing the same, in the master bathroom. No way would she let Evan see her in that condition.

As Jack paces between the two bathrooms, I ask, "What the hell happened to them? Was it food poisoning? Should we take them to the hospital?"

Frowning, he replies, hesitantly, "No, and no. They're…um…drunk."

"What? …But—how?" I stare down at Jeff as if I'm seeing him for the very first time. Rebellion and puberty seem to go hand-in-hand, but he's always been my sensible child; the one who looks before he leaps into any abyss his peers run toward like lemmings. "Did Mary cajole him into—"

"No, Mary did nothing wrong. They were tricked into drinking it."

"By whom?" My heart takes a leap. "Evan wouldn't have done this to them—"

Jack puts a finger to his lips and motions for me to join him in the hall closet.

When we're inside, he answers, "While we were at the opening ceremony, the producers put cameras in every room but the bathrooms, as per the contracts we signed."

"In other words, we have to wait until we're taking a shower before having a private conversation?" I ask.

"They didn't think to put one in the playhouse or the kitchen pantry. If any of these secure places are inconvenient, we're to use the code phrase, 'We're running low on olive oil,' at which point Arnie will turn off the audio and turn on a pre-recorded feed of an empty room."

"Just dandy." I close my eyes to wish away my fatigue, if not our situation.

"And, for the record, Evan had nothing to do with Mary and Jeff's conditions. I'm sure he would have picked up on it instantly if he had taken the so-called sodas that Lucy was passing around to the kids."

"She spiked their drinks? That isn't legal!"

"Ironically, she's off the hook because of the roundabout way in which she did it: allowing Cheever and Adam to see where she hid the key to the liquor cabinet. The only thing the camera picked up is the two boys' complicity. After they had spiked everyone's sodas with vodka, they goaded Jeff into a chugging contest."

"So, Cheever has a new minion? How depressing."

"Frankly, it's the other way around. Adam is clearly the top dog in that relationship." Jack rolls his eyes. "If he told Cheever to jump off a roof, my guess is the moron would do it."

"Lucky Adam. He has his mother's dark side," I mutter. "And Mary played chug-a-lug as well? It's so unlike her!"

"Adam went out of his way to make sure she drank as much of it as she could. And Evan felt so sorry for Jenna that he paid more attention to her than to Mary—"

"Let me guess. Mary got jealous and decided that flirting with Adam would get her Evan's attention again." I cross my arms at my waist, if only to keep from slamming a fist against the wall. "And where were you all this time?"

"The husbands were asked to hang out with each other for another half hour. When I brought up that it was a school night, we were told that the children would be escorted home within the hour."

"Okay, I get it. You did what anyone would have done: trusted Addison and his producers." I grab my phone. "We're calling Ryan and telling him game over—"

Jack lays both hands on my shoulders. "Honey, I've already talked to Ryan about it. He asked that we keep to the game plan."

"No way! Not when our children's wellbeing is at stake!"

"Donna, listen." Jack always runs his fingers through his thick dark hair when he knows he's got to convince me of something. I steel myself for what he has to say. "Arnie thinks he can isolate the ISP sending and receiving messages to ISIS, but he needs more time. If we pull out now, we may not get another chance. To assure that we're comfortable with the situation, Ryan has given us his word that he will personally monitor the producers' interaction with the children so that they will never again be put in another compromising position."

I shrug. What am I supposed to do, shoot the messenger? If I'm sighting anyone in the crosshairs, it's Brin and her odious hench-woman, Lucy. "So, the producers have accomplished their goal: they've got the children playing cruel games with each other, just like the adults."

"Shouldn't we tell the kids about the camera-free zones?"

Jack thinks for a moment before nodding. "But we have to warn them to keep it to themselves. If they share it with the other children, I'm sure it will leak back to Brin, and we'll lose our secure spaces."

"Agreed." I take a deep breath. "I guess we should watch the video feed of our children's nationally televised public humiliation."

Jack kisses my forehead. "They've both been through worse—and survived."

He's got a point. When the mean girls on Mary's high school basketball team decided that she threatened their positions on the team, they spiked her water bottle with a roofie. As for Jeff, the peril of being beheaded on national television was a life-changing event. No doubt, what was done to them tonight is unconscionable. But they are mature enough to put it in perspective.

On the other hand, I am now out for blood.

Jack flips on the video feed.

I watch as the children—Evan, Mary, and Jeff, as well as Cheever, Adam, Sami, Jenna, Jason, Jordan, and Jody—circle each other warily.

To Mary's credit, her attempts to warm up Jenna are heartfelt and insistent, despite being met with flat one-word responses and indifferent shrugs.

Evan has been chatting up Adam, who, like he, has just started his senior year at Hilldale High. Adam's way of convincing Evan to leave him alone is to leer at Mary and smirk, "You're one lucky dude, living with her. I'll bet you tap that thing every night." Seeing Evan's scowl, he adds, "What, she won't let you? Don't worry, I'll warm her up for you." As he says this, he looks directly at one of the three cameras in the room.

Why, that little creep!

Evan's fists clench, but he manages to keep his temper in check.

Brin must have seen this too, because she grouses, "Some boyfriend! Damn it; maybe that Adam kid is right and they haven't done the dirty deed as of yet. How boring is that?"

In contrast, Sami eagerly bonds with Jeff over fantasy sports stats. Jeff suggests, "Hey, why don't we start a fantasy league?" To Cheever's chagrin and Adam's annoyance, Sami nods enthusiastically. "Sure, okay."

I wonder, why would Adam want his brother to be ignored by the others?

Apparently, things aren't happening quickly enough for the producers. About twenty minutes into the gathering, Lucy makes her way into the media room. She's carrying two boxes. One is filled with liquor, whereas the other holds sodas. As she walks toward the bar, she asks Cheever and Adam to help her unload them. Unlocking the liquor cabinet, she adds, "Just put the hard stuff in here. You can pass around the sodas." She leaves the key to the liquor cabinet and walks away for ten minutes.

By the time Lucy returns, the boys have set up a tray of drinks spiked with vodka. She must have already known this, since there is a webcam pointed directly at the bar. Lucy smiles, makes a big show of locking the liquor cabinet, pockets the key, and then motions them to pass the drinks around.

At this point, Evan is looking for any excuse to ditch Adam. He finds it in Mary's exasperation with Jenna.

Unfortunately, his method—trying to draw Jenna out of her shell with a few flattering compliments—gets under Mary's skin. Caustically, she mutters to him: "Why do you have to play Prince Charming to every charity case?"

The camera zooms in as he pulls Mary to one side. "Don't you see how sad she is? Grow up! Look outside yourself!" he chides her.

She's hurt that he thinks she can't do so.

Needless to say, when Adam flirtatiously offers Mary a drink, she takes it. "Down the hatch," he exclaims as he tips his glass toward hers in a toast. As she downs her drink, he gives Evan a thumbs-up.

Evan frowns. He doesn't know what just transpired; and yet, instinctively, he doesn't like it.

Cheever, now in his cups, boasts, "My dad makes more money than anyone else's in this room…"

Jordan—Jenna's brother who is closest to Jeff's age—is just as sloppy from chugging his ginger ale. He retorts: "So what? My dad has killed more people than anyone else!"

Mary shakes her head at Jeff. He nods back. He knows enough to keep his mouth shut about the real profession of his parents.

Cheever's eyes narrow at the claim. "Oh, yeah? You're from Nevada, right? What is he, a Mafia hit man?"

"No. He's a drone pilot," Jordan retorts.

Cheever shuts up—but only after a long loud burp.

Cute.

"He's not that anymore," Jason rebuffs his younger brother. "He's just an asshole."

Jody, feeling no pain, giggles at her brother's proclamation.

"He retired, didn't he?" Evan asks.

"Ha! He wishes," Jason mutters. "He—"

Before he can finish his sentence, Jordan throws up on his brother's shoes.

"Shit!" Jason shouts. Angered, he pounds his brother with both fists.

Cheever, revolted by it, upchucks as well.

Soon, Jeff and Mary are barfing out a duet.

Adam laughs so hard at them that he practically falls on the ground.

"Can you turn that off?" Jeff's voice, sounding as if it's underwater, comes from behind us.

I do so before turning around to get a good look at my son: his head hung low, his skin is as wan as parchment paper.

"I'm...sorry. I didn't realize...that..."

"That your drink had been spiked with vodka," I reply. "You're not to blame. It was done to you—by Cheever and Adam."

"I'm going to kill them—" Jeff hiccups loudly, unable to finish his sentence.

"No, you're not," Jack tells him firmly. "We've got it under control."

"Oh...kay, if you say so." Jeff winces, not entirely convinced. "Mom...there's something I saw that seems odd...but...I can't remember what it is now. About one of the kids." He shakes his head, as if hoping this tidbit will be loosened from the fog now clouding his memory.

When it doesn't reveal itself, he sighs.

I kiss his forehead. "Go on to bed. Maybe it'll come to you in the morning."

Jeff nods listlessly as he plods his way up the staircase.

Jack and I follow.

Our cell phones buzz with a text from Brin:

Gentlemen: On the agenda, tomorrow, 10 AM, GOLF, so dress appropriately! The winner doubles his audience votes. And at 7 PM, gentle ladies: there will be a potluck at Cassandra's place: luau theme! Here's a chance to show your culinary skills—and win over HHH's audience. Again, we'll double your family's audience votes!

Jack sighs. "Just great. Four hours of watching Peter take mulligans while Roger and James try to one-up each other with macho asides about…never mind."

Never mind? Like hell. "About what?"

"They…are a couple of rude assholes. Let's just leave it at that."

I give him a sidelong glance. "And you? Are you doing your best to fit into the show's model of DILFiness?"

"Yeah, sure, I'm doing my best to stay in the game—and keep a shred of my dignity."

I snort. "Sadly, I think those goals are mutually exclusive."

He takes my hand and kisses it. "Why don't we let the *Hot Housewives* audience decide that?"

I nod, but I don't think he gets the premise of the show. The audience isn't watching to cheer us on; they're waiting to see how low we'll go.

From what I saw tonight, mud wrestling may be in my future.

I'm glad the day is over, but I don't look forward to tomorrow. The best thing that can happen is that my break-in to Ariel's home provides us with our terrorist so that my family can pull out of this damn TV show.

It's also the worst thing that can happen—for Ariel.

Well, on the upside, I may be proving her right that he's just a sweet husband and father with a heart of gold—and they'll live happily ever after—

A much better reality than living with a terrorist and never knowing it.

Been there, done that.

9

Californication

"Despite all evidence to the contrary, I am a gentleman."
—Hank Moody

The term "Californication" refers to the influx of the state's former residents to other western states. (So get your mind out of the gutter. Yes, I mean YOU.)

Afraid that these hot tub-hopping free-lovers may be seeping over the borders of your fair state too? Not to worry! California's population keeps growing at a rate of least five percent every ten years. This has something to do with its free beaches, beautiful vistas, clean air, mountains, lakes, tech jobs, the entertainment industry...

Does any of this entice you to move west, young woman? By all means, go for it! Don't let these urban myths scare you away from being a California Girl:

- *Myth #1: It never rains there. (Granted, it happens only in certain months. And yes, when it rains, it pours.)*
- *Myth# 2: Earthquakes will reduce it to rubble, or will eventually untether it from the North American continent. (Like ants and Cher—both of which you'll find here—the odds*

are in your favor that you will survive a shake. And no need to worry about floating off anytime soon. Should that ever happen, the Human Race will be long gone from the face of the Earth.)

- *Myth #3: Everyone owns a hot tub. In fact, according to the Hot Tub Availability Index, Nevada and Arkansas have far more of them per one thousand households, followed by the states of Utah, Colorado, Wyoming, and Idaho.*
- *Myth #4: The guy standing behind you only sort of looks like Jake Gyllenhaal. Nope, he doesn't just look like him; he is him.*

Yes, while in the Golden State, you will spot a movie star at least once. Eventually, you'll notice this happening so often that it will not matter. (Hint: In other words, prepare to be underwhelmed.)

- *Myth #5: Dying is optional. Ha! If that were the case, it wouldn't just be the most populous state in the union; it would be the* only *state.*

As lovely as Trisha's voice is when singing in harmony with Katy Perry's latest single, I don't blame Mary at all for covering her ears and grousing, "Aagh! Why couldn't we sleep in today?"

I prod her gently with one of the two glasses of tomato juice that has been blended with raw egg and paprika. "Sweetie, please! Take one more sip. That's my sweet girl! You too, Jeff." There is a smile in my voice and on my face, but not in my heart. Having had hangovers myself, I feel for both Mary and Jeff. Hopefully, this experience will stay with them through their college years. When they'll both reach drinking age, I pray they are smart enough to practice moderation in any and all vices.

Jeff groans but does as asked before ducking below the seat in front of him.

Because Ariel's mommy meet-up is from ten to noon and Jack's golf game doesn't start until eleven-thirty, he's driving everyone to school today so that I can get ready for the task at hand: snooping around the Powell residence. And because he doesn't need Mary and Jeff throwing up on the way to school, maybe I should take Jack's advice and not push so hard about this sure-fire hangover remedy.

Any other day, Evan would have driven to school. But yesterday a jealous enemy scratched the word PLAYER on Evan's car. He'll take it to Hilldale's automotive repair shop this afternoon to get it rubbed out and repainted: not exactly an expense he'd wished to incur, what with college looming in his future. I insist that he do so. We will pay for it, and he can pay us back when he feels the time is right.

As they drive off, I glance down at my watch: eight forty-five.

"You ready?" Arnie asks through my earbud. He's watching via my webcam lenses and satellite. Whereas the Bings', Farnhams', and our household were made camera-ready yesterday, Arnie informs me that the Powells will be getting the same treatment later this afternoon, as well as the Garrett and the Pembroke homes. That way, my break-in won't be seen or heard.

"Let's take a hike," I murmur back.

And I'm off.

I'VE DRESSED FOR A JOG. IN A HIDDEN POCKET OF MY YOGA PANTS ARE tiny scanners that I will insert into any and all computers and cell phones I find on the premises. When connected to the device's audio port, it reads the phone's passcode, opens the device, and releases a Trojan virus that accesses any secure cloud. Acme will then be able to trace all emails, texts, and voice correspondence.

Also, strapped to the small of my back is a tiny device that will detect bomb-making materials, should any be present.

Just in case someone is watching, my route takes me up and around Hilldale Park, before I duck into one of the back alleys used almost exclusively for twice weekly refuse pick-ups. The first of these back alleys puts me directly behind the Powells' large Italian villa-style mansion.

Before coming here, I was able to scrutinize the home's floor plan because Peter Bing was too lazy to take down these schematics from his website after the sale of the house closed. Franklin's office is downstairs, as is the kitchen, a guest powder room, formal living room, formal dining room, and the media room. Upstairs there are four bedrooms, each with an *en suite* bathroom. There is also an upstairs hall powder room. The bedroom used as a nursery is next door to the master suite, which is at the end of the hall. Two other guest rooms are closest to the magnificent double staircase.

Ariel has turned the bonus suite over the garage into her private workout room and home spa. Her husband's handiwork gave her a face and figure that is the envy of every woman who knows her and the fantasy of every man who sees her. She wants to keep it that way.

I put on latex gloves before picking the lock on the door between the alley and the Powell estate. It opens quickly.

The lock on the back door into the kitchen is also a cinch. I step inside—

Only to hear a guttural growl.

I lock eyes with a young mastiff. The dog bares its teeth.

"I didn't know they had a puppy," I mutter to Arnie.

I hear the click of his fingers on his computer keyboard. "Ah… sorry! They got a mastiff when they moved in. A male named Caesar. He's only three years old…but he's been obedience-trained, so…"

In other words, run.

But then I notice the dog door. The flap is exposed so it can go in and out. The wood slat that slides over it is up against the wall beside the door.

I look around. The kitchen counters are spotless. The only food on it is a bowl of fruit. I grab a pear and hold it out to the dog.

My action confuses him. I guess it's not used to Ariel feeding him human food, let alone anything off the counter.

"Caesar! Fetch!" I toss it through the dog door.

Tail wagging, he leaps out after it. I slide the wooden slat over the door's plastic flap.

"Well done!" Arnie's enthusiastic approval makes me smile.

I take a moment to walk the bomb detector through the kitchen. Its alarm stays silent.

I then do the same in the garage, which flanks the alley. Again, nothing.

However, there is a car in the garage. "It has a baby seat in it, but I don't know if the vehicle is Ariel's and she strolled Connor to the mommy meet-up, or if it's the good doctor's. Any idea, Arnie?"

"They both drive the same make and model, and it's the same color as well: a black BMW SUV, which doesn't help matters," Arnie explains. "We stayed with Franklin's vehicle until he cleared the Hilldale entrance gate. By now he should be at his surgery center, or doing hospital rounds before making it back to Hilldale Country Club for the show's golf game later today."

Silently, I make my way to Franklin's home office. The door is shut. I put my ear up to it: again, I hear nothing. I take a moment to look through the keyhole. From what I can tell, the room is empty.

The knob turns soundlessly. I make sure to close the door behind me, just in case Ariel or Franklin comes home unexpectedly.

I'm not at all surprised at the tidiness of Franklin's sumptuous office. The walls are a honey-toned mahogany. There is not a speck of dust on any of the surfaces, let alone the floor-to-ceiling built-in bookcases. They hold medical journals, Franklin's framed university degrees, and photos of him with several celebrities, whom, I suppose, were beneficiaries of his often-touted surgical skills.

One of the pictures has me looking twice: Franklin stands beside the nation's First Lady, Babette Chiffray. At the time it was taken, she wasn't pregnant, and from the way she wears her hair, the photo is at least a couple of years old: more than likely during her widowhood and before her relationship with Lee. It would make sense for a wealthy thirty-something socialite to get a little work done before going back on the market.

Having her as a former patient is certainly a testament to Franklin's surgical skills. Babette's features are flawless. Anyone would guess her age as ten years younger.

Even more impressive are the framed photos of before-and-after pictures of Franklin with indigent child patients, taken both here in the United States and in war-torn Third World countries.

"He must volunteer overseas," Arnie reasons.

A collage shows patients in varying stages of recovery. In one of the photos, a little girl, held on her mother's lap, smiles sweetly despite the bandage over the hole that once was her nose. Three more of the photos document her progress. Another three show progressive results of a burn victim's skin grafts.

A third photo shows Franklin with another IED victim whose face was partially blown away. A tent shields them from the hot white desert sun. Something is written on this picture. I look closely to read it, but I can make out only part of the scrawled words: Franklin's surname. The photo is dated from five years ago. Was it sent to Ariel for the family scrapbook? Or was it previously used for promotional purposes of some charitable work on Franklin's part?

"It looks as if he's serious about giving back," Arnie exclaims. "The guy must be a saint."

"Yes, it's truly impressive," I concede. "Well, the quicker we vet him, the sooner we can cross him off our suspect list."

I continue my search for his computer and cell phone. I guess both items are with him because they aren't on his desk or in any drawers. I also run the bomb detector around the room as well, but it reacts to nothing.

Finally, I reply, "I guess you're right. He's quite a guy."

I walk out the door, but what I hear next causes me to freeze in the foyer:

Noises are coming from upstairs.

Who else is here?

As silently as possible, I climb the stairs, following the sounds —moans—which come from one of the guest bedrooms.

I peek inside. I see Franklin—

And he's making love to someone:

Cassandra.

Arnie whistles loudly in my ear. "Well, what do you know!"

She and Franklin are sitting up in the bed. Their legs are entwined, and their orgasms are spontaneous. His back is to me. Thank goodness Cassandra's eyes are closed. Her sleek chignon has been unfurled. For the first time, I realize how long her hair is: its dark coiling tendrils reach almost to the small of her back.

His cell phone sits on the dresser.

I get on my hands and knees and crawl toward it. When their love calls are at their loudest, I reach up and grab the cell. My fingers fumble to insert the scanner cord, then count off the few minutes needed for it to do its thing…

"Uploaded," Arnie finally whispers.

I've just raised my hand to replace the cell on the dresser when Cassandra opens her eyes.

I freeze.

Her lids shut tightly again as her groans grow even more ecstatic. I take this as my cue to scurry silently downstairs.

"She didn't see you," Arnie assures me. "She's blind without her glasses, which were on the bedside table."

Thank goodness for that.

As I slip out the back door, I grab another pear: right instinct, since Caesar whines so loudly for it that I think he may interrupt their lovemaking. I toss the pear into a bush before running toward the gate and out into the alley.

For the first time, I notice that Cassandra's car is parked in the alley, but a few houses away. A big fat black cat sleeps on its hood.

It's a tribute to the safety of our neighborhood that she left her cellphone in the front center console.

Damn it! When I unlock her door, the alarm goes off.

Startled, the cat arches its back and leaps off the car and onto a garbage can, which then topples over. Still, the cat is curious enough to peek out from around it as I work quickly to scan Cassandra's phone.

"Get away, fast! Cassandra is coming out the back door," Arnie warns me.

I duck behind a garbage dumpster just in time.

Arnie is right: she's now wearing her glasses.

And a smile on her face—

Until she realizes that it is her car's alarm waking the neighborhood to her presence behind her competitor's home.

Seeing the spilled garbage, she curses the cat. It responds with a hiss as she tries to shoo it away.

It misses being run over by a mere few inches.

After she drives off, I jog home as fast as I can.

10

Mad Men

"Fear stimulates my imagination."
—Don Draper

Dear Sir, I have no idea why you are so angry! As for which of us has a right to be morose, let us compare notes:

No matter how much Pilates, yoga, weight training, cross training, or cross-country skiing I do, you will always be the physically stronger sex.

Whereas your hard work will assure you of a fast-tracked career, the fairer sex must leap through twice as many hoops to touch—let alone break—the glass ceiling that blocks her from the executive suite.

The same lascivious phrase coming out of both our mouths can position you as a stud but will brand me as a skank.

I must network, lean in, and put out. When it comes to my acceptance, will any of this turn your shrugs into admiring nods?

No? Well then, I give up—

Not on my goals, dreams, or schemes, but on trying to impress you.

As for whether you can impress me? Well, sir, how fast can you run? Is it faster than a speeding bullet? Just give me a second to load up.

You see, I aim to please: myself.

WHEN I PICK UP THE KIDS FROM SCHOOL, THEY ARE SUBDUED. THIS isn't attributed to any remnants of their hangovers but the ribbing from their classmates as to their new status as television celebrities.

"Apparently, we're all over the news!" Jeff grouses. "The *Today* show ran a segment on underage drinking and used us as their example!"

"That's nothing," Evan grumbles. "*E! Online* is claiming that Adam and I are duking it out over Jenna."

"Well, aren't you?" Mary asks bitterly. "There are photos of you with her posted all over Twitter! The sadder she looks, the more it looks like you want to kiss her—"

"Mary, come on! Can't you tell they've been Photoshopped?" Exasperated, Evan throws up his hands.

"Well…okay, maybe." She shrugs. "Frankly, what's even more embarrassing is that *Cosmopolitan* is running an online poll as to whether I am still a…"—Mary's hesitation is accompanied with burning cheeks—"well, a virgin."

"How dare they! Of course you are!" I nod emphatically to her through the mirror.

She blushes and turns away.

Oh…no.

I shift my stare to Evan.

When his eyes meet mine, they grow wide. He shakes his head emphatically.

Is he signaling, "No, I haven't dared touch your daughter because I know you'd skin me alive and let wild animals feast on my entrails?"

Or is it, "No, she's not a virgin, but even though it's my dastardly doing, please don't kill me and then cut up my body into tiny pieces so that I'm fish food when you dump me in the middle of the Pacific?"

Or perhaps it's, "Okay, her virginity is a thing of the past, but I had nothing to do with its untimely demise because I respect her and you too much—and besides, I've seen how you slice up raw steak, and I'd never want to get that close to you when you have a knife in your hand?"

In any regard, I find it hard to ignore my oldest daughter's deep pink blush, especially when my youngest daughter asks, "What's a virgin? Can I be one too?"

I jerk the car to the curb so quickly that the car behind us barely has time to swerve to miss us. The driver rudely keeps his fist on the horn as he revs his way to the next stop light.

The way the kids stare at me as my head whips around, you'd think I was Linda Blair.

No. Right now I am much, much, scarier…

"Mom! You don't think…" Mary's complexion darkens to the hue of a ripened eggplant.

"I…don't know…unless…" I blather incoherently, "Is there a reason why you'd think that I might have a reason to believe…"

With a quizzical frown, Trisha's head swivels back and forth between us.

Finally, I stutter: "Oh…never mind!"

"So, the answer is no?" Trisha asks.

"No!" Mary and I shout in unison. And then: "I mean yes —you are!"

Satisfied, Trisha wipes her brow. "Good…I think."

We make the rest of the trip home in silence.

Neither Evan nor Mary notices I see as he slips his hand into hers.

Have they?…

Seriously, I can't think about this now.

It's almost five, but Jack still isn't home from the golf game. And, although the first hour of every show is taped, edited, and aired right before the live-on-air last hour, he's still cutting it close.

In the meantime, I've had time to make my contribution to the Hawaiian luau potluck: a pineapple upside-down cake and coconut beer-battered shrimp on skewers.

I've made double of everything so that the kids can have it for dinner. Now that we have the paparazzi camping out on our doorstep, I warn them, "Stay inside and lock the doors."

Frankly, I wish I could lock them in their rooms—alone. Instead, I do the next best thing: As I point to the cameras positioned over our heads.

They take the hint. Big brother is watching. Worse yet, so is Mom.

I shower for the cocktail party that takes place in an hour. Afterward, I slip out into the playhouse to make my call to Ryan regarding my earlier reconnaissance. "Was his cell phone clean?" I ask.

"Yes. And so was Cassandra's." Ryan's sigh echoes mine. We'd both like to find our bad guys and wrap up this mission.

"How's the golf game going?" I ask.

"Jack is scoring—with viewers, too," Ryan assures me, albeit I detect a note of hesitation in his voice.

"Good to hear…I guess."

When he doesn't take my hint for more of an explanation, I add, "Is there something we should be concerned about?"

"Nah. Not really." Hmmm. He's doing a lousy job of convincing me otherwise. "Of course, just because Cassandra is clean doesn't mean Gerald is, too. And he seems to have taken a shine to you."

I snort at that supposition. "Since when?"

"Apparently you've got a couple of admirers. Besides him, James is also a bit…smitten. And Roger has indeed expressed…interest."

"Oh?" I murmur coolly. What the hell is happening out on that golf course?

"It may make things easier to vet them…if you catch my drift."

His drift stinks.

"Yeah, okay," I agree grudgingly. "I'll play up to the producers."

"I know I can count on you to do whatever it takes. From what I gather, Cassandra's party will give you a great start." Before I can respond, he's hung up the phone.

What the hell is happening on that golf course?

I text Arnie a request to put all the cameras watching our house on a video loop before accessing the secure cloud to watch the latest footage on the show—

Oh. My. God. *What the…*

I can't believe what I'm hearing.

I watch the segment until it ends—and yes, it only gets worse.

How dare they!

I don't mean the producers; I mean the husbands.

Okay, yes, and the producers for going along with this hair-brained scheme because it's going to be ratings dynamite.

Grrrr. Wait until Jack gets home.

BY THE TIME JACK FINALLY APPEARS, I'M ALREADY DRESSED FOR Cassandra's cocktail shindig.

When he kisses my forehead, I don't bother to look up; instead, I focus on the task at hand: putting on my make-up.

His face and arms are sunburned, and he's sweaty. "You didn't wait to shower with me?" He's teasing, but he's also disappointed.

"Why should I?" I retort. "With all the 'ample meat on my bones,' there may not be room for both of us in there."

He stops short at my remark. "Oh…um…I guess you downloaded some of the videos from the golf game." He blanches at the thought.

"You betcha." I reach for the bedroom's TV remote control. "Just the edited highlights, mind you," I assure him.

He glances up at the camera in our bedroom. "Are you sure you want to—"

"Don't worry; Arnie has us looped." I shrug. "Huzzah! You won the game, so the Craigs earn a few brownie points! Great for us! And you'll be happy to know that Brin was tickled pink with your little he-man outing overall. However, I don't think the wives will feel the same way."

I flick the remote and fast forward to when the men have reached the third hole and Roger nudges Franklin, who is pulling his putter from his golf bag. "So, tell me: what's it like, being married to a Barbie doll?"

Franklin shrugs but smiles proudly nonetheless. "Yeah, boy, I'm living the dream…but so can you."

Roger stops mid-putt with a smirk. "Are you suggesting that we share and share alike?"

Franklin laughs. "Tell the truth: if Sienna were perfect, would you want to share?"

James, on the edge of the green with his arms crossed, murmurs wistfully, "She's not so hard on the eyes. For that matter, neither is Donna."

Jack, who is pulling his putter from his golf bag, grips it tightly with both hands but says nothing.

Roger shrugs. "There's always room for improvement, right?"

Gerald adds, "If we're talking an attitude adjustment, then yeah, for sure." He then snorts at the thought.

"He wouldn't be laughing if he saw what I did today—his wife in the throes of passion, thanks to the good doctor," I mutter.

Jack's brow raises at the thought, but he keeps mum as I tweak the volume up a notch to catch Franklin's next statement: "I'm saying that every one of your wives could look as gorgeous as Ariel."

"Let me put it this way: they don't all have her 'bone structure,'" James growls. He must be thinking of Patty because he misses the cup by six inches.

"A little liposuction would take care of that," Franklin assures him. "And a tummy tuck. I'd do a breast reduction and raise them, too."

Peter sighs as he watches James line up his ball for a bogey. "Let me tell you: Penelope could use a little lift—both there, and on her ass."

"Yeah, well, you can afford to give it to her," James points out sourly. "We aren't all real estate moguls, you know."

"You don't have to be," Franklin insists. "I'd do it for free."

"Seriously? For free?" Hearing this, James's putt misses the cup again. But from the look on his face, he couldn't care less.

"Sure. The producers have already agreed to my making the offer to all of the Housewives—for a good cause, in fact. The usual cost of the procedures will be matched by the show to my charity, Plastic Surgeons Without Borders."

Roger frowns. "Never heard of it."

"Its mission is to provide lifesaving surgeries to patients who are victims of war. I founded it in honor of my brother, who died while serving overseas." He looks down at his feet. "In fact, *Hot Housewives of Hilldale* will also match, two dollars-to-one, any donations made to the charity from the audience. It's a win-win for everyone, don't you agree?"

Peter's eyes open wide. "But…wouldn't the show have to stop filming for the women to recover from surgery?"

"Not really. The latest procedures are laparoscopic. You can hardly see the incisions, and healing is quick. They'll have around-the-clock care so that they'll be up on their feet in a couple of days, tops. The producers will intercut the Housewives' recovery shots with ones showing how we husbands are picking up the slack with the children." His wink to the other men is barely perceptible by the camera.

On the other hand, to Jack's credit, his poker face would give him a winning hand at a Vegas card table.

"What do you say, Jack?" Peter asks hopefully.

Jack says nothing. Instead, he makes his putt.

The ball curves toward the cup and circles it slowly before it drops in.

Finally, he replies, "I say if any of the wives want to do it, they should go for it."

Roger laughs suggestively. "I think what Peter is asking is if you want in on this very generous offer—for Donna."

Jack shrugs. "It's true that no one's perfect. Granted, Donna has ample meat on her bones. But, no, I don't see anything wrong with my wife."

Roger smirks knowingly. "You wouldn't want to see some of the fat carved from that sweet meat?"

Jack, bemused, shakes his head. "Beauty is in the eye of the beholder, right?"

"I get it. You actually like those luscious love handles! Pushing on the cushion, and all that, eh?" Gerald asks insistently.

I stand up and point to my hips. "Pinch an inch! I dare you!"

Jack smiles as he pinches one of my cheeks—on my face.

"Sienna and I are tying the knot. She's already looking at skin-tight wedding dresses. Convincing her to accept Franklin's very generous offer will be a cinch," Roger predicts.

Peter rolls his eyes. "I'll get no flack from Penelope. Hell, she'll be first in line!"

"Patty won't say no, either," proclaims James. His grimace suggests he'll make her life hell if she does.

Gerald thinks for a moment. "I'm all for it, but I think Cassandra will need a little convincing."

"I'll have a talk with her," Franklin promises him. "In fact, let me announce it to all the wives at the luau tonight. I'm sure the producers would appreciate it, and the women will be more receptive with the cameras rolling." He turns to Jack. "And what about Donna?"

Jack shrugs. "It's not my decision. You'll have to ask her yourself."

Franklin pats him on the back. "There's got to be one little thing about her that bothers you."

Jack shakes his head adamantly. "Nope, not a thing."

"You know, hate is a form of love too. Whatever you point out may be the one thing she loathes about herself. If you're more honest with her as to how she can be a wee bit more beautiful in your eyes, you'll be giving her your permission to act on it."

The camera doesn't pick up the dark shadow that crosses Jack's eyes—the one that I've seen while he's choked a man to death.

But instead of rebuffing him, Jack stoops to retrieve his golf ball.

Thank you, Jack.

Roger and James exchange knowing smiles. Any doubts the men have that their wives—and I—may finally encompass their wildest fantasies and feminine ideals are now reflected in their slight smiles and their dreamy gazes.

Brin must have seen it as well, because she shouted, "Boo-yah! I'll bet we'll get some masturbation scenes that make the American Pie franchise look lame!"

"They *are* lame," Emma murmurs.

"What was that, New Girl? Did you say you want to monitor the men's audio feeds when they step into the little boys' room?" I can't see Lucy's smirk, but I can hear it.

"No...I...didn't say a word," Emma mutters.

"Hey, now, that's not a bad idea!" Brin exclaims. "Get on it, New Girl. But give us moans, not grunts and groans... Hey, did I just rhyme? Does that make me a rapper?"

I can't stomach any more of this crap. I click the OFF button on the TV remote before facing Jack. "How dare he suggest I don't want to help out a great cause! Hell, I'll give money not to be butchered by the illustrious Dr. Frankenstein—I mean Dr. Franklin Powell."

"Donna, hon…calm down! It's not as if he's some hack or something—"

"Don't tell me to calm down!" Despite my hyperventilating, a dreadful thought hits me: "Oh, my God! …Jack, be honest now: is there anything you'd change about me?"

He thinks for a moment. "Okay, yeah."

Here it comes…

"I'd like it if you smiled more. I don't see that as your fault. It's more mine."

But of course, he knows how to calm me down.

And to make me smile.

No, make that laugh until it hurts. Better to bruise my funny bone than my ego, right? "Agreed, it's all your fault," I mutter. "I think the best solution is that we have sex more often."

Jack laughs as he pulls me down onto the bed on top of him. "I thought you'd never ask."

We've arrived late to Cassandra's shindig. My bad. The thought of being told I need a nip/tuck in front of an audience of several million doesn't exactly have me running out the door.

For the luau, I've wrapped a red floral sarong low on my hips. It hugs every curve. Above it, I wear a white lace strapless bandeau top. It is cropped high enough to expose my midriff. (Okay, yes, I want to prove to anyone watching that I am practically perfect in every way.) To complete the look, I have a white lei around my neck, and a bright red hibiscus flower in my hair.

Except for Patty who wears a polka-dotted muumuu, and Aunt Phyllis who wears a grass skirt and a couple of coconut half-shells over her breasts, the other women are also in form-fitting sarongs, including our hostess.

And yes, I fought the good fight to get Aunt Phyllis into something less showy, to no avail.

"Don't give me any lip, young lady!" she retorted. "I'm competing with you and every other housewife bombshell for air time, so I've got to pull out all the stops!"

"Aunt Phyllis, please! Do you really think this is the best way to go about it?" My voice drops into the gentle but firm tone I use with my children when they are stubbornly set on getting their way.

As my aunt's shoulders sag, her coconuts droop almost to her waist. She tightens the grass shoulder strap with one hand but uses the other to shake a finger at me. "Ha! if this were *Survivor*, I'd be tossing boulders off cliffs and onto the rest of you—naked— if that's what it took to stay on the show!"

"Well, then, thank God it's not," Jack muttered under his breath.

Amen.

Cupping her coconuts, Aunt Phyllis huffed, "You'll thank me later for wearing this getup."

As for the husbands, they're wearing Hawaiian shirts and shorts or slacks. Jack comes in a very tight T-shirt (because it belongs to Evan) with the slogan, SURF'S UP. I'm sure he—we— are racking up bonus points for his effort to be extra-hunky.

We're all mic'ed and the cameras are rolling: at least the one following Penelope and Sienna. And apparently, there's some drama going on between the Garrets as well. Patty's eyes are swollen from tears, and James is reading her the riot act.

Did he give her a heads-up on what to expect? In a way, that would have been kinder on his part. If she's dead-set opposed to the idea, catching her disgust on camera will only give him a reason to bully her into it—in front of the show's audience.

I'm speaking for myself. Despite having a heads-up on

tonight's drama, I still don't know how I'll react when Franklin begins his detailed analysis of my physical imperfections.

I might just give him a few imperfections of his own. A broken nose would be a start.

Before we followed Aunt Phyllis into the luau, Jack convinced me that my initial reaction—a knife to his heart—might be a bit extreme. "Remember, it's live television, and you'd have a lot of explaining to do to the kids, not to mention to Acme"— he points out—"especially since you have just cleared Franklin as a suspect."

I sighed grudgingly. "I see your point. It might be considered an overreaction."

"You think?" Jack smirks.

On the other hand, a sufficient dose of Saxitoxin in his morning Starbucks grande cup would be a bit more subtle—

Nah. Just kidding. Heck, the man is practically a saint! And besides, there are others more deserving of a quick and painful demise…

Stay focused…stay focused…

Right now I force myself to tune into the calypso band playing *It's a Wonderful World* in the only corner of the pool area not already taken up by one of the three bars that have been set up by the cater-waiters. Abu tends the one that Arnie has predicted will be closest to the drama. I'd like to know how he figured this out.

Okay, maybe I really don't want to know.

Our hostess sees us and waves us over.

Jack presses me in the small of my back in her direction. Why do I feel as if I'm being led to my last supper? And who'd have guessed it would include poi?

11

Nip/Tuck

"Beauty is a curse on the world. It keeps us from seeing who the
real monsters are."
—The Carver, in *Nip/Tuck*

Don't recognize the person staring back at you in the mirror?

No, she isn't your mother—

She is you.

*And while it's too late to stifle the mortified groan elicited from this
realization, or to stop the tears rolling down onto your hollowed out
withered cheeks, before your look of horror hardens permanently in your
already finely lined face, do the following:*

*First, ask around for a competent plastic surgeon. Consider seeking
out the one or two doctors whose patients use such accolades as
"Excellent," "Highly skilled," and "Made me perfect!"*

*(However, if these proclamations are ushered forth from a newly
sculpted mouth which is as wide as that of the killer clown in your worst
nightmare, cross the referral off your list.)*

*Next, put together a list of interview questions for potential doctors.
For example, you can ask to see pictures of his successes—and his botched
jobs. If he refuses to show you the latter, or claims there have been none,*

don't just take his word for it. Instead, do an Internet search. (Suggestion: By using his name and the keyword "lawsuit," you'll have your answer quickly enough.)

And finally, don't expect things to go without a hitch. However, if said hitch has you crying every time you look at the "new you" in the mirror, it's time to search for a lawyer who can surgically remove some of the compensation from their malpractice insurance.

"Your shrimp is a big hit." Cassandra's compliment is a grudging tribute at best.

Her roast pig on a spit was ignored by Sienna, who is apparently pescatarian. Penelope followed her lead. Apparently, she has decided that clinging to Sienna and copying everything the bride-to-be does is endearing, and she'll be chosen as Sienna's matron of honor.

Their snubs of the main course, made on camera, were not well received by our hostess, who barely contained her urge to hoist the whole pig off the spit and slap their retreating backsides with it.

Truly, Cassandra's restraint was admirable. I'm sure her afternoon delight has something to do with it.

"The roast pig is delicious too," I offer. "You've done a great job pulling this off on such short notice."

"I can't take all the credit, nor would I. In fact, I plan on resisting every attempt this show makes of turning us into Hilldale's version of *The Stepford Wives*." With a triumphant smile, she declares this directly to the camera covering us: Abu's. "My guests are lucky. One thing Hilldale has over a Middle-Eastern war zone is a few good caterers—and pork." She nods toward the plate in my hand. "I miss it."

I glance down at her plate, which contains just a few spinach leaves and some carrot sticks. "Pork?" I wonder out loud. "Well... there's plenty of it here tonight, so dig in."

Ouch. Is she wincing because I've reminded her about Sienna and Penelope's snubs?

As if in answer to my question, she flicks a wrist at the hubbub around us. "I was referring to the Middle East. It's so much more real than any of this."

"I'm truly sorry you're not happy here," I muster. You certainly seemed joyous in Franklin's bed. "Cassandra, if, like you said, that Gerald was asked to stay in Dubai, why not return there?"

Her brow furrows. "You of all people should understand a craving for some semblance of normalcy."

"I don't get your implication," I reply coolly. "I've lived here in Hilldale for almost eight years. If it's anything, it's normal to the point of boring."

Her laughter rings hollow in its bitterness. "Your pal, Penelope, makes it sound anything but! In fact, if we're to believe her, you're a—"

"Okay, wifeys and hubbies, gather round!" Brin's omnipotent bellow blares through the speaker system. "Let's start with the good news! Last night's ratings were through the roof in all categories, Women 18-34, Men 18-54, Teens 14-19…you name it! We were not only number one in our time slot, but for the evening as well! And already in tonight's first hour, we've had a fifteen percent increase in viewership! And there's a three-way tie for first place between the Craigs, the Farnhams, and surprise, surprise, the Bings! The viewers must feel that there's an intervention in your future, Penelope!"

At first, Penelope's response is ecstatic—until Lucy tosses her a copy of *People* magazine. A small photo of her being carried out over the shoulder of her Chippendales-worthy waiter at the Casa del Mar is dwarfed by the cover picture, which must have been taken when the *Housewives of Hilldale*'s cameras caught me in Jack's arms as we came out of the bathroom. His robe is sloping off my shoulder, and there is a humongous bulge under the towel wrapped around his waist.

Even Jack does a doubletake at what he sees. "Wow! I'm that, er, gifted?"

It's up to me, his wife, to break the news to him. "Sorry, darling, only in your dreams. You've been Photoshopped."

"Now, the rest of you laggardly Housewives better bring your A-Game tonight! Your mortgage payment is counting on us," Brin warns us. "Can you redeem yourselves? We'll make it easy for you! Our illustrious host, Dominic, has an announcement that is sure to 'perk' you up—and I do mean this in the best way possible! Everyone who plays along will get that much closer to winning our little competition."

The show's competitive couples exchange glances: the wives are inquisitive, whereas their husbands, already in the know, smile supremely.

"We're live in THREE...TWO...ONE!" Brin's voice fades into oblivion.

If only she'd do the same.

Dominic, in one of his new tuxes, makes his entrance onto the tiki lamp-lit ramp over the Olympic-sized swimming pool to a frantic drumbeat worthy of the Skull Island natives' announcement of their human sacrifice to King Kong. The ear-splitting pounding stops only when he reaches the center of the span. He then turns to stare directly into a camera that has floated down over our heads on the long-arm of a jib. "Welcome back to the second consecutive night of *Hot Housewives of Hilldale*, where the question on everyone's mind is surely"—he pauses, in order to raise a brow at the camera—"How far will she go to please him?'"

Oh, brother! Can't he come up with something more original than "the question on everyone's" whatever?

"We have an offer that no woman can refuse—at least not if they want to earn their families the much-needed bonus points to win the equivalent of one year's mortgage paid in full!" Dominic's arm swings in the direction of Ariel and Franklin. "One of our contestants, Ariel Powell, is married to one of the prominent plastic surgeons in the world: Dr. Franklin Powell—"

Another camera goes in close on the couple.

"—And, ladies, he's got an offer you'll find hard to refuse." Dominic smiles broadly. "Take it away, Dr. Frank!"

"—enstein," I mutter under my breath.

"Donna…" Jack's warning comes with a squeeze on my arm.

Or maybe he's getting ready to restrain me from kicking in the good doctor's teeth when he begins detailing all my imperfections.

To his credit, even Franklin frowns at Dominic's nickname for him. But when he sees the camera's red light, he turns that frown upside down and takes a step forward, his hand still in his wife's. Ariel looks just as surprised as the rest of the wives, so I doubt she's in on the joke.

Yes, I mean joke. Should be interesting if any of the other women feel the same way.

"Each of us is here on the show for different reasons, and every one of those reasons is important to you," Franklin replies. "Mine happens to be the need to help a charity near and dear to my heart: Plastic Surgeons Without Borders. It's a relatively new organization, but it has an incredible mission. It goes into war-torn countries to help victims recover from their debilitating injuries."

He pauses to let the cameras capture the head nods and murmurs of admiration before adding, "Everyone should feel good when they look into the mirror. I'm offering the show's Housewives the chance to all look their best—at no cost to any of you. Instead, the show's producers will give a donation equal to the standard cost of each procedure you choose to undergo. Additionally, during the seven-day run of this show, every dollar that viewers donate to Plastic Surgeons without Borders will be matched by the producers as well."

Needless to say, at first the women are too stunned to talk.

Penelope is the first one to react. She squeals, "I am so in!" She practically runs to Franklin. "I know my procedures won't be many, but anything for, er, a great cause, right?"

He leans into her face for a really good look. Taken aback, she frowns. "What? Why are you looking at me that way?"

"Oh…nothing." He shrugs, but his eyes haven't left her face. "If you want my opinion—"

"Of course I do!" she assures him emphatically.

"Well, then," Franklin takes a step back to get a better look. "Your face is wonderfully proportioned, so nothing as drastic as, say, any facial contouring—you know, rhinoplasty, or chin or cheek implants."

Penelope practically preens at his compliment.

"As for facial rejuvenation, you've got about, say five years before considering a facelift," he continues. "I'd even forego an eye lift or brow lift for another year or two. If you sign up now, the offer to do it for free still stands, since the producers are willing to donate the equivalent of the costs to the charity—and match viewer donations as well."

"Sure, okay, sign me up for the works—I mean, for whatever I can do to help such a worthy cause and improve my appearance." She stumbles over her obvious mistakes.

"In fact, I can say that about every woman here," he adds.

That alone is enough to wipe the smile off her face.

"But every one of you could use a little body contouring: a tummy tuck for, say, you, Penelope; and maybe Cassandra. Indeed, Donna." He smiles apologetically to those he's named.

Is my slow burn picked up by the cameras? How about my sleight of hand as I slide the icepick off the bar beside me?

"And if Patty wanted it, I'd perform liposuction," Franklin adds nonchalantly.

"She wants it alright," James growls emphatically.

All eyes—and cameras—turn to his wife.

She purses her mouth but nods reluctantly.

No, the decision is not hers.

Sienna raises her hand slowly. "Can this be done before our wedding?" She raises her head supremely. "It takes place on the last day of the show."

Franklin nods. "As for a breast lift or enhancement"—he looks pointedly at her waif-worthy chest—"I can schedule you and the rest of the ladies as early as tomorrow. I've cleared my schedule to accommodate the show's schedule. And because it's a laparoscopic procedure, I'll have you on your feet in no time. In fact, Ariel had her enhancement just two weeks ago."

All eyes slide toward the incomparably beautiful woman at his side.

At the unwanted attention, her cheeks pink up and her mouth puckers downward. Her sarong is strapless, and yet despite the deep dip between her ample breasts, they are magically elevated and outward over her wasp waist and slim hips.

Gerald is practically salivating.

"The producers are excited about the opportunity to keep tabs on your recovery as well," Franklin promises. "They feel that helping women feel good about themselves is important."

"I don't care if the whole world thinks I'm ugly! I won't do it," Cassandra proclaims bluntly. Her glare is directed at Franklin.

For a second, his smile levels out into a grimace. He forces the grin back into place.

Gerald puts his arm around his wife's waist. Tepidly he murmurs, "Franklin is only asking that you think it over, dear."

"You're not serious, are you?" She turns toward him and squints as if seeing Gerald for the very first time. "Look, I'm aware of what you see as my 'limitations.' Rest assured, dear husband, I've never let yours stand in the way of our marriage."

Way. To. Go.

He stutters before finding what he hopes are the right words: "I was only suggesting that you take advantage of his very generous offer for a good cause."

"Were you?" The arch of her eyebrow belies her belief in this. "I see no reason to mutilate my body for anyone's so-called cause. If you feel differently, feel free to consider a tummy tuck or liposuction." Her eyes drop pointedly below his waist. "By the way, I hear they're also making incredible inroads with penile implant surgeries."

Her harsh words pierce what little bravado Gerald has left. He shrinks before our eyes.

The visual leaves a lot to be desired.

Despite the fact that it's Cassandra's home, she thinks nothing of making her exit up the foyer's grand staircase.

Brin hoots with glee. "Way to go, Caustic Cassandra!"

Lucy snickers, "Make that Castrating Cassandra."

"Love it! Yes!" Brin screeches. "I'll offer Gerald a bonus if he can make her change her mind between now and tomorrow's show. Knowing their money problems, it should be a cinch." She chuckles deviously. "Who wants to take a side bet that he'll do it?"

The rumbling in the control room doesn't give her much hope, nor do the head shakes of the production crew who hear her every word.

As much as I'd love to follow Cassandra upstairs with a bottle of bubbly for a round of sistah solidarity, my mandate is to stay in the game—

But I don't take that to mean that I have to go under the knife—

Unless the knife is being held to my throat, in which case I wouldn't be worried about how pretty I was when I woke up, but whether I'd be waking up at all.

I'd sure fight like hell to make sure I do. Here, I do the next best thing: I clap, slowly and loudly. "Smart woman," I say just loud enough for the audio boom to catch it.

"Oh, hell," Lucy sighs. "We've got a mutiny."

"Want to bet?" Brin retorts. "I'll make Hunky Hubby the same deal. He'll make sure Delicious Donna plays ball."

Sienna says in a loud voice: "What time would you like me at your office, Doctor Powell?"

Penelope shoves her aside. "I said yes first!"

"Not to worry, ladies. Penelope, I'll see you at seven, sharp. Sienna, let's shoot for eleven."

James nudges Patty forward. "Will you have time for me as well?"

Franklin takes both her hands in his. "I'll always have time for you, Patty," he assures her. "Why don't we say two o'clock tomorrow?"

Dominic turns to the cameras. "That's four takers, and two who have elected to stay au natural." He rolls his eyes.

I'd like to push a boulder on top of him, then sit on it while he squirms and begs for mercy.

"How about you, *Hot Housewives* audience?" he continues. "Are Cassandra and Donna passing up a great opportunity? Just text us at the toll-free number at the bottom of your screen with the word 'niptuck' and the name of the Housewives you feel could use a little tender loving care—despite their stubbornness."

Stubborn—me? That dumbass, Dominic, will need a little TLC when I get through with him…

Ryan proves he's of like mind when he mutters into my earbud: "What's he trying to do, get you Craigs kicked off the show? Not that you aren't doing a good enough job on your own."

I steel my lips to keep from frowning. Jack has to turn away from the camera to hide his scowl.

Dominic smiles obliviously at the camera. "And after our fabulous Hot Housewife make-over, you, our audience, will vote on which transformation was the most beautiful! The winner will earn the equivalent of triple bonus votes toward the grand prize!"

Well, isn't that great? There go our piddly double bonus votes for my skewers and Jack's golf game…

Aunt Phyllis points to her chest. "Hey, Doc, I'll let you perk up these puppies too!"

Franklin grimaces uneasily before nodding reluctantly.

She's so excited that she runs to him for a hug. But then a brisk breeze blows the fronds of Aunt Phyllis's grass skirt toward the outdoor fire pit. The next thing we see is it going up in flames—

Franklin sweeps her up in his arms and jumps into the pool with her.

Jack jumps in as well.

The rest of us run to the pool's edge. The steam rises so thickly that we can't see how much damage has been done to my poor dear aunt—

Apparently not much. She's still in Franklin's arms as he makes his way to the pool's steps. As he walks up, she hugs his neck and exclaims, "My hero!"

Frankly, I'd say Abu deserves the title. He's kept the camera on their faces, as opposed to Phyllis's hips, which, now skirtless, reveal every bulge fighting through her flesh-toned Spanx.

The show's closing credits are now rolling across the screen.

"Unwittingly, the old broad may have kept the Craigs in the game," Lucy declares from the control room.

Lucky us.

"Nah," Brin assures her. "I mean, sure, we'll grant them a few bonus points for her going under the knife. But it's still up to Hunky Hubby."

By the time Brin's loud shout, "Cut!" echoes through the speakers above our heads, Jack has climbed out of the pool.

I grab two pool towels. After tossing one to Jack, I wrap the other around Aunt Phyllis.

As the on-set doctor and nurse team shuttle her to the poolside cabana for a quick check-up, I nudge Franklin to one side. "Thank you for saving my aunt. She might have been burned alive!"

He shrugs. "Burns at her age don't heal quickly. Besides, I have a full enough day tomorrow without having to take time out for skin grafts."

"Why, of course," I retort dryly. "How does that Hippocratic oath go again? Oh, yes! 'The show must go on.'"

To his credit, his usual mask of bland geniality never slips.

Only the tenor of his voice betrays his anger. "Your aunt's foolishness is charming to some, but it could also be dangerous. In this instance, at the very least it could have cost her years of pain, and at the very most, her life. If you assume my reasons for being here are any less noble than yours, let me assure you, Mrs. Craig, they are not. The producers have given me the opportunity to turn a very bright spotlight on the victims of the world's wars, and I plan on using it."

He doesn't feel the need for me to respond. Instead, he walks away.

Jack waits until Franklin is out of earshot before coming over. "Whatever you said sure got under his skin." Noting my grimace, he adds, "Sorry, hon, for the poor choice of words."

"Yes, well, I had the audacity to question his pureness of heart." I shrug. "Shame on me."

"First you rudely turn down his offer to make you my ideal woman, and then you hurt his feelings?" Jack shakes his head in mock anger. "Just wait until I get you home, young lady!"

I nuzzle his neck with my lips. "The sooner, the better," I murmur.

"Don't tell me that the Craigs are into a little discipline role-playing! How adorable is that?" Brin chortles behind us. "How many lashes will it take to get her to agree to a boob job? No, no, don't tell me, lover boy, don't tell me. Let's just catch it on video, shall we? Oh!...And before we air it, we'll let the viewers take bets! For every smack over ten, we'll double your viewer votes just to sweeten the deal."

I close a hand over Jack's clenched fist before it moves in the direction of her face.

He takes a deep breath before speaking. "Brin, you know as well as I do that Donna makes her own decisions. As for Franklin's offer, she's given her answer. Case closed."

The gaiety in Brin's dark chuckle sends a shiver up my spine. "Okay, I get it: the Comely Craigs aren't into making stag films. If only the Bings felt the same way." She rolls her eyes. "If I have to hear Peter choke out 'mistress of madness' through his ball gag one more time, I may have to cut them from the show. I'll let you in on a little secret: it's turning me off to porn. Can you believe it, me?" She shrugs. "But I've got to give them credit. They'll do anything to win this thing"—her smile disappears—"unlike the two of you." Her eyes shift to me. "Donna, would you mind if I had a private conversation with Jack? I promise to release him in"—she looks at her watch—"an hour, tops. Feel free to mosey on home."

"Say yes," Ryan's voice, coming in through my earbud, isn't a suggestion. It's a command.

Of course, Jack hears it as well. His mouth, hard and fierce, opens—

But I speak first. "Sure, Brin, you can have him for as long as you need."

I pull Jack into a lingering kiss and then walk away without a backward glance.

There is nothing Brin can do or say to change Jack's feelings toward her or how we are handling this mission.

And besides, I can hear and see what's happening.

"Thank you, Donna," Ryan says. "Now, if you don't mind, I'd like to see you. I want to discuss your next task—in private."

Not a good sign.

"And by the way, we'll be going dark on Jack now," he adds.

What the…why?

He doesn't wait for me to protest. Jack's audio and video feeds vanish to my ears and eyes.

Yes, I'm angry.

I look forward to telling Ryan so in person.

____

12

Breaking Bad

____

"There's no honor among thieves…except for us, of course."
—Saul Goodman

The term "breaking bad," is a Southern colloquialism that means challenging authority.

You know, raising hell.

When in fact playing the hell raiser, here are a few do's and don'ts:

Do embody the role! (A tepid stance on being a bad ass makes you a half-ass. In other words, no one will cower. Instead, they will snicker.)

Don't let the law stand in your way! Some people are above it, proving that there are always ways around it. (Unfortunately, most of these paths can put you six feet under.)

Do remember that no one likes an outlaw, but everyone loves Robin Hood! (In other words, share the wealth.)

Finally, don't expect to live a long and prosperous life. It's not true that only the good die young. Those who live hard and fast seem to go belly up at a good clip as well.

And, as we all know, only Superman is faster than a speeding bullet.

∽

You catch more flies with honey than with vinegar.

I've heard that homily all my life. I'm about to put it to the test.

Apparently, so is Ryan. He's smiling when I open the door to his private office.

Great, yeah, two can play this game…

"Hi, boss. What's up?" I practically giggle as I plop down in one of the chairs in front of his desk.

His smile broadens, but his eyes are wary. "Thank you for joining me after such a long day. And congratulations on the clearances of Franklin and Cassandra."

I bat my eyes. "All in a day's work."

"Tomorrow may be easier. Brin has put Emma in charge of ferrying the patients to and from the medical office."

"Why?" I smirk. "Is she afraid they'll bail on Franklin's marvelous offer?"

"Perhaps." He shrugs. "In any regard, it allows Emma to scan their cell phones while they go under the knife, which is a plus for us." He leans in slightly. "It still leaves us to scan Ariel's phone, not to mention James's, Gerald's, Peter's, and Roger's—which is where you come in."

Always the team player, I nod enthusiastically. "But of course."

"All of the patients are to be picked up by seven tomorrow, which gives you plenty of time to make the rounds. If you're looking for an excuse to meet with their husbands, why not do the neighborly thing and drop off a casserole? That way, you can get them, er, talking."

"Yeah, right." Or whatever. "So, who's first?"

"Ideally, James." Ryan pauses. "I…have a gut feeling about him. Something is just…well, not right with him."

"You can say that again," I mutter. "Who would you prefer next?"

"Roger. If he's involved in a National Security leak, POTUS will want to know as soon as possible."

"But of course."

"Speaking of POTUS, he'll be in town toward the end of the week." Ryan shifts uncomfortably in his chair.

I can't say that I blame him. With a terrorist in the 'hood, having Lee in our midst only complicates things. "Surely you'll talk him out of it!"

"Why waste my breath? Only you have that super power."

I blush because he's right. "Would you like me to try?" Say no…say no…

Ryan's brow creases in contemplation. "Let me think about it. As much as I don't like using him as bait, it may come down to that, if you don't turn up any clues in the next few days. With a big fish swimming within reach, our suspect may make a mistake and show his hand. In the meantime, I have no doubt you'll do every-thing within your power to get our man." He stands up. It's my cue to take my leave.

Suddenly, I realize that Ryan hasn't brought up my refusal to take Franklin's offer. Now, why is that?

"One more thing," I begin nonchalantly. "I want to thank you for honoring my decision not to go under the knife for this stupid show."

"No need to thank me. It was always your decision to make. However, if you had felt you needed some, er, enhancement, I'm sure you would have taken the good doctor up on his offer." Ryan smothers a smile. "As it turns out, such a drastic measure isn't necessary."

"Oh, yeah…because Aunt Phyllis wants the operation." Until I can talk her out of it.

"No." He looks down.

"Because the Craigs are leading with points?" I press.

"You aren't, but I've no doubt you'll catch up."

Funny. He doesn't sound like it. "So, why then, Ryan?" I ask impatiently.

He hesitates. Finally, he answers: "Brin and Jack have come to…an understanding."

My heart seems to want to jump out of my chest. Just what the hell does that mean?

"It worked out better for Acme," he assures me.

"Sure, okay." I check my nails for chipped polish.

Later, I may be flicking blood off of them. Brin's.

Maybe I'll torture her on the air. I'm sure if the ratings go through the roof, she would think it was worth it. But since a life outside of prison walls is my end game, I'll forgo any fantasy I have of making her pay for all the misery she's caused me these past couple of days.

A hot bath is waiting for me at home—and hopefully, a husband who is still just as upset at her as I am.

I PULL INTO THE GARAGE BY ELEVEN. I HEAR THE MUSIC COMING FROM Evan's room, right above me. He must still be studying for his trigonometry exam tomorrow. In passing, he mentioned that both Jenna and Adam are also in his class, and that she whizzes through the equations without even trying. On the other hand, Adam is struggling. But instead of working harder at the course, he taunts his classmates and charms his teachers.

Aunt Phyllis is fast asleep. I don't hear a peep in the children's rooms. Still, to assure myself that all is well, I peek beyond each of their doors, one by one.

Just seeing Trisha's lips bowed into a gentle smile has me breathing easier.

Jeff has fallen asleep with his math book on his chest. After kissing his cheeks, I place the book on his bed stand and turn off his light.

Mary has her iPhone's earbuds in, but her eyes are closed, and her lip quivers with what I hope are sweet dreams. Gently, I pull out the earbuds, brush her forehead with my lips, and extinguish her light.

My room is dark.

My bed is empty.

Brin's requested hour with my husband ended forty minutes ago. So, what's keeping him?

I climb out of my clothes. I prop up my pillow with the intention of staying up until Jack comes home…

OH, HELL, I MUST HAVE FALLEN ASLEEP.

Only one eyelid responds to my attempt to open either or both. The bright face on the nightstand clock reads 3:21 a.m.

I reach out behind me, hoping to pat Jack. Instead, I hit the flat mattress covered in nothing but a cold sheet: smooth; undisturbed.

I am alone.

I lay in bed, watching the clock flick off the early morning minutes like green lightning bugs on a steamy summer night. Finally, a halo of light forces its way along the border of our bedroom curtain.

Jack isn't coming home.

BECAUSE I CAN'T SLEEP, BY FIVE O'CLOCK I DRAG MYSELF OUT OF BED. I need a cup of coffee.

But, first things first. With my cell phone, I head out to the playhouse. From there I call Arnie.

"What…what's up?" His voice is thick, weighted by sleep.

"I need you to keep our home's webcam on a generic loop."

He clears his throat. "Already got it covered—last night, in fact. I've shuffled some time-appropriate footage of the happy-pappy Craigs intermingled with empty home shots. Unless someone looks closely, they won't notice that they've seen the stuff before. I'll upload it now. It'll play through the run of the show."

"Perfect! Thanks."

"Don't thank me. Thank Jack. It was his idea."

Before I can ask him when he heard from Jack about this, I hear Emma's sleepy murmur followed by Arnie's exclamation, "Whoa, baby! Again? Sheesh! You've got to quit watching those Penelope outtakes! You're wearing me out—"

His cell phone falls with a clatter before clicking off.

I guess Jack is expecting a row. Why else would he ask Arnie to put the show's webcams on a loop?

AUNT PHYLLIS TRAILS INTO THE KITCHEN A HALF-HOUR LATER, yawning. When I offer her a fresh cup, she waves me off. "We're not supposed to eat or drink anything for eight hours before the operation."

When I set down the mug, my hand is shaking. "Aunt Phyllis, I wish you wouldn't go through with that stupid operation."

She crosses her arms below her ample chest. "But—I'm doing it for us."

"If that's the case, then I vote no. So does Jack. And if we were to ask the kids, they'd say no too."

"Ask us what?" Trisha's voice, hazy with sleep comes from the stairwell.

Phyllis blanches. "Nothing…" She sits down at the kitchen banquette. "Okay, yes. I'm having an operation today."

Trisha's eyes open wide. "What kind?"

My aunt waves her hands at her chest. "It's for my…heart."

Trisha runs to my aunt. Crawling into her lap, she asks, "Is your heart sick?"

"No! …It's just that…" She peers down at the little girl cradled in her arms. "I mean…you hope you can change other people's hearts so that they see you like you want to see yourself."

"You look in the mirror all the time!" Trisha points out. "Don't you like what you see?"

"Not always. Not…anymore." She frowns as she stammers to relay her thoughts. "What I'm trying to say is…Sometimes, you want to change something about yourself so that…well, so that others will like you better."

Trisha's brow wrinkles with worry. "Who doesn't like you, Aunt Phyllis?"

"I don't mean just 'like.'" Phyllis sighs. "I mean…I mean love."

Trisha grasps her great aunt as if she'll never let her go. "Everyone loves you—because you love everyone and everything."

Aunt Phyllis blinks back her tears. "Well, little one, thank you for that. But…I want some special someone to love me."

Some special someone.

Yes, Aunt Phyllis deserves someone who loves her completely.

And unconditionally. We all do.

Shocked at the implication, Trisha covers her mouth. Still, a giggle slips out. She pats my aunt's face gently. "Aunt Phyllis, you are so silly! You're the most beautiful aunt I know! And the kindest. And the funniest. Any man who doesn't fall in love with you is an idiot! He'd be the one that needs the operation on his heart. Not you." She waves her hand dismissively. "If he can't see and feel what we do, we wouldn't want him as an uncle anyway!"

Aunt Phyllis buries her face in Trisha's hair. She doesn't want my daughter to see her cry.

And because I don't want Trisha or Phyllis to hear me bawl my head off, I leave the room.

"Pass the toast, please," Mary asks Jeff, who isn't sitting close to it.

Evan is, but for some reason, Mary is ignoring him. Tit for tat.

When Evan came downstairs, he said good morning to everyone but Mary.

There is trouble in Paradise.

Usually, Aunt Phyllis has a way to get them to kiss and make up, figuratively if not literally. (At least, not in front of the rest of the family.) But by seven o'clock she'd been whisked off to Franklin's sumptuous Beverly Hills offices. I know this because I was stepping into the shower when I heard the honk of the show's limo in front of our house.

So now it's my turn to spread soothing oil on the water roiling between Mary and Evan.

I've gotten into the habit of scanning all of the online celebrity news. As I do so now, I run across an item in *US Weekly*. The headline reads:

#HHHilldale Update! Mary Makes Jenna Cry—Again!

The accompanying photo shows Jenna at her school locker. She stares into the camera, teary-eyed. Mary, at the next locker frowns. She has her back to Jenna. Her arms crossed at her waist.

I recognize the picture of Mary. It was taken last spring after her basketball team lost a game. She was not standing at her locker at all, but in the gym.

"I presume you've already seen this," I hold my iPad up to Mary so that she can see it too.

"Oh, yeah, you bet!" With a scowl, she nods toward Evan but doesn't look at him.

"The picture of you was PhotoShopped!" I exclaim.

Evan whips around to me. "It was?"

Mary turns to him. "See? I told you! Now will you quit believing everything that girl says about me?"

Before he has a chance to respond, she storms out of the kitchen.

"What has she been telling you?" I ask him.

"She says…lots of things. Not necessarily about Mary, though. She just needs a shoulder to cry on."

"I know Mary has tried to be her friend. Why won't she let her?"

Evan grimaces. "Because…what I'm trying to say is that it has nothing to do with Mary—although I can't convince Mary of that! She believes too much of this stuff online." He rolls his eyes. "And her girlfriends aren't helping things by reporting every time Jenna and I pass each other in the hall—"

"Evan, I know that you're…loyal to Mary." I put my hand on his shoulder. "In a few days, all of this will be over, and you and Mary can go on with your lives as they were."

God, yes, please!...

I think.

"And I understand you're concerned for Jenna," I add. "What is it exactly that has her so traumatized?"

"It has something to do with her family." He shakes his head. "It's made her brother, Jason, even angrier than usual. He hates his dad and blames him for everything that is wrong in their lives. And Jordan is…well, he's just strange."

Jeff nods. "Yeah, boy. He never opens up in class. And he's obsessed with…war."

Not a good sign.

Nonchalantly, I ask, "How are the Garrett kids holding up under all the notoriety from the show?"

Evan shrugs. "I can't say. I don't hang out much with Jason…or Adam."

"They've started to hang together?"

He holds up his right hand. He has crossed his middle and index fingers. "They're thick. They're also assholes. You should hear how they talk to girls—and then about them behind their backs. It's disgusting."

"Does Mary…" I want to ask if she's still enthralled with Adam, but I'm almost afraid of Evan's answer.

"No! After he tricked her into chugging her way to a hangover, she steers clear of him. Unfortunately, he's interested in Jenna." Evan shakes his head at the thought.

I lay my hand on his shoulder. "I take it that you're protecting Jenna."

"Well, yeah! Someone has to! Her brother certainly isn't! In fact, he's…he told Adam that…that she's no longer a virgin." He shakes his head. "Even if that were the case, why would he say something like that?"

Good point. I shake my head in wonder. "It sounds as if all this notoriety has had an awful effect on the Garretts. How about Sami? Is he acting out, like his brother?"

"Sami's okay," Jeff replies. "I just wish kids would quit making fun of him. Yesterday, some of the juniors put him and his wheelchair in one of the gym showers and left him there with the shower running until one of the coaches heard him screaming for help. Mrs. Farnham was so angry that she pulled him out of school. I'm going over there later today to help him with his Geography homework."

"That's despicable," I declare. "How could those boys be so mean?"

"It's called high school," Evan points out the obvious.

"It's sweet of you, Jeff, to stand by him." I pat his cheek gently. "Both of you are doing your best to stay grounded. I know Mary is as well." I sigh. "You boys had better grab your bags if we're to get to school on time."

Trisha shouts, "I call shotgun!"

"I'd love that," Aunt Phyllis's voice comes from behind us.

I turn and stammer, "But…I thought you went to—"

"Nah." Aunt Phyllis shakes her head adamantly. "When the limo pulled up, I told New Girl and those hottie housewives to take off without me. I'm already perfect, am I right?" She looks down at Trisha.

If she's looking for proof, her grandniece's hug is all she needs.

She takes mine, too. And Jeff's, and Evan's.

"Mary!" Evan shouts. "Get in here!"

Mary peeks out from the great room door. "Why should I?" she says sulkily.

"Group hug. And despite your misdirected anger, you're still part of this family." His demand leaves little room that he'll take no for an answer.

"Ha!" she mutters.

But a moment later, I feel her arm around me.

All too soon, our arms loosen. Bodies, relieved of the tension the last few days have brought us, pull away reluctantly.

"I can't believe we have another three days of this crap!" Mary exclaims.

"Four," Jeff reminds her. "This is only the third day. The finale is on Sunday."

Not for us—if we apprehend our suspect before then.

For my family's sake, this is now my sole goal in life.

I keep the benign smile on my face until the children are out the door with Aunt Phyllis.

Then, I cry.

For Jack.

Because I know he'll go as far as he has to, to complete this mission.

And I will too, which is why I walk upstairs and into my costume closet.

13

Gunsmoke

"He draws trouble like a summer melon draws flies."
—Festus Haggin, in *Gunsmoke*

Yikes! You're caught in the middle of a gunfight! What's a gal to do?

Before hiking up your skirt and tearing off a piece of your petticoat and waving it in tepid surrender, do this instead:

- *Tip #1: Duck—preferably behind something bigger than you. (Yes, it can be a person, particularly one who doesn't quite strike your fancy. Human shields are always in fashion!)*
- *Tip #2: Fight back. You may be outmanned. You may be outgunned. But you're far from being outsmarted. If you can't shoot, ambush. Once you're close enough, you can punch, gouge, kick, and stab. Do you see a pattern here? Your life is worth fighting for, so don't just lay down and play dead!*

Or worse, let some stranger alter your reality.

Remember this: anything can be used as a weapon. A belt is ideal for strangling. A trash can lid will give your opponent one hell of a concussion when slammed into the side of his head, so may the force—

and lots of it—be with you! Even a high heel, when broken off the sole of your shoe and crammed into your opponent's jugular will extinguish the light in his beady little eyes.

(When you take the shoes back to the store, tell them they didn't hold up as promised. They will replace them, no worries! They probably won't notice the little bit of blood you forgot to wipe away…)

- *Tip #3: Get the hell outta there. Because there is only one way to quote-unquote live to fight another day:*

STAY ALIVE.

FOR MY SURPRISE VISIT TO JAMES, I CHOOSE SOMETHING I HOPE WILL turn his head—away from me long enough to scan his phone. My frock is vintage: white with red polka dots, with a short flouncy skirt and a collared halter-top that plunges between my braless, albeit already generous and never-been-enhanced-yet-still-perky breasts.

The blood red bow in my hair matches the hue of my kitten heels and the dress's wide patent leather belt, where I tuck the cell phone scanner next to the portable stiletto knife already secured there.

Still, something is missing…

Ah, yes, the red polka-dot thong purchased in some sleazy sex shop on Melrose Avenue.

The final touches: I heavy up on my eyeliner and oxblood red lipstick to match.

Am I right to think that this outfit subtly suggests fun and sexy flirtatiousness, despite being a thirty-plus married woman with three kids?

In other words, it screams MILF.

No need for subtlety. I mean, hey, if this outfit doesn't get my target slobbering, I'll give Franklin's nip-tuck offer some serious consideration.

A few local fans catch sight of me as I enter the Hilldale Woodlands Market. One couple insists I take a selfie with them.

When the wife heads off in search of pomegranate seeds, her husband asks me for my phone number. I give him one to a porn addict hotline instead, and then I glide toward the deli to peruse which prepared foods will entice a hungry hubby eagerly awaiting his new and improved wife.

Finally, I select a whole roasted chicken, garlic mashed potatoes, grilled broccolini, and chocolate mint brownies, which I'll tuck into the picnic basket along with a note that reads GET WELL! —THE CRAIGS

Here's hoping James appreciates what he gets—

In the basket.

Because as far as I'm concerned, it won't be much else. Some flirtatious adoration? Perhaps. A little slap and tickle? (Sigh…) If I must.

But if James reaches for a breast, leg, or thigh that isn't attached to something that once laid an egg, he'll find himself in traction.

It should be interesting hearing them explain that to their already sore wives.

As I promised Ryan, I make my way to the Garretts' ranch-style home, located in the back of our planned community in the older section of town.

Here, random vehicles are few and far between: only the people who live on this cul-de-sac, or delivery trucks.

The Garretts' lot is one of the biggest in Hilldale. A regiment of Italian cypresses flanks the deep front yard, creating a sky-high barrier that makes the house itself hard to see. Perhaps it's for the best. The Garretts haven't lived there a year; still, it's been long enough for the wear and tear that comes with six children and a husband who seems to lack a green thumb. The grass planted by the builder has already browned out. Weeds line the sidewalk to the front door.

Both James and Patty's cars are in the open garage.

I make the decision to pull into the driveway. I won't be here long, so the likelihood of someone seeing my car—let alone knowing that it is mine—is slim.

Patty is asleep on some operating table in Beverly Hills, and Arnie assures me James is home. "He hasn't left the house since he dropped the toddler at daycare."

"Arnie, have you modified the show's webcam feed?"

"Yep, I put it on a loop a half-hour ago." Arnie sighs. "Jesus, what a crap storm! He picks fights with her all the time. If her eyes aren't red from crying, they're black and blue from his punches. Lucy made the decision that it was too much of a downer for the audience to see."

"My, my! Isn't she a sport," I mutter. "One of her contestants is getting beat up, and she can't do the right thing and call the police?"

"I should have done it myself." Arnie sounds embarrassed. "But we're not supposed to get involved."

"That's not an Acme regulation."

"No—it's Brin's, for her staff. And if Lucy learns it's been broken she'll blame 'the New Girl.' We can't afford to have Emma tossed off the show."

True. Still, no one is stopping me from having a conversation with Patty.

Or breaking a few of James's fingers. Maybe then he'll feel Patty's pain.

I ring the doorbell. No answer.

I knock hard. Again, no wary hello, let alone the sound of footsteps.

I try the knob. Locked.

I have the right tool to pick it, hidden in the fold of a napkin in the picnic basket.

A few seconds later, I'm inside.

~

THE PLACE IS AS DARK AS A TOMB.

The foyer seems devoid of air. I'm surprised that it is painted dark gray instead of the usual Realtor Beige. Even the molding around the ceiling and floorboards is flat gray—

Like a military barracks.

"Hello?" I call out. "Anyone home?"

No answer. Where is James?

I glance into various rooms—the kitchen, dining room, formal living room, great room—before making my way down the long hallway. Yes, barracks is an apt description. In each room, the furnishings are modest: metal or unadorned wood; and neat with military precision.

There are bunk beds in the children's rooms. I don't see toys or video games, let alone computers of any kind. They could be occupied by soldiers.

The thought sends a chill up my spine.

There is one more room, at the end of the hall. I presume it's the master bedroom. I stop to contemplate if I should enter. I'd hate to walk into a scene like the one I found in the Powells' home.

A hand grabs me by the wrist and wrenches my right arm behind my back.

Cold hard steel snuggles against my temple. "You're just the person I wanted to see," James whispers in my ear.

I attempt a smile. "If you're so happy to see me, why are you holding a gun to my head?"

His laugh spews spittle on my neck. "Because you broke into my home. And I caught you snooping around." He digs the gun deeper into my temple. "Why are you here?"

"I left food in the kitchen—a roasted chicken. I figure Patty won't be in any condition to cook for you tonight."

He laughs. "I don't let Patty cook, period. Besides the fact that she stinks at it, I'm afraid she might poison me one day. My oldest girl, Jenna—now she knows her way around the kitchen." He chuckles again. "She knows how to please me."

"Great. Well then, surprise, Jenna gets the night off! Now, if you'll excuse me."

When I move, he wrenches my arm even more tightly.

"You didn't come here to play Welcome Wagon. We've lived in enough new towns for me to know that." He puts the gun under one of the halter straps of my dress. "And Welcome Wagon ladies don't wear fuck-me dresses."

I turn to face him. That puts the gun right between my eyes.

But I don't stare at it. Crossed eyes is not a sexy look, so I look directly at him. I part my lips just wide enough to lick them. He rewards me with a ghost of a smile.

Finally, he lowers the gun, a Sig P320—

To my left breast.

He circles my nipple with the barrel of the gun.

I feign a shudder. "Do you know what you're doing with that thing?"

"What do you think?"

"I think…it's a turn-on." I lick my lips. "They make a woman look sexy, and a man look strong."

He relaxes the gun. "Can you shoot?"

"I wish," I lie with a sigh. "Can you teach me?"

"Shooting a gun isn't a game. War isn't a game. Killing isn't a high. It puts you in the gutter." He frowns. "I know this first hand."

"But you're a war hero! At least, that's what your wife and kids claim."

"A hero…" His voice is so low that it sounds a million miles away. "Yeah, well, that depends on who you ask. Not when you miss the target. Not when you take innocent lives. They call it 'collateral damage.'"

His gun is now on the side of my skull. He wants to wipe the smile off my face. He wants me to be scared.

"Bang, bang, Donna Craig. You're dead." He pulls the trigger.

Click.

"Empty." He shrugs. "Rule Number One: you've got to clean a gun before you use it."

I want to punch him in the throat. I want to gouge his eyes out.

Instead, I look up at him, doe-eyed, and smile. "So that's a yes? You'll teach me?"

The darkness leaves his face. His leer is back in full force as he gives me the once-over. "Sure, darling Donna—but it will cost you."

That's what I was afraid of, I think, as he flips me so that I've now got my back against the wall.

His mouth presses against mine. He forces my lips open with his tongue.

Yes, I know I could make my getaway now. I could bite down hard. He'd be in such pain that instinctively, he'd pull away from me—

Far enough away that all it would take is an elbow to the gut and then a fist to the neck to bring him to his knees. Ah, how nice it would be to put that gun against his crotch and listen to him beg for mercy—

Just like he's waiting for me to do.

But, nah. I'll survive this little tongue tango. I'm having too much fun seeing where James goes with this.

And, besides, I've got a job to do.

Oh, joy, he's hardening against me. Time to get to work.

As my right hand cups the tent rising in his pants, my left hand inches toward his cell phone. I relieve him of it. With my free hand, I take out the scanner secreted in my belt and insert it into the phone. I slip both of them into my belt again, and pray he won't hear the faint buzz when it's done.

A hand slides under my dress and up toward my ass. The realization that James doesn't feel panty, just skin, has him breathing heavier. His finger moves between my bum cheeks but stops when it hits my thong. "Ha, ha! A whore's token attempt at modesty!"

The first yank takes it down around my thighs.

The second drops it to the floor around my heels.

To retrieve it, he lifts the left leg first, on the calf. He puts just enough pressure on it as if to warn me: Don't try anything.

He drops that leg only to lift the other and collect his prize.

I steel myself from cringing as he holds it up and sniffs it like a dog.

"You know you aren't going home with these, don't you?" His right brow rises with his leer.

I shrug. "Why? Do you need a trophy to show the other husbands?"

"Now, that's a thought." His smile widens. Instead of answering, he reaches behind his back—

And the next thing I know, I'm being handcuffed.

Shit.

James laughs raucously as he goose-steps me toward the mysterious door.

When he opens it, at first, all I see is darkness. When my eyes adjust, a staircase beckons.

"Watch your step," He whispers. He shoves me forward. To what, I can only imagine.

The faint buzz of the scanner sounds all the louder in the stairwell. James halts. His hand tightens on my arm. "What was that?" he asks suspiciously.

"My watch," I stammer. "I have to go pick up my youngest, Trisha, in a half hour."

I can't see his face, but I can hear his labored breathing. "A shame. Your lesson may not be over by then. She may have to wait a while."

I think of all I know about his family: his wife's submissiveness; his oldest daughter's apprehensions; his sons' surliness.

No, I don't like the sound of that.

We are in the Garretts' basement.

Or I should say, we're in the Garretts' indoor shooting range.

We entered through an air-locked corridor. The concrete walls have also been baffled for sound.

The range has four lanes, which, I'm guessing, are twenty-five yards in length. Every lane has a target tract system. A different kind of target—all human forms—is hooked onto each one.

From the smell of it, he was having target practice when I broke into his house. Not all of it has been cleared away by the humongous HVAC vent, which sits at the far end of the room so that the smoke and toxic lead particles from the discharged rounds are sucked out of the room.

Hate and fear are toxic too. If only it could be dissipated just as easily from the lives of the Garretts as well.

Against the closest wall is a vast collection of artillery and ammo. Semi-automatics fill the meticulously arranged rows: M-14, HK417, and Mod 0 rifles, to name a few. The bottom row is filled with handguns of all makes, including smaller ones: an S&W Shield 9mm, a couple of Glock 43's.

James nods toward another wall, which is filled with used targets. Most have a cluster of bullet holes around the target's hearts. A few have them in the head or neck. "Everyone in this family knows how to shoot. These are my kids' latest kill shots. Pretty impressive, huh?"

I take a closer look. I nod. "I'll say."

"How about you?" he asks. "How's your aim?"

I chuckle. "You're kidding, right?" Wide-eyed, I take a step back.

My meekness emboldens him to place his hand on my waist and pull me toward him. His tongue darts around my molars. Seriously, if I had any gold fillings, I'd be wondering if he were pilfering them.

When James is done, he vows, "I don't play games, remember?"

He strolls back to his wall of arms. "Time for your shooting lesson. Here's how it goes: you choose a weapon. I'd suggest one of these little girly guns that my daughters like." He points to the lower shelf. "I'll help you position your luscious little body and your gun. You'll get three practice shots. After that, any shot outside of the 7-ring and you lose."

I purse my lips into a pout. "I lose what, exactly?"

"Like I said, I get to keep something of yours." He holds up my thong. "Since your virginity is already a distant memory, I'll take this instead. Sort of like strip poker."

"Those are pretty high stakes. This happens to be one of my husband's favorites." In truth, Jack has never seen it—and I intend that he soon will.

"Is that so?" The thought has James salivating. "Well then, you better listen carefully. Otherwise, you'll walk out of here without it. I don't think you'll want to explain to him how you lost it."

I bat my eyes. "Yes, Teacher," I whisper.

My submissiveness has him grinning ear to ear. "Go ahead, choose your weapon."

"Hmmm..." I saunter over to his munitions wall and feign fascination at all the choices, but I've already made up my mind. "Can't we just use that one, in your hand? I already love the feel of it."

My guess is that he's the type of disciplinarian who times his children's ability to lock and load their weapon of choice at every lesson, in which case the other weapons are empty. Works for me. I only want one weapon in play: his.

He takes a minute to think about it. Finally, he nods. "Yeah, okay, sure. No need to get you all worked up on how to load one of these killing machines when the objective is to get you shooting in the right direction." He points to the target: a knee-to-head photo of a menacing man. He chuckles. "I bet you'd hate to tell ol' Jack that you lost your panties to that fella."

"Wouldn't you prefer I said I lost them to you?"

He sobers up at the thought. "You better hope he doesn't find out the hard way that there's a new rooster in the henhouse. My guess is that he's stupid enough to fight me for taking what's his."

Our eyes meet.

I drop mine meekly and nod.

He chuckles again, all smiles. The next thing I hear is the click of the handcuffs as they are unlocked.

As I rub the soreness from my wrists, he walks over to the munitions wall and opens one of the many ammo drawers that line it.

While he's got his back to me, I take his phone from my belt. It takes a second for me to pull the scanner from its audio jack and tuck them both separately into my belt again. A bigger issue is how to put the phone back into his pocket without raising his attention.

I'll figure it out when the time is right.

It better be soon because he's turning around. He holds the gun low. "Face your target," he commands me.

I saunter over to the shooting lane and turn in the right direction.

"Look straight ahead," he demands.

James waits until I do so before walking over to me. He holds the P320 in his right arm, which is stiffened close to his side and downward: around the four-o'clock.

He stands behind me. I feel his hand on my calf, correcting my stance by positioning my right leg a few inches further away. Why he then feels the need to caress my ankle is beyond me.

Finally, he straightens up behind me again. Too close. And too hard. "Stretch out your right hand, thumb up."

When I oblige him, he places the gun in my hand. "Grip it high on the strap—here." I allow him to position it accurately: four fingers on the fore-grip, which allows my palm to butt up against the rear grip. My thumb is up, as if I'm stroking the barrel's left side.

James takes my left hand and moves it into the support position: cradling my right hand even as it covers the rest of the grip. He takes a moment to place my left hand's four fingers under the trigger guard. He presses the highest—my index finger—hard beneath it.

"Now, move your right hand's index finger to the side of the gun so that it's parallel to it."

Feigning ignorance, I move my left one instead.

"I guess you're as dumb as you are pretty," he mutters.

"Is that supposed to be a compliment?" I taunt him.

With his free hand, he grabs my hair. As he jerks my head back, he growls, "Guns are not toys. This is not a game."

Seeing the anger in my eyes, he coils my hair even tighter and yanks it even harder. "Do you have a problem with that?"

I frown, but I drop my gaze to the gun. "No."

"No, sir."

I stay silent.

He tosses my hair away to shift his hand to his shoulder. But before he has a chance to backhand me, I reply adamantly, "*No, sir!*"

His hand stops just an inch from my face. "That's better. But because you felt the need to sass me, you now get only two practice shots."

"What do you mean by that?" I fake the tremor in my voice.

"I mean what I say. You've been a bad girl. I'm taking away

your third one." He scowls. "If you want to hold onto that little patch of heaven, you'd better behave yourself—and pray you can shoot straight."

Soon he'll be begging that I don't. But for now, I nod meekly.

He moves my left thumb next to the right one. "See how your hands fit together? Like two pieces of a puzzle." The leer is back. "Like when a woman is a tight fit—around the right man. How do you think we'd fit together?"

My blush is not faked. However, it is anger-induced.

Temper…temper…

"Okay, keep your eye on your target. I'll give you a break by keeping him still on the track."

"Thank you." I sound so grateful that you'd think he just offered me a million dollars.

Feeling magnanimous, he gives me a pat on the ass.

Again, a blush (from anger). *Temper…temper.*

"Okay, now here's the important part. When you're ready to shoot, just squeeze the trigger—gently," he warns me. To make his point, he strokes my nipple gently. "Just like this," he whispers in my ear.

I'd like to make my point too—maybe not so gently.

Instead, I nod. "Yeah, I get it."

"What did you say?" His militant bark comes with a grimace that is supposed to scare me.

Okay, I'll play along. "Yes…yes, sir." I think my quivering lower lip is a good touch.

He must think so too because he nods his approval. "Now, look at the target and take your first shot. Remember, aim for the heart."

Don't. Tempt. Me.

I frown as if the task is beyond me. No ring below eight, eh?

I shoot just wild enough that I hit the 2-ring.

James clucks his tongue. "Shame, shame, shame. If you want to hold on to your thatch patch, you're going to have to do better than that."

I nod meekly. "Yes...sir. I know." I eye him coquettishly. "Listen, as bad as I am, can't you give me that third practice shot back?"

He draws me close to lick my face. *Ewwww.*

"Let's say I thought about it, but sorry, no can do," he replies. "In this man's army, there is no leniency."

I may take him up on that policy.

"Now, take that second shot. That's an order."

So that he thinks he's scaring me, I nod frantically, take a couple of anxious breaths, center myself—

Oops, the shot goes wild and bores the target in the shoulder.

"I...I...missed again." I make sure my eyes open wide. "Please? Can't you be lenient—just this once?"

"Sorry, you know the rules." He points to the target again. "Go ahead, take the shot that counts."

"But...but...sir..."

He stares at me with dead eyes but raises his palm to within a few inches of my face. "Donna, do not ask me again. That is an order."

I nod silently. I take a deep breath. I position myself again.

This time, the shot misses the target completely.

James's hand holds up his prize: my thong.

"No...please! No..." I'm whimpering as I back away. "This was a mistake! I...I just came to tease you—you know for the show."

"No. You really like me." One way or another, he wants his fantasy to be a reality. "You want me."

"Okay...yes."

"Yes, sir."

"Yes, sir," I'm now nodding emphatically. "I...want you."

"Even though you know your husband will never forgive you?"

I whisper, "Yes, sir."

"Your 'friendly little Fraulein' act here: have you pulled this on any of the other men?"

"What?" I shake my head emphatically. "No!"

"What did you say?" he shouts. We are now nose to nose.

"No, sir!" I scream back.

He stares down at me. "Good. They wouldn't know how to keep you in line like I do. Hell, it's obvious that ol' Jack doesn't know what to do with you either! I suppose he's too soft on you." He smiles at the double entendre. "Say it! 'Jack is too soft.'"

"Jack…is too soft." *And you are soooo lucky we cut the video feed on this.*

"This asshole is a fucking sadist," Arnie says in my earbud. "Seriously, you deserve an Academy Award."

Oops! I forgot that we're not really alone. I smother a smile, but in my head, I'm taking a bow. Okay, now time for the finale:

"James! …I mean sir, all I ask is that you"—I drop my voice to a whisper—"that you…reconsider." I cast my eyes downward.

"You're begging." He tries to turn his grin into a frown and fails miserably at it. "When you do that, you look pathetic, Donna. I have no sympathy for pathetic women."

"I…can't go home without it! Jack is sure to be home by now. If he sees me in this dress…well, he'll know what I was wearing under it." My lip trembles. "Perhaps we can come to some other sort of understanding?"

I can't see his face, but I hear the delight in his voice. "I'm not opposed to some negotiation."

"Okay…um, how's this? If this next shot is better, I can leave with it?"

"And if it isn't?"

I take a deep breath. "I'll…we can…"

"Fuck. Say it."

"Yes, sir. Fuck." —you, asshole.

He pretends to ponder this. I squirm as if my life depends on it. If only he knew whose life is really at stake.

"Sure, okay. One more shot. And if it hits the eight-ring or better, you're free to go with your ass floss."

I nod. "Thank you!" I show my gratitude with a fervent kiss—

And by brushing against his boner.

His arms are all over me. Tit for tat: mine are all over him, too—

Which gives me the opportunity to replace his phone.

By the time I pull away and take my stance, he's almost bent in half at the thought of collecting on my promise.

I raise the gun, but I don't need a second hand to steady the shot that goes cleanly through the target's heart.

"Tah-tah." I head for the door.

He's so stunned at the shot that he stands there long enough for me to make it to the door before he runs after me. When he grabs for me, I duck just out of reach—

For the most part. He succeeds in ripping my dress's halter strap.

Fuck that! It's *vintage!*

When I whip around, the gun is pointed at an easy target: his heart.

He stops dead in his tracks.

"Kiss the floor," I command. "Feel free to lick it."

He's seething, but slowly, he falls onto the concrete.

I put my knee in the center of his back and then pull the cuffs from his rear pocket, jerk his wrists behind him, and snap them shut. "Jesus, you still have a hard-on?" I roll my eyes.

At that second, he lifts up—

Tossing me off of him.

I drop the gun. James scrambles for it, but so do I.

I reach it first. I slam it into his thick skull.

He falls backward. His head wallops the concrete floor. He's out like a light.

I stumble to my feet, breathing heavily. James is still out cold when I pull the handcuffs' key from his pants pocket. I take off the cuffs, but I take them with me as a souvenir. Why leave them so that he can use them on poor Patty or one of the kids?

And, of course, I take my thong.

I slam the door behind me.

I put on my thong before heading toward the front door. But I stop when I reach the kitchen because it hits me: I was never here.

I mean, let's face it: he'll never admit to it, so why should I?

I walk out the door with the picnic basket. Tonight, we'll have chicken.

I HUSTLE TO MY CAR, UNLOCK IT, DROP THE PICNIC BASKET ON THE back floor, and then sink into the driver's seat.

I'm still breathing so heavily that, at first, I don't hear the tap on my window.

When I jump in my seat, I almost drop my hand holding up my halter top, but I catch the falling strap before it slips out of my hand.

It's Ariel.

Busted.

She's dressed for a run. Connor is cooing in his BOB Ironman jogging stroller.

"Did you forget our coffee meet-up today?"

"I...got tied up." I feel my cheeks flush at my lie. More like shackled. *Tomato, to-mah-toe...*

"Yes, I...I know. I saw you leaving the Garretts' home just now." Ariel uses little Connor's fussiness as her excuse to avoid looking me in the eye. "It's okay. I get it. You'll do whatever it takes to win. I just wished you'd have had the courtesy to call me so that I wasn't sitting around for an hour, looking like some celebrity idiot who...who had been stood up."

"I'm so sorry, Ariel! Truly I am. Since Patty was in surgery, I thought dropping off some chicken and fixings would be appreciated—"

"Please, Donna, don't take me for a fool!" She taps the side view mirror. "Your lipstick is smeared."

I check the mirror. Egad, she's right. I look like a crazed clown. "James…tried to take some liberties."

"Let me guess. Next, you're going to try to tell me that you put up a fight." She rolls her eyes. "I suppose what Penelope said about you is right. You have no boundaries."

"Speaking of no boundaries, are you aware that Franklin—"

Ariel holds up her hand. "Stop right there! Are you going to claim now that Franklin came on to you too? Have you no decency? Do you truly believe that being the most lascivious person on the show will help you win it?" She shakes furiously. "You won't be sullying my sweet, decent husband with unmerited claims of extracurricular activities with you!" She steels herself, then adds: "I feel sorry for poor Jack. He's so kind, and yet you're ruining his life—all because of your greediness!"

Okay, that does it. To open the door, I must let loose of the strap—

Ouch! I flash Ariel…

Mortified, she shakes with anger as I fumble to grab my broken strap. On the other hand, her son reaches toward me, begging, "Bobba! Bobba!"

I guess he'll take what he can get since Mama's wells have run dry.

And are made of silicone gel.

Furious, she runs down the street with the stroller.

No doubt, my little escapade will be the talk of the next *House-wives* coffee klatch. As the topic of conversation, I don't expect an invitation.

Still, it's her word against mine. And certainly, James will deny it. Without video footage to back it up, whom would they believe: the woman they aspire to be, or the one they fear will damage their marriage?

Don't answer that.

I start the car and head home.

JACK'S CAR ISN'T IN THE GARAGE.

Yes, I'm angry. It's past noon. At some point, you'd think Brin would have to get back to the control booth to supervise the editing that makes the rest of us look as nasty as she is.

I hold my halter top while carefully getting out of my SUV. I don't need the cameras catching a nip slip.

Thank goodness I'm able to unlock the door from the garage into the laundry room with one hand. My body aches from the struggle with James, so I climb the stairs slowly to the bedroom.

Strange. The door is open—

Because Jack is in there.

His shirt is off. Just above his hip is a bite mark.

My God, Brin plays rough.

He catches my eye in the mirror. He walks toward me, but no. I'm not ready to discuss anything right now, so I turn and head down the hall.

He grabs me by the elbow of the arm that holds up my halter.

"Donna, please! We need to talk."

No shit.

I don't turn to face Jack until I hear his sigh.

At least he doesn't flinch at my glare. "Okay, start talking."

14

Full House

"You're in big trouble, Mister!"
—Michelle Tanner

Ah, the joys of large family! Let us count them:

First, since there are never enough bathrooms in a home filled with children, you are forced to learn how to hold your water like a camel. (This also comes in handy wherever you'll find long lavatory lines, such as on airplanes, sports stadiums, and port-a-potties at outdoor wedding venues.)

Next, you are resigned to accepting hand-me-downs. (Yes, you went Boho before it was fashionable! Pat yourself on the back for being ahead of the fashion curve, even if it lasted only through the years the Olsen Twins were fashion mavens.)

And, finally, you have an exceptional cast for your online reality show.

Now, if a network comes knocking with a contract, the real family feud begins!

~

Jack leans against the wall. For Jack, this is a defensive position, allowing him to keep his back from any possible adversaries.

Right now, I am the adversary. The nail file in my hand makes me so, as does the doubt in my eyes.

"Where is your car?" I ask nonchalantly.

"Down the block. Too many cameras out front. I didn't want anyone seeing me enter the house."

To document that he hasn't been home all night.

Noting my scowl, he goes right to the point: "Brin had a proposition for me."

"I've no doubt about that," I mutter.

"And...I didn't say no to it."

"Oh." I feel as if my heart has stopped beating altogether. Slowly, I drop onto the bed.

"She wanted to...okay, now, how do I say this?" He looks up at the ceiling as if he'll find the words floating somewhere up there. Finally, he takes a deep breath: "When the show ends this Sunday, she wants to spin the Craigs off into our own show."

She...*what?*

The breath I thought had already left my body gathers into a gale force when I declare, "I hope you told her 'HELL NO'!"

"In fact, I told her we'd give it serious consideration. We've got to do all we can to stay on the show." He shrugs.

"And?" I'm waiting for the other shoe to drop. Make that pants. His.

"She was appreciative."

"I'll just bet," I mutter.

"You'll be delighted to hear that Brin Patterson is all talk and no action."

"Yes, truly delighted!" Oh, dear! The way I'm holding my nail file could be misconstrued as a weapon.

Or, in Jack's case construed. He takes a step back.

"Did it take you all night to figure this out?" I purr.

"I was in Brin's office an hour and a half, tops. It would have been shorter, but the show's assistant producers interrupt her constantly. Seriously, I didn't realize that there were so many decisions to make when producing a television show that is partially broadcast live. And to think they have to do it for another four nights, too!" He shakes his head in wonder.

"And with the possibility of some terrorist assault taking place too," I remind him.

"Yeah, well, I guess it's why Addison pays her half-a-mil per episode. Which brings me to why I also get paid pretty handsomely as well—albeit, not half a mil." He holds something up. I recognize it immediately: a scanner, like the one I've used to hack our suspects' cell phones. "On the other hand, I do get numerous opportunities to get shot at, drugged, or blown up." The thought makes him wince. "Jesus, maybe I'm in the wrong business!"

"Has her cell phone checked out?"

"Arnie's on it now."

I take a deep breath. Now, for the at least half-a-million dollar question: "So then, how did you spend the rest of your night?"

"Like I said: getting shot at, drugged, and blown up."

I feel my jaw dropping. "Who? Where? What the hell happened?"

Jack paces the room. "As I was walking out of Brin's office, Ryan called. We got a mysterious lead—an anonymous text message suggesting that we'd find our suspect in a warehouse facility in Long Beach. Instead, we walked in on the owners of a meth lab divvying up their latest deal. Let's just say that mayhem ensued." He points to his lower back at the bite I had presumed was a love nip from Brin.

I take a closer look, and then I shrug. "She hides the fact that she's a little long in the tooth, but even Brin isn't this much of an animal."

"A Doberman. His master shot him up by mistake—along with the rest of the lab. It'll be on the evening news tonight." He winces from the pain. "I'm just glad he was high enough that it affected his aim. So were the DEA agents who cleaned up after us. The blast took him out, so one less asshole the state needs to prosecute."

"I'm just glad you walked away in one piece." I try to keep the tremble out of my voice.

He hears it anyway. He takes me in his arms. "So, I'm forgiven?"

"Sure—as long as you aren't becoming addicted to the fame and fortune that comes with having your very own reality show."

"Like you, I can't wait until we're incognito again—and under-cover." He grins wickedly at the double entendre. His adoration shines in his eyes—

Until they hone in on the hand that holds up the broken halter.

Ouch! Here it comes…

"Why do you feel the need to hold up your strap like that?"

"It…broke."

"Ah." He nods slowly. "Not while you were at the grocery store, I take it."

"Thank goodness, no! If it had, Brin would have the lead-in for the show tonight."

I force a giggle, but Jack isn't buying it. He takes the few steps he needs to be at my side.

Instinctively, I take a step backward toward the dresser so that he can't see the bruise on the back of my arm.

Jack sees it anyway, through the mirror behind me. He grimaces. "James did this? I take it you didn't run into him in the condiments aisle of our local supermarket." He frowns as he strokes the bruise gently with two fingers. "He's not very subtle, is he?"

I flinch. "Abusers never are. It's okay. I made sure he got the hint that, unlike Patty, I wasn't just going to stand there and take it."

"Good." Jack's relief shows itself in the tightness of his hug. He sighs. "Did you get near enough to his cell phone to scan it?"

I nod. "And, lucky me, I also got to check out James' arsenal."

"Is it large enough to put him on the INTERPOL Watch List?"

"Let's just say he's a bit paranoid." I shake my head. "As much as I despise him, I also feel sorry for him. Jack, I think he has PTSD. My guess is that it cost him his job and"—I pause to find the right words—"makes him such a bully to everyone in his life. It's why his wife and children are giving up hope." I hold up the scanner. "I guess we'll know soon." I glance at myself in the mirror. "Before I hit up our next suspect, I'd better change into something a little more presentable, and then mosey on down to the store again and fill up my picnic basket."

Jack takes my broken strap. Fingering it gently, he asks, "Who's next on the agenda?"

"Roger." I roll my eyes. "What do you think? Should I use his books as an icebreaker? Aren't authors always hungry to hear praise about their books?"

Jack laughs. "Considering his ego, you could talk about the color of his eyes, and he'd think you were putty in his hands. Unfortunately, you won't find him at home—or Peter or Gerald, for that matter. They're in Beverly Hills, getting fitted for their wedding tuxes—on the show's dime."

"You weren't invited?"

"I passed on the honor. I told them I had a hot wife to go home to."

"Yeah, well, too bad James passed too." I shudder. "Gee, thanks for burnishing my reputation as Hilldale's Number One 'ho-tart."

"We're in it to win it, right?"

I tap my chin in mock contemplation. "Then maybe we text Arnie to take the bedroom off his fake webcam loop."

"Just the bedroom?" he chides me "Why stop there? Do you think the love we have can be contained in just one room?"

"You're so right. What the heck are we waiting for? We don't have to be at the *Housewives'* mansion until nine, right? Between all the operating room drama and the husbands getting fit for tuxes, we've got the whole afternoon off!" I let my halter strap drop.

"Ah, there they are!'" He sighs admiringly at my breasts. "I've missed you, my fair ladies! Even one night away seems like an eternity!"

I double over with laughter.

"And let's not forget the best lady part south of the border—" He lifts my skirt, and then nods approvingly of what he sees beneath it. "Hey, when did you a buy this cute little polka-dot thong?"

I curtsey. "I've been waiting to wear it with just the right outfit. Who knew I'd find it in my slut gear collection?"

"The way she pilfers your clothes, probably Mary. I'd guess Aunt Phyllis has coveted it too." Jack circles me approvingly. "It is the crowning height of whore couture."

"Yeah, well, in any case, I'm sure Penelope would approve because it makes her case. It screams 'neighborhood harlot'."

He laughs. "She'd be so jealous that she'd run out and get one herself." He picks up the halter's ends. "Although, I doubt she'll fit into it now. From what Brin said, she'll be so inflated that it looks as if she'll be walking behind two zeppelins." He shakes his head at the thought. "For that matter, Cassandra will be unrecognizable too."

"What do you mean? She was adamant that she wasn't going!"

"She changed her mind. In fact, I was there when Brin got her call. Apparently, Franklin convinced her that it was for the good of her marriage, if not the show."

I frown. "How noble of him." Suddenly, the thought of Ariel's anxiety of the effect of the show on her marriage saddens me. Stroking Jack's chest, I whisper, "Was a one-in-six shot for a year with no mortgage payments worth it? How many marriages will break up because of this show?"

Jack tilts my face toward his. "I know one that will survive, no matter what."

His kiss is so tender that it moves me to tears.

As he wipes them away, I think about the others who have been competing against us. They seem so desperate; so disconnected from each other—

So lonely.

On the other hand, we share a love that grows with each passing day.

We revel in our adoration for each other.

Our mutual respect is demonstrated by each loving act.

And our love has been tested in too many ways to count.

Not even twelve million viewers can get between us.

Suddenly, the realization hits me: we've already won.

Each other.

The buzz of our phones breaks the silence in our bedroom.

The most Pavlovian of all instincts kicks in: simultaneously we reach for them.

"Ryan," we mutter in unison.

"I'm not disturbing anything, am I?" he asks.

Something tells me he knows better.

By the way in which Jack's head rises to the webcam in the ceiling, he must think so too. "Nah. Donna and I are just shooting the breeze," he drawls nonchalantly.

"Good. Then she won't mind making it over to Roger and Sienna's place. Another direct text correspondence was traced from the terrorist—this time to Roger's home ISP. Since he's getting fitted for a tux, she shouldn't have to worry about, er, running into him."

"Works for me." *Not.* I sigh. "I'll get right over there."

Jack waits until Ryan hangs up before muttering, "I guess you should change into something more…appropriate."

Black yoga pants and a zip-up jacket that matches will have to do.

And thank goodness, no picnic basket.

If I'm too late, Jack promises to pick up the kids.

I don't plan on it. I'd like to go with him. If they've had as rough a day as us, they'll appreciate seeing both their parents.

Together. And still in love.

BY THE TIME I JOG ONTO ROGER AND SIENNA'S STREET, ARNIE HAS done his bit: the security system is off, the camera feeds to the TV show are looped, and he has verified that they don't have a dog.

"Just a cat—a white Persian that they keep indoors," he warns me.

"Duly noted," I say, as I jimmy the door.

The house, a post-modern monstrosity, boasts curved walls of glass to take in the view of Hilldale's hills and the ocean beyond. Between all the sun streaming in and the all-white color scheme, I have to shield my eyes to the abundance of light.

Roger's office is in the loft above the living room. Windows are on three sides. The fourth side consists of a wall with a double door that leads to the master bedroom suite. Both spaces share a terrace. As I make my way to the other side of Roger's desk, I hear a cat: a fat white Persian. It stares up at me from one of the two large tufted leather easy chairs facing Roger's desk. When it stretches up and out, I scratch it under its chin.

It purrs appreciatively. The cat could do this all day. Unfortunately, I can't.

I glance down at the desk: dark mahogany with ball-and-claw feet, it's an antique from the nineteen-twenties. The top is covered with a green blotter. But there isn't a computer on it– just an old Underwood typewriter.

"No computer? How can that be?" I ask Arnie. "I thought we'd tracked the ISIS text to this address!"

"We did," Arnie insists. "Maybe it's on a bookcase or the

credenza? Look for a smaller device as well—either an iPad or a second cell phone."

"On it."

Beside the typewriter is a three-inch stack of yellow paper: Roger's current work in progress.

I slide open the middle desk drawer to see if it holds any wireless devices. Nope, just a bunch of bills—and a rejection letter from his editor:

Sorry, Rog, old chap. Despite a stellar premise and your typical elaborate plot for an incomparable hero, we must pass on the book. The lackluster sales of your last novel....

Yikes.

And considering the mortgage on this place, no wonder he and Sienna are scrambling to win the show's prize.

The desk drawers on either side of the middle one yield nothing. Nor does the bookcase, or the small table behind Roger's desk.

I enter the master bedroom. Again, nothing on the bookshelves in there, or in the nightstands—

However, the nightstand on the right has a drawer containing an extensive collection of dildos of all lengths, girths, and tactile sensations.

"I think I've found Sienna's happy place," I murmur.

"More like a little shop of horrors," Arnie retorts. "Doesn't say much for Roger's ability to please his lady. Ha, funny! If you read that dude's books, you'd think he was hung like a—"

"*Shhh*! I hear something...voices!" I run to the door and peer down the spiral staircase. "Arnie, give me eyes—pronto!"

"Shit!" he exclaims. "Roger is home—with Sienna, and two medical orderlies. They're bringing her into the house!"

If I go back out into the loft, I can be easily spotted, so I stay in the bedroom. The massive round bed sits on a platform too low for me to slip under it. The door leading to the balcony is locked, and its key is nowhere to be seen. There are two other doors. I open them: closets, damn it. Unfortunately, they are my only choices for a hiding place. Now, which is the one least likely to be opened?

I choose hers.

The voices are getting closer. "Jesus, New Girl, she looks as if she ran into a boulder! Can't you and your goons be more careful with her?"

"We're doing the best we can, Mr. Pembroke." Emma's voice sounds tired. Kowtowing to these pseudo-celebrities is taking its toll on her.

They are now in the bedroom. I peek through the door.

Sienna is certainly out of it. Her delirious groans are heartbreaking, but no louder than the grunts from the orderlies who gently position her onto the bed.

"You're not leaving her there in—that thing." Roger is pointing down at Sienna's hospital gown.

"Despite my explicit directions, the only other thing she brought with her was a flimsy negligee," Emma counters. "We couldn't very well wheel her into the surgical suite in that! The network censors would have had a tizzy fit—not to mention it would have distracted the medical staff."

"Well, she's home with me now, and I can't have her upset over something so important as sleeping in something other than silk." I duck just as he whips around to the closet. "In there you'll find a collection of chemises."

Emma rolls her eyes but heads toward the door.

I leap out of sight just in time—

But she's already gasped before I've had a chance to cover her mouth with my hand.

"What is it?" Roger asks crossly.

"Nothing…It's just…that her wardrobe is so, er, stunning! Not to worry, I'll be right out. Mr. Pembroke, please listen carefully to the orderlies' instructions on how to take care of Sienna over the next two days." Emma's eyes open wide, looking for an explanation from me.

Time for charades. My hand signals indicate one word, three syllables. I mimic typing on a keyboard.

She shakes her head and points toward the other side of the door.

"Tell her to put on her Acme earbuds," Arnie suggests.

Duh. I pull one of mine out and stick it in Emma's ear.

In the meantime, Roger is hyperventilating. "What? But...aren't you going to stay and look after her? I need her awake, and fast— or I can't complete my book!"

"Please, don't panic!" Emma's screech isn't that reassuring. She's finding it hard to reply with Arnie shouting in her ear COMPUTER! WE'RE LOOKING FOR A COMPUTER OR OTHER WIFI DEVICE. "The show will have a nurse here twenty-four-seven until she's back on her feet—as good as new!" She turns to me, hissing, "First things first—I've got to shut him up. Help me find a gown for Sleeping Beauty."

While Emma rummages through all the hanging clothes, I fling open drawers, looking for anything long and see-through. I slap her arm when I hit the jackpot: a drawer filled with sheer nude chemises and see-through lace gowns.

Even more interesting: in the drawer underneath all of Sienna's lingerie is an iPad. Its top is also a keyboard.

Hmmm. Why hide it in here?

There's only one way to find out. I insert the scanner, and then signal Emma: Five minutes.

She nods, grabs three or four of the gowns, and heads out of the closet with them, but leaves it open just wide enough for me to glance out.

"How about these?" she asks Roger.

"That one? No! It will never do. Considering what she's just gone through, it may be too small now...okay, maybe this one... No, no, this one is much better! Now, help me put it on her."

Emma stammers, "But…that's what the orderlies are for!"

"They're men! I'll not have them gawking at my fiancée!"

"They were the ones who put her into this hospital gown in the first place! Believe me; they've see it all," Emma argues. "Haven't you?"

I can't see, but I guess the men are nodding.

"Don't argue with me!" Roger screeches. "Or I'll have you fired —and the two of them as well."

"We'll wait downstairs," one of the orderlies mutters. The next thing I hear is the sound of their footsteps going down the stairs.

"Now see what you've done? She's waking up! Quick! I'll hold her up while you replace that rag with something decent!"

The scanner's buzz comes not a moment too soon. I pull it out and then upload it to Acme's secure cloud.

"Got it," Arnie assures me.

Good, because I'm out of here.

I nudge the door open a few more inches and peek out. Now that Roger has propped up his fiancée, Emma is straddling her to place the gown over poor Sienna's head. Getting down on my hands and knees, I crawl out of the closet—

Only to run into Sienna's white Persian cat.

Its *MEOW* is loud enough to turn Roger's head in my direction. I hit the floor. At the same time, Emma pulls the negligee over Sienna's head, purposefully tangling her charge's arms through the holes as well. Standing up to block his view, she declares, "Hey, um, Roger! I could use a little help here!"

I smack the cat on its ass. It shrieks. Realizing now that I'm more foe than friend, it hisses before bounding onto the bed—

To burrow in its naked mistress's lap.

Instead, it gets tangled in the gown along with Sienna, who screams deliriously.

"That is some…er, mean pussy," Arnie murmurs.

It's hard for me to appreciate his pun—not now that Sienna's eyes are open wide, and staring straight at me.

"Don…Donna…there…how…"

Before her moans make sense, I roll out of the room.

I can hear the orderlies waiting at the base of the staircase, talking and laughing about something: photos of Penelope and Sienna, apparently taken while escorting the unconscious women to their homes. The men are comparing notes on their sales of celebrity patients to the various gossip rags.

I don't want to be around my competitors when photos of their black-and-blue bruised and surgically inflated chests hit the newsstands. As it is, I've overstayed my welcome at Casa Pembroke.

So how do I get out of here without running into the two mercenary orderlies?

"There are some photographers out front," Arnie warns me.

Shit.

I run to the terrace. At this height, I'll break my neck in a jump—

Unless it's into the large kidney-shaped pool in the backyard.

As I take off in that direction, I measure its distance from the house with my eye. Can I make the leap from here?

Arnie is on my wavelength: "If you're thinking of jumping into the pool, I'd suggest—"

Whatever he has to say next doesn't matter since Roger is coming through the bedroom door. He's arguing with Emma. "What do you mean, you don't have her meds! Don't you hear her? She's hallucinating! My God, she's accusing me of having an affair with the one who's a slut…what's her name? Oh, yeah, Donna—"

I leap.

It's a clean jack-knife, making barely a splash.

I wish Jack had seen it.

Then again, he probably has, if he's been monitoring the video feed coming in from my contacts.

As I swim silently to the side of the pool, I wonder how the action will stack up against tonight's show.

I guess we'll see in a couple of hours.

The sun broils overhead. In a moment, any damp handprints I leave as I hike myself over Roger's back wall will soon disappear without a trace.

I hear an appreciative whistle. Ah, it's Jack. He waits on the hill overlooking Roger and Sienna's house.

Jack has a large beach towel in his hand. Better still, he has the picnic lunch I'd packed for the Garretts.

As my man wraps me in the towel, he asks, "Dark or white meat?"

I kiss him before reminding him, "I'd like a bit of both, please."

Up here, Hilldale seems peaceful.

As if reading my mind, Jack reminds me, "Four more days."

Each one will seem like an eternity.

All the more reason to savor this little moment together.

15

Big Love

"I don't know that a marriage based on love can go the distance:
the sacred holiness of the institution; the sanctity of marriage.
Without it, it's just random couplings, with no purpose or stick-to-
it-iveness. How will we survive the bad times on just love?"
—Nikki Grant

There is no definition of marriage.

For some, it is a convenience.

For others, it is a commitment.

*Still others strive to turn a temporary state of infatuation into their
own reality show.*

*Reality Check: You're just a couple of people stumbling through life
—together.*

*You want him to slay your dragons. He hopes you can cast out his
demons.*

*You are not the princess waiting for her savior. And he isn't some
Prince Charming who has been looking for you all of his life.*

*For you to sustain your happily ever after for a lifetime, remember one
rule: you're in this thing together.*

THE KIDS ARE HAPPY TO HAVE US HOME WITH THEM, BUT NO MORE than we are. It's a relief to not have *Hot Housewives of Hilldale*'s harsh spotlight trained on us, if only for one night.

Along with the rest of the competitors, Jack and I already received texts from Brin:

We look forward to seeing you tomorrow, Day Four, no later than 6 p.m. sharp! By then, we anticipate that all of the brave Housewives who were generous enough to donate (their bodies) for charity will have recovered sufficiently to watch the videos of support that have been pouring in from your devoted fans! You'll also hear your husbands' awe and adoration for the sacrifice you made to become their ideals—and you'll catch up with their adventures as well! Afterward, we'll tally up your points! For those who have disappointed their fans with a lackluster performance, extracurricular tasks are available to boost your vote counts.

"She might as well have added, '*Donna, this means you*'—exclamation point!" I grouse to Jack.

"Hey, quiet in the peanut gallery!" Phyllis hushes me. "The show is about to start!"

All eyes turn toward the screen. In anticipation of doom, Jeff squints out of one eye. Trisha, also expecting the worst, covers her eyes with one hand, but the fingers are spaced so that she doesn't miss one horrifying moment.

The opening credits are a montage of jaw-dropping moments in the Housewives' lives. Intercut between lovey-dovey moments between husbands and wives are hair-raising shouting matches caught on camera when the couple thought they were in private. And yet, Penelope's drunken escapades at the Casa del Mar are the most groan-worthy.

The montage fades away to a shot of Dominic in yet another new tuxedo, standing beside the full-length television screen in the media room of the *Housewives'* mansion. "Welcome to *Hot House-wives of Hilldale,* where the question on everyone's lips is surely, how big are my neighbor's"—he pauses in order to leer directly at the camera—"fibs? And what will she do when they are exposed to the public?" He shifts his gaze to a second camera. "Tonight, you'll see several acts of courage, all for a great cause: the very noble charity founded by one of our competing families: Plastic Surgeons Without Borders."

The camera follows him as he walks to the coffee table in order to pick up the television's remote control. "And tonight, you'll be shocked to learn that we'll be saying goodbye to one of our competing families." He pauses, as if anticipating the gasps heard around the world. "The reason for their leaving is outrageous, as it was caused by the actions of a competing Housewife." As the camera comes in for a close-up, Dominic raises a brow. "Stay tuned to find out who's been naughty to one who has been nothing but nice…"

"Emma!" Ryan's bark comes in so loud through our ear buds that both Jack and I sit straight up. "Should we be concerned?"

"Um…I don't think so, Boss," Emma mutters. "Let me see what's up…"

Mary pats my arm. "Mom, are you okay?"

Shit! Was I caught on camera somehow?

I nod. Forcing a smile on my lips, I add, "Yeah, sure. I'm just anticipating the worst with this show."

She frowns. "Me too. Um…I should warn you. He may be referring to something that I said…to Jenna."

I hug her. "Honey, don't worry. My guess is that it has nothing to do with you."

She turns her head in order to whisper into my ear fervently: *"Why? What did you do?"*

I put a finger to my lips.

She sighs, frustrated and anxious.

We'll learn about the culprit soon enough.

EXCEPT FOR A MINUTE-AND-A-HALF CLIP OF "THE ONE HOUSEWIFE WHO elected out of surgery but who's always available to pose with adoring fans" (a.k.a., me, in all my retro polka-dot slut gear glory, posing for a selfie with the couple at the grocery store) for the most part tonight's show focuses on the women who opted for Franklin's breast enhancement offer.

To build tension as well as to fill the show's first hour, the patients are given six-minute personal profiles that begin with mournful stares in full-length mirrors. They then give soul-searching monologues as to why they think their decisions will be "a chance to wrong a few rights" (according to Penelope) or "because looking good means feeling great!" (Sienna) or "because my husband deserves the best wife in the world..." (Patty) or "I changed my mind because it's for a good cause..." (Cassandra).

They are then taken in hand by Franklin, who describes completely but gently what the operation will entail; and how best to facilitate a speedy recovery. He ends each interview by showing them "before" photos, along with ones with their heads superimposed over computer-generated fantasy breasts.

A gal can dream, right?

Ironically, it won't affect the one part of the chest he cannot touch: their hearts. Any doubts or feeling of self-loathing they have still swells somewhere deep within that organ.

I take that back. His ability to convince Cassandra to change her mind speaks volumes as to where her heart lies:

Firmly within his grasp.

The patients' profiles then move to quick overhead cuts taken of their operations. Each of the women is honored with a music playlist chosen specifically for her: Katy Perry for Penelope, whereas Sienna gets a Taylor Swift mix. Patty's operation is performed to Rhianna, while Cassandra goes under the knife with some old-school Beyoncé: *Dangerously in Love.*

The women's faces and bodies below the chest are sheathed. Still, the viewing audience is surely gasping over Franklin's terse commands for sharp or probing instruments. It must also be gulping back any bile that rises with each expert incision. As Franklin's operating team *oohs* and *ahhs* over his deft skills, I'm sure that, like my family, viewers are also awed by his skills.

And when he finally declares, "Beautiful! That's a wrap..." after each operation, no doubt applause can be heard around the world.

After the last operation—Cassandra's—Aunt Phyllis sighs loudly. I imagine she's wondering if she made a mistake by walking away from his offer.

To assure her that she didn't, Mary clasps her hand. "I am so worried about them. When all is said and done, what if they still don't like who they are?"

Aunt Phyllis shrugs. "How did you get so wise at such a young age?" When she hugs her grandniece, she misses Mary's smile at me.

I slide over to throw my arms around both of them.

But a moment later I'm tossed back into the alternate reality of my life when Ryan barks, "Emma?"

All he gets is radio silence.

He sighs loudly.

Like me, he's realizing that a bombshell will drop any moment —if not literally, then figuratively.

THE NEXT TWENTY MINUTES OF THE SHOW IS DEVOTED TO ROGER, Peter, and Gerald as they pick out their tuxes for Sienna and Roger's wedding.

At first, the men stay on cue (per Lucy's ominous warning, which rings through our Acme earbuds) and use their time on camera to win over the audience by talking about what they love and cherish about the women in their lives.

As Peter preens in front of a full-length mirror, he takes the opportunity to point out the obvious about his wife: "Penelope will do anything to win—just like me. You just wait and see. She'll be the one with the biggest boobs of all the women."

"*Argh!*" Jeff groans. "As if that's some sort of accomplishment! Poor Cheever!"

"Something tells me he'll make the most of it," Evan retorts.

Mary nods in agreement. "Knowing him, he'll figure out a way to cut a hole in the wall of her bedroom and sell tickets to the peep show."

Jeff's face turns bright red. "That's disgusting!"

I agree, but Mary makes a good point: Cheever has a way of turning others' bad decisions into lucrative opportunities for himself. If it's the first time he does so at his mother's expense, it won't be the last.

"Bigger isn't always better, old boy," Gerald murmurs as he straightens a cuff. "Do you ever wonder how Penelope would do in a war zone? How would she react at the sight of heads blown off?"

"Yeah, yeah, okay we get it: your wife is a saint." Peter rolls his eyes.

Gerald quits tugging at his sleeve as he contemplates his fellow groomsman's retort. "She is, in fact. It's why I love her. And why… Cassandra is right that we must always do things that make us bigger than ourselves."

"Yeah, well a boob job will certainly make her 'bigger,'" Peter snorts.

It's Roger who gives the most touching declaration of all: "Without Sienna, I'd be nothing—I'd be no one. She made me who I am today."

His eyes glisten tearfully.

He truly loves her.

I lean into Jack and whisper, "Roger isn't our suspect."

"What makes you think so?" he asks.

I shrug. "It's just a feeling I have. He's too…Oh, I don't know —*soft*, I guess."

It takes a moment of contemplation for Jack to see my point. "You're right. He's besotted. No one who's that much in love will risk losing everything."

With the children around, Jack stops there as opposed to saying: *by blowing himself up to prove a point. By doing something that might get him a life sentence. By doing anything that might turn her away from him.*

Which begs the question: who is our man?

THE MOMENT EVERYONE IS WAITING FOR COMES RIGHT BEFORE THE LAST commercial break.

To ratchet up the tension, the producers have placed Dominic outside, by the pool. He is lit in such a way that the dimple in his chin looks even deeper. Thanks to the show's exacting make-up artists, his cheekbones jut even more prominently from his superciliously handsome face.

His stare, directly into the camera, prefaces some ominous doom.

Like a good host, he waits until the last rousing flourishes of the show's theme song have faded. "And now, it is with great sadness that we say goodbye to one of our own." He beckons someone forward:

Ariel.

Despite the efforts of the show's make-up artists, it's obvious by her red-rimmed eyes that she has been crying.

"Ariel Powell, please—tell us why you've made the decision to leave the show?" Dominic's plea is so ardent that it could be coming from a heartbroken lover.

Ariel sighs mightily. "Believe me, Dominic, I wish my experience with *Hot Housewives of Hilldale* had been everything Franklin and I had hoped for. But unfortunately, not all the wives are playing by the rules."

He leans in closer to her. "What do you mean, Ariel?"

Anticipating the worst, the camera comes in close on Ariel. She stares directly into it as she proclaims: "One of the Housewives is having an affair with the husband of another!"

"Really?" Aunt Phyllis shakes her head in disbelief. "Just *one* of the Housewives?"

"*Boo-yah!*" Brin crows through the control room. "You see, people? That's how you stay *numero uno* in the ratings, night after night! Way to go, Lucy, for convincing her to reveal this on camera."

"Piece of cake," Lucy boasts. "I told her it was her civic duty to reveal the whoring housewife. She said she'd do so, but only if we promised to toss the harlot off the show."

Yikes. There goes our mission.

Dominic is smart enough to shut his yap so that the squeals taking place in living rooms around the world—including my own —don't drown out what he says next:

"Who is it, Ariel?"

I sink into the couch.

I can feel Mary's eyes on me. And Jack's.

Still, I keep my eyes directly on the TV. The camera is now so close on Ariel that her freckles can be seen even through her thick pancake foundation. She purses her lips. It may be just a few seconds, but it seems like eons before she finally exhales. "I...I won't say her name here."

Dominic's mouth drops open. Unsure of how to handle this, his eyes shift off camera.

"You—Hottie Host: don't just stand there looking brain dead!" Brin shouts into the crews' earpieces. "Appeal to her sense of morality! Use that old chestnut—what is it? ...Oh yeah: 'Sistah Solidarity!' Hell, remind her of all the money we just paid her husband's damn charity, for God's sake—"

"No, don't do that," Emma counters. Her voice is calm. Coolly, she adds, "We should keep the audience guessing about it until the very last show!"

"New Girl is right!" Brin proclaims. "If our mystery whore thinks she's gotten away with it, she may hookup with Wayward Hubby again—and this time, we'll be ready to catch it on camera. Quick thinking, New Girl!"

"I second that," Ryan adds for our ears only.

No one is more relieved than me.

Finally, Dominic finds his voice. "Ariel, your discretion is… well, there is no way to describe it except noble. It is a trait our audience has come to identify with the Powells."

Ariel's eyes harden. "I guess I should thank you for that." She shrugs. "But let me assure you: I don't presume we Powells are grander, or as you put it more 'noble' than anyone else. That woman…I imagine she is doing what she feels is best for her family. And by walking away from this so-called reality"—Ariel's hand sweeps out toward the mansion's luxurious surroundings —"I know I'm doing what is best for mine."

She then does just that: turns her back to the camera and walks away.

"Bravo," Jack murmurs.

I know what he's thinking: *If only we could do the same.*

With a hesitant smile, Dominic turns back to the camera. "Think you know which of our housewives is also a home-wrecker? Text your guess to the number at the bottom of your television screens! Press 1 for Donna, 2 for Penelope, 3 for Sienna, 4 for Cassandra, 5 for Patty, and 6 for Phyllis—"

"Yes! I have a number! Yes! Yes!" Phyllis shouts jubilantly.

"You're proud of that?" Jeff shakes his head in wonder. He rises and heads for the stairs. "That's it for me. Back to the real world."

Evan laughs. "Oh, yeah? And what would that be?"

"I'm helping Sami develop an app that will track the creeps who are bullying him."

"That's kind of you," I reply. As I stand to stretch, Mary touches me on the shoulder. "Mom, can we talk?"

I nod and then follow her up to her room. I assume it's about her most recent altercation with Jenna.

After she closes her bedroom door, she takes the time she needs to find her words. Finally, she blurts out: "Did you…was it you who had the affair with one of those deplorable men?"

I'm so stunned that I sink onto her bed. "Why would you even ask me that?"

"Because…I would imagine your job means you have to…you know…be a tease—or something…worse." Her eyes dart around the room because she can't look me in the eye.

Our pact rings in my ear: *no more lies.*

And yet, I need to salvage so much with what I say next:

The realities of my life as a covert operative and assassin.

The compromise Jack and I accept as part and parcel of our marriage.

My daughter's respect for me.

I reach for her in order to tilt her head so she can look me in the eye: "I have never betrayed your father—and I never will."

The words I speak are simple. They are also true.

Relieved, she smothers me with kisses. As we both cry, she stutters, "I'm so sorry. I'm ashamed I even asked…but…"

"You needed to know." I shrug. "It's okay. Because of what I do —and how I must do it—you'll always hear rumors. But the perceptions of others…well, it's just that: they see what I want them to see."

Her smile fades. "So…sometimes you have to be…that way?"

"Yes. Sometimes I have to make them think I'm someone I'm not. It's the only way I'll get whatever information I need from them."

And the price is very high—sometimes their lives.

Her shrug indicates she doesn't need to hear any more. My guess is that she doesn't want to anyway. To change the subject, I ask, "You mentioned some issue Jenna has with you."

Mary nods. She walks over to her desk and opens her computer bag. She pulls out a note. Walking it over to me, she says, "It's from Jenna."

The note is handwritten. The letters are wild. It reads:

Dear Mary,

I'm sorry I keep reaching out to you, but I think it's important that you know that I'd never intrude on your relationship with Evan. Not that I even could. He loves you too much.

I just appreciate that he's kind enough to be my friend. I don't know why he does it. If I were him (or for that matter anyone) I'd run as far away from me as I could! I don't like me either. So no, I don't blame you for thinking I'm weird.

Before the show, no one noticed me. I can't blame them. If they did, they would loathe me, and not for any reason you might think. But now everyone thinks they know what my life is like, just like they think they know yours. Only you understand what bullshit that is.

If my real life didn't suck so badly, I might even enjoy all of this. But it does, and I don't.

Which brings me to why I'm writing you:

I hope you'll let me spend the weekend at your house. I don't know how the show will end. I just know that my parents will never win. People don't like them, just like they don't like me.

When they lose, he will blame Mom. I feel sorry for her, but I can't take it anymore.

I hope you'll let me stay. It would be so great to hang with some normal people.

Jenna

"I called her already and told her no. She got so upset that she started begging me, but…I just can't!"

"Why not? It sounds as if she just wants some space from her family. The show is hard on everyone." *Say yes! The poor girl's life is scary and miserable…*

"Believe me, it's not because she wants us to be friends." Mary shrugs. "If you ask me, she's using the show as an excuse to get closer to Evan! When he heard I told her no, he made me feel like such a…well, a *bitch*."

I know Mary isn't looking for me to talk her out of her decision. She wants validation instead.

She's given it to me. I owe her that in return. "I trust you to do what you feel is best."

She throws her arms around me again. "Thank you! You're the best mom in the world—even if you're not the most normal one."

You can say that again.

Is there such thing as a "normal mom?"

I'd argue no. Every mother is unique. Every mother must do what she has to, in order to protect her family—no questions asked.

No regrets.

Hopefully, she'll never learn the extent to which I was never her ideal.

House of Cards

"A great man once said, everything is about sex. Except sex. Sex is about power."
—Frank Underwood

Okay, kiddies, time to talk about sex! Here's what it is—and what it isn't:

Sex means never having to say you're sorry. (Unlike love, which is always about saying it—and with gusto.)

Sex comes from the gut. (Unlike love, which comes from the heart.)

Sex isn't pretty, but it's satisfying. (Unlike love, which is beautiful, but always leaves you hungry for more.)

Sex shouldn't be work. It should be fun. (Unlike love, which takes hard work, and is a constant challenge.)

And finally: no matter what age, sex should always be in your life. (Unlike love, which will stay with you for eternity.)

JACK AND I WAKE TO TWO TEXTS. THE FIRST, FROM BRIN, IS A GROUP missive to all *Hot Housewives* couples. It reads:

Congratulations, ladies, on your speedy recoveries—and your incredible overnight ratings! Because of your heroic sacrifices, once again we were Number One for the night!

We realize you may still be a bit tender, so we've devised an easy challenge task: a Hot Housewives Book Swap, here at the mansion. Please show up an hour earlier than airtime to get into makeup—and a new wardrobe, courtesy of the show! Feel free to bring your favorite book to share with the other housewives—and our audience! In fact, the audience will demonstrate its support by weighing in on your choice!

Speaking of which, as of this morning, we have a new vote count! I guess you've already figured out that Ariel's departure works in everyone's favor. Still ONLY ONE OF YOU CAN WIN. And as of right now, here are your vote counts:

Sienna: 739,665 (Way to go, girl! You moved up because you got the most votes for the night! Viewers can't wait to see your new bod in your bridal attire!)

Penelope: 641,940 (Stuck in second place—again, Penelope! But if you want to win, you better up your game!)

Cassandra: 540,302 (Looks like she made the right decision to "pump it up" after all!)

Patty: 432,594 (FINALLY out of last place! And wait until they see the "new you" out of that awful muumuu!)

Donna: 331,976 (Well, girl, what do you expect? Sadly, not everyone agrees with Jack that you're perfect. But if it's any consolation, so far most viewers are convinced that you're the whoring Housewife! Congrats!)

Remember: Sadly, none of these are higher than Ariel's last count: 884,221. YOU NEED TO UP YOUR GAME!

Including tonight, only three more days on the air, so EVERY VOTE COUNTS.

"And it won't be a day too soon," Jack mutters. "What book are you bringing?"

"Gee, I don't know. Most of the stuff I read nowadays is classified case files. It's been too long since I've read for pleasure." I think for a moment. "Maybe *Pride and Prejudice*? How can you go wrong with that?"

"Remember: every vote counts. Do you think the show's audience is into Jane Austen?"

"If they're not, I feel sorry for them! It's got everything: romance, unrequited love, great pageantry, a gossip-hungry small town, and it ends with a wedding—oh, and a real bitch trying to ruin things for the heroine—"

Jack laughs. "You're right. It's the perfect read for viewers of *Hot Housewives of Hilldale*."

He glances down at the second text: this one, thankfully, not from Brin, the pit viper. "It's from Arnie. He wants to remind you that Ryan asked you to hone in on Gerald, and the sooner, the better. Somehow the CIA got its hands on Farnham's file with Al Mukhabarat Al A'amah—Saudi Arabia's intelligence agency."

"Does it explain why he left the country under such secret circumstances?"

Jack texts my question back to Arnie.

A minute later, we're reading his answer:

Hard to say. As soon as we can read between all the redaction, Abu will translate—but it doesn't look good for Farnham.

I frown. "Interesting. I would guess our suspect is tending to his missus as she recuperates."

"As a matter of fact, Arnie wrote that Gerald is teaching at Hilldale State University. Keeping his morning classes was part of his deal with the show. However, he has a break between classes from noon to one."

"Lucky me," I groan. "Oh, well. I'll head over after I drop the kids at school."

"No, I'll do drop-off today." He pauses before sheepishly

adding, "And then I'm heading over to Beverly Hills. Brin wants me to meet some network execs."

I prop myself up on an elbow. "My, my! She's pulling out all the stops to get you onboard."

"You mean, to get us on board. No hard feelings, right? We both know I've got to keep her in play—just a few more days."

I shrug. "Sure, all good. While Gerald is chasing me around a desk, you'll be having a power lunch at Mr. Chow's."

Jack laughs. "Okay, yeah, something like that." He moves in the hope of getting to second base.

I roll out of bed instead. "Sorry, no time for fun and games. I've got to pull together some sexy schoolgirl costume." A thought stops me. "Hey, would an instructor bring his cell phone to class?"

Jack contemplates my question for a moment. "Maybe not, since it sets a bad example for students. Maybe you can get to his office early enough that you don't have to see him at all."

"Jack Craig, move to the head of the class!" I kiss Jack firmly on the lips. "Thank goodness no roleplaying today!"

"No slutty student role play?" Jack mutters. "Darn it! I should have kept my mouth shut."

"No, sorry. I'm sticking to jeans, a T-shirt, and a hoodie, just like every other co-ed."

Still, here's hoping I don't get recognized by any of Gerald's students. After last night's show, the last thing I need is to validate any rumors that I'm Ariel's housewife whore.

That role honestly belongs to Cassandra, even if neither Ariel nor Gerald realizes this—yet.

As planned, I arrive at Gerald Farnham's office on the third floor of Hilldale State University's Law School building just as he starts his ten-thirty class. He has no secretary, and it only takes me a minute to pick the lock on his office door. His class runs fifty-five minutes, so I should have plenty of time before he walks back in.

Frankly, his office is a dump. The only difference between it and a supply closet is that it has a window: now open, thank goodness, since the room doesn't appear to be air-conditioned. A two-foot wide ledge hangs a few feet beneath it.

It doesn't look out on much: an alley filled with dumpsters. They contain the remnants of lunches tossed into the student center's trash cans. And in this heat, boy do they stink!

The office is so small that it barely has room for his cracked leather chair and aging oak desk. Crowding it, even more, are two file cabinets topped with all manner of books that almost reach the ceiling. A couple of guest chairs are crammed in front of the desk.

Disappointingly, his computer isn't here. However, I do find his cell phone in the top left drawer. Bingo! I insert the scanner into the phone.

It doesn't take long before I hear the buzz. I've just disconnected the devices when I hear voices:

They are speaking an Arabic dialect.

One of the voices belongs to Gerald.

I toss the phone back into the drawer and shut it.

"Donna! Out the window!" Arnie shouts.

I crouch on the ledge and pray that Gerald and his friend don't look out.

"I'M TAPING THE CONVERSATION SO THAT ACME CAN TRANSLATE IT later," Arnie informs me.

"Just dandy. And what are you doing to get me off this ledge?" I mutter.

"Don't worry, the cavalry is on its way," he replies. "Whoa, they're now speaking in English! Hey, see if you can get closer to the window. I've pumped up the volume all I can."

I sigh, but rise to my knees and inch closer to the window:

"—the minister. I'm sure you understand that nothing has changed, as far as he is concerned."

The man speaks with a slight Middle-Eastern accent. From what I can tell, he's sucking on a cigarette. So much for adhering to the school's no-smoking policy.

"However," the man continues, "if you're willing to follow through with the minister's request—"

"No! I'm sorry, but…" Gerald's words stutter to a halt. "Look, I told you: it was all a mistake! I've made amends already! You know I have. As far as this very last thing you want—I…I just can't! Please, you must understand what it would do to my family—!"

"Mr. Farnham, don't misunderstand me. You will follow through on our wishes. Your life depends on it—and that of your family."

I hear the man's footsteps coming closer. Is he looking out the window? Does he see me?

Apparently not. He walked my way to flick out his cigarette butt—

Onto my back!

I smell it before I feel it as it burns through my hoodie and T-shirt before singeing my skin.

I leap off the ledge—

And into the dumpster.

As I lie on a soft spongy bed of rancid spaghetti, salad, and sandwiches, I try to think of a way this might be worse.

Nah, I can't think of anything.

Well, then there you go.

I stay still enough to see if I'll sink any further into this muck. When it looks as if I'm as low as I can go, I'll find a way to climb out of this crap.

It's the story of my life.

"Sorry it took me so long to get to you," Abu apologizes. "I had to slip out when Lucy wasn't looking."

I sigh. "Frankly, it was kind of you to let me into your car. I know this stench won't be easy to get rid of. I hope it doesn't affect your Uber driver rating too much."

"Nah, don't worry about it. I'm thinking of giving up the gig. All I need is another forty hours behind the camera and I can join the union." Abu smiles proudly.

"Gee, well, congratulations! But that doesn't mean you're leaving Acme, does it?"

"Heck no. Unless Scorsese calls. Or Spielberg. Or Tarantino. And, okay, yeah, David Yates—"

Seeing my shock, he laughs. "Donna, don't worry. There is no greater thrill than working at Acme. We both know it." He looks at me sideways. "Isn't that why you came back after your attempt at retirement?"

I laugh. "What retirement? It was a week off, tops." I stick my finger through the burn hole in my hoodie. "Hey, do you think Ryan will reimburse me for this?"

"You can ask him yourself. I'm taking you there now."

"Smelling like this?" I shake my head adamantly. "Oh, no, you don't!"

"Donna, POTUS is in town. In fact, he's meeting with Ryan now, and there's no time for a detour."

I slump into the seat.

Well, if anything will break Lee Chiffray's schoolboy crush on me, smelling like a pile of week-old garbage should do it.

Ryan raises his nose in the air. "What's that smell?"

No hello. No "Glad you survived a two-story fall"—nothing.

Slowly, I raise my hand; the one that isn't smeared with peanut butter and jelly.

Ryan rolls his eyes.

Emma, Arnie, Abu, and Dominic seem to be holding their collective breath. On the plus side, this keeps them from outright laughing.

As for Lee, he hides his grin behind the Acme report of our mission thus far.

"Where's Jack?" Ryan barks.

"Um…Mr. Chow." I shrug. "Taking a meeting. Studio suits. For, um…a spin-off."

Ryan frowns.

Lee's smile widens.

"The president's time is tight. We'll just have to start without him," Ryan growls. He taps his iPad screen.

We now see headshots of all the Housewives and their husbands on the conference room monitor. Ryan says, "To recap: we firmly believe that ISIS has indeed infiltrated *Hot Housewives of Hilldale*. In fact, on the first night of the show, Acme intercepted texts from a known terrorist cell to a cell phone on the set. We're now going through a process of elimination. So far, all of the show's crewmembers' cell phones and computers have been scanned, the text and email data vetted, and the devices cleared. The same process is taking place for the contestants."

As Ryan taps a photo of a male contestant, the picture lights up. "Thus far, Donna has secured access to the phones of the following male suspects: Franklin Powell, James Garrett, Roger Pembroke, and Gerald Farnham."

Lee nods. "Other than Donna and Jack, there are five couples in the show. Who's missing?"

"That would be Peter and Penelope Bing," Emma responds.

Lee winces. "I'm all too familiar with them. Frankly, I'd be surprised if they turned out to be our targets—"

"Agreed, sir." I'll say anything to get them off my plate if not out of my life.

Lee glances over at me. "As I was saying, in any event, they may be pawns on some level, so let's keep them in play."

I nod. Well now, there's the cherry on the cake of my day.

"Emma secured the phones of these female suspects while they were in surgery." He taps each picture. "In order, they are Penelope, Patty Garrett, and Cassandra Farnham. The last woman is Sienna Woodruff. She is Roger Pembroke's fiancée. Their cell phones were also vetted and cleared."

"One woman is missing," Lee points out.

"Yes, that would be Dr. Powell's wife, Ariel," Emma replies. "Last night, they took themselves out of the running. She found it too stressful."

"Despite her husband's efforts to secure viewer votes and funding for his cause?" Lee's wariness comes through in the tone of his voice. "That's certainly an interesting turn of events. Well, I guess he accomplished his goal."

Lee now leans in. His focus is Sienna's photo. "I've met her. She accompanied Pembroke to a recent White House dinner. Apparently, Babette reads his thrillers." He shrugs. "What did your reconnaissance show on him?"

It's my turn to wince. "At the time I infiltrated their home, Roger was gone, along with his cell phone. And apparently, he doesn't use a computer." It's time for a positive spin. "However, we were able to scan an iPad in the house. We believe it belongs to Sienna."

Lee's eyes narrow. "Why hers? If he doesn't have a computer and needs one to write, wouldn't it logically belong to him?"

"He uses a vintage Underwood, and…" I blush. "I found the iPad in her lingerie drawer."

"I see." Lee coughs to cover his chuckle.

"Our TECHINT team is trying to break the iPad's encryption as we speak," Arnie adds. "Unlike Dr. Frankenstein's computer and the other contestants' cell phones we've scanned, it has unique security software."

"'Dr. Frankenstein'?" Lee frowns at the nickname.

"Well, um, yeah!" Now that Arnie is in the hot seat, he sits straight up. "By that I mean Dominic called him Dr. Frank on the air, and then Donna added the '—enstein.'" He chuckles in the hope that the others will too.

No one bites.

Ryan's scowl deepens.

Lee frowns. "In other words, Acme has come up empty."

Arnie gulps. "For now. We're still assessing Gerald's cell phone, and will soon hack Sienna's iPad—"

Lee waves him into silence. "Then get on it. Don't let me keep you." He rises.

So do the rest of us. As we stream out of the room, Lee says, "Donna, I'm on my way into Hilldale. Would you like a lift?"

I stop in my tracks. I think before turning around. "Sir, if you're talking about the presidential limo, you may have to fumigate it afterward." I can just imagine what Babette would think. The last thing she needs is a reminder that I'm still in Lee's life.

Lee laughs. "We'll go in one of the decoys." He shakes Ryan's hand. "We'll talk later."

He escorts me out the door.

As we walk out, his Secret Service detail sniffs the air, but say nothing.

"So, when I tune in tonight, what should I expect?" To Lee's credit, he's not hugging the door on his side of the decoy SUV. I'm sure he sorely wishes he could roll down the window.

I've got to make it up to him somehow—only not in the way he'd like. He's gotten the message: I'm a one-man woman.

"The Housewives who had surgery will be treated to videos of their fans' reactions to their new physiques."

"Thrilling," Lee mutters.

"And in the second hour, the Housewives will have a book swap. I'm reading from *Pride and Prejudice*."

Lee pretends to snore.

I smack his arm. "Not funny," I warn him. "By the way, what brings you back to Hilldale?"

"Babette insists on having the baby in her own bed. She doesn't want photos taken surreptitiously in the hospital."

Knowing how the Housewives were treated, I can't say I blame her.

"You know that you're the biggest target a terrorist cell could ask for."

He nods. This time, though, he's not smiling.

"Don't worry. I plan on staying out of its way." His hand reaches out for mine. "Does that mean I have to stay out of your way too?"

"At least until we've got a suspect in custody." It's a reasonable excuse.

He squeezes my hand. "Are you talking for you, or for Jack?"

"For both of us." I turn to face him. "Lee, you're a dear sweet friend. I'd hate to lose you."

"I feel the same way about you." He opens my palm to stroke my fingers. "I don't like the thought of you so close to some bomber—"

"You forget—this is my job."

"Donna, I'd never forgive myself if I lost you!"

The decoy vehicle takes a sharp turn as it enters the wide street leading to Hilldale's guarded gate.

I pull my hand away, but he holds tight. "Donna, please—"

"Lee, don't! Babette…she's delivering a child any day now."

"Not my child!" I feel his thumb pressing on the center of my wrist. "You and I—we both know that."

I nod bleakly. "But we also know that you love her—and I love Jack."

Still, Lee doesn't let go of my hand. Instead, he kisses it.

When I stroke his cheek, his other hand stills my palm. I guess it's his way of showing that he doesn't want my sympathy.

I pray he'll still accept my friendship.

The SUV screeches to a halt.

I look out the window. We are parked in front of my house.

Jack's car is in the garage. Worse yet, he's sitting on the front porch, reading the latest issue of the *Hilldale Signal*.

Yes, he glances up when we stop.

And yes, his perpetual grin fades when he sees us, and our entourage.

Finally, Lee allows me to pull away, but not without fair warning: "I'll always have your back."

"I know," I whisper, as I open my door.

Jack is certainly surprised when I get out of one of the SUVs as opposed to one of the many limousines.

My disheveled appearance also surprises him.

He waits until I'm beside him before asking, "I take it things aren't going so great."

"Hold me," I command him.

He does as requested—until his nose gets the better of him. "Whew! Let's get you in the bathtub," he suggests. "You can tell me all about it."

"Only if you go first."

He nods. "Deal. If you scrub my back, I'll scrub yours."

It's the best offer I've had all day.

No, I don't need to reinforce in Jack the notion that Lee is still in love with me. Instead, I tell him only what he needs to know:

Lee and Babette are home because she's due any day now, and she insists on having the child in her own bed at Lion's Lair;

Yes, he's as frustrated as us about the lack of progress being made in identifying and capturing the terrorist cell;

And no, my *Eau de Pepe le Pew* did not turn him off completely.

"What a shame," Jack mutters as he sponges my back. By his tone of voice, I know he means it.

"How about the studio moguls?" I ask, hoping to change the subject. "Did they smell money when you walked into their midst? Did you reek of ratings success?"

He sniffs the air and then shakes his head. "I doubt it. Now, if I'd had you tagging along—"

I splash him until he's gagging for air. "For the record, I don't 'tag' along! And as of this moment"—I sniff an armpit–"I'm as fresh as a daisy." I rise from the tub. "I'll need to keep it that way if I'm going to entice Peter to turn over his cell phone to me."

Jack's snort has nothing to do with the amount of water I splashed up his nose. "That's easy. Just promise him a few X-rated selfies, and he'll gladly hand it over."

"My God, you're a genius!" I exclaim as I wrap myself in my robe. "For once, Brin is right. You're wasted in this mundane spy work. But forget her play to make you a reality show star. You're devious enough to be a producer!"

Jack splashes in my direction, but I'm already out the door and laughing.

17

I Love Lucy

"Ever since we said 'I do,' there's been many things we don't."
—Lucy Ricardo

What is love?

Is it an action based on attraction, or does it build slowly, through a friendship based on trust?

Is it a hot romance, or is it a long-term commitment?

Is it defined by grand displays of affection, or is it proven with random acts of caring?

Can it be just some of these, or must it be all of these?

Here's the deal: love is not just one thing.

It is many things to each person because it is unique to each relationship.

It is perfect despite its flaws.

In other words, it's as human as you and your loved one.

It's why Lucy strived to be in the show.

And it's why Ricky finally let her onstage.

A life well lived has just one mandate: Make sure you find love before you take your final curtain call.

ALTHOUGH THE HUSBANDS AREN'T PARTICIPATING IN THE BOOK CLUB, they've been asked to accompany their wives.

James glowers when he sees me. Noticing this, Jack puts his arm around me and waves him over. "Howdy, neighbor!"

"You're waving a flag at a bull," I warn him.

"He doesn't have the balls," Jack counters. "He's just a bully."

"That's my point. With his type, someone always pays." I nod toward Patty. She's still a bit wan after the operation, but her transformation is impressive. I barely recognize her.

Jack understands. Someone has to do something—and soon.

Somehow, we'll make sure it happens.

Soon the men are rounded up. "Drinks and pu pu's are waiting out by the pool, boys!" Brin proclaims as she shoos them outside. "When you next see your gals, they'll all be prettier than a picture!"

Thanks to Franklin, these recent patients don't need much improvement. Even without makeup, the women look sleek, fit, and above all, sensual.

Patty smiles shyly when I take the makeup chair beside her.

"Patty, you look gorgeous," I exclaim.

"Doesn't she?" Mona, the stylist, gives Patty a hug. Undoubtedly, Mona adores her.

She blushes. "Thank you, Mona! Donna, I feel as if I'm in a dream!"

I nod. "I'll bet the children were surprised."

Her smile falters. "Yes, well, it was an adjustment."

"And James? He must be pleased with your—well, I guess the best word is transformation."

From the way the tears well up in her eyes, apparently not. "He needs more time to get used to the new me."

Mona gives Patty's hand an encouraging squeeze. "Let's show off that beautiful face with an upsweep, shall we?" she coos.

Patty nods and leans back in the chair.

But when Mona lifts Patty's hair off her shoulders, we both see something that scares us: the bruises around the back of Patty's neck and shoulders.

When Patty catches our expressions, she quickly says, "Those are from the operation."

The stylist knows better. She shakes her head at me.

By the time the hair stylists, make-up artists, and wardrobe mistresses are done with us, we at least embody the role of celebrities. Our floor-length gowns are Oscar-worthy. Hair is either upswept like Patty's, or flows to our shoulders in silky waves, like mine. Along the décolleté, make-up is used to cover up any bruises still visible from the operation.

As we move toward the living room, I'm concerned enough to pull Lucy to one side. I'm blunt and to the point: "James is an abuser. The show should protect Patty and her children."

Lucy shrugs. "You're leaping to conclusions."

"Bullshit. You've known since Day One!" I point my hand in the direction of the make-up trailer. "Don't lie and say the staff hasn't already mentioned it to you. As the assistant showrunner, you need to alert the police."

When Lucy is fibbing, her eyes dart from left to right. At the speed in which they're moving now, she's making me dizzy. "We can't do anything unless she asks," she insists.

"At least talk to her about it!"

"Sure, okay—*after* the show." She turns to walk away.

I grab her arm. "You like ratings, right? Don't you see? If you expose him on-air, the producers are heroes. The ratings will pop!"

Lucy's eyes shine at the thought, but then she shrugs. "I don't know. There's good drama and then there's bad drama. Abuse falls into the latter category."

"Since when is saving a life a bad thing?" I argue. "Never mind, don't answer that. I can guess: when it hurts the ratings." I shake my head. "You people are sick."

She winces because she knows I'm right. When she says, "Let me talk it over with Brin…" I know the conversation will never happen.

Damn it! I hope James turns out to be our man. Putting him away for life may be Patty's only salvation.

~

THE SHOW'S FIRST HOUR IS MADE UP OF AUDIENCE VIDEOS congratulating their favorite Housewives.

Except for James, the men smile proudly at the beauties by their sides. But the audience's favorite is soon apparent. Whereas all of the patients receive accolades, it's Sienna who wins the night. Most of the videos are addressed to her.

Roger is ecstatic—and from the peek I got at his financial problems, relieved as well. "Their votes only validate what I've known since the moment I met you," he exclaims more to the camera than to Sienna. "You are the most beautiful woman in the world."

The other women's disappointment doesn't show in their unlined Botox'ed faces and Collagen-inflated lips, but their grinding teeth are loud enough for one of the boom boys to whisper, "Where is that sound coming from?"

Hopefully, Season Two will hire a dental surgeon who can supply porcelain implants to any teeth ground to the root during the run of the show.

~

"—WHICH IS WHY EVERYONE SHOULD READ *MIDDLEMARCH*," Cassandra concludes. "I'm sure you agree—don't you, Penelope?"

Apparently not, because Penelope's eyes are closed, and she is yawning.

"Argh! Will someone shut her up already?" From the way Brin is groaning in the control room, I guess that the second half of the episode—our little book swap—is putting the show's audience to sleep as well.

Lucy must be wincing. After all, the book club was her idea. It was her night to shine. Instead, the ratings must be dropping with each character description given by Cassandra of the classic tome few have ever read.

Ergo, Brin will have Lucy's head on a platter if things don't perk up—and soon.

Donna to the rescue! I raise my hand. "Granted, a good case of tuberculosis always makes for riveting prose, but I think the levity of *Pride and Prejudice* would be better appreciated by our—"

"Really—Jane Austen?" Cassandra looks heavenward. "Hasn't she been done to death? Seriously, who hasn't read her?"

Patty raises her hand.

"What is it, Patty?" Cassandra asks impatiently.

"I haven't," Patty whispers meekly.

"You haven't what?" Cassandra demands crossly.

"I haven't…I haven't read Jane Austen."

Her tepid attempt at boldness is to turn to the camera. "But I have read *Bridges of Madison County*, and I can say unequivocally that—"

"My God!" Cassandra exclaims. "How can you even mention that sentimental dreck in the same breath as *Middlemarch*?"

Miffed, Patty exclaims, "But I didn't!"

Cassandra sighs loudly. "What? What did you not do?"

"I didn't mention it regarding *Middlemarch*. I was referring to Jane Austen."

Sienna snickers. No doubt Sienna's book club choice—*Fifty Shades of Grey*—still resonates with the show's audience, while also burnishing her brand as the show's not-so-blushing soon-to-be bride. We'll know soon enough when the votes are tallied later tonight. Since I am currently in last place, you could say I am sweating it.

Still, I resist the impulse to stick my tongue out at her. Instead, to take her down a peg, I mutter, "I'm surprised you didn't bring one of Roger's books here tonight. Why not? Not enough kinky sex in it?"

Sienna's back stiffens at the mention of her supposed beloved. "No, not at all! I just feel that *Fifty Shades of Grey* is more realistic to women's lives than *Middlemarch* or *Pride and Prejudice*—and certainly more erotic than *The Bridges of Madison County*."

It's Patty's turn to snort. "There's nothing real about *Fifty Shades of Grey*."

Sienna frowns at her. "Oh, yeah? How would you know?"

Patty's face is now beet red. "You don't think I've read it? Of course, I have! And let me tell you, that girl in the book knew nothing about the life of a submissive. She and her billionaire boss were just playing at it!" She stands up, shaking. "Do you actually believe that women like to be beaten—to be abused? They don't! A woman who lives with an abuser dreads it. She's ashamed to say anything because no one wants to get involved. So she lives with her bruises for days, and with her broken bones for months—and with the pain for years!" Her words spew out in fits and starts. "For her, it's not a game! It's survival!"

Sienna doesn't realize her mouth is wide open. She is too awed to say anything.

"Well, what do you know?" Brin exclaims. "Some real drama! Finally, Fatty Patty's votes are climbing! Look at the texts coming in… OH. MY. GOD! She's surpassed Sienna! *Middlemarch*, Schmiddlemarch! It's Fifty Shades of Fat all the way! Hey, New Girl, make a note: we do this book club thing every season!"

"Why should she make a note?" Lucy mutters. "I'm the one who thought of it!"

Patty's little speech has even wakened our sleeping beauty, Penelope. She stares up at Patty, stunned. Finally, she retorts, "Look, if you hate being on the receiving end, you should try being a top. No pain, all gain. And, besides, you get to wear some incredible leather outfits."

Patty's face crumbles. Her cry for help has fallen on deaf ears. She flees the room.

"What did I say?" Penelope asks wickedly.

"As always, nothing of substance," Cassandra murmurs. "And you do it so well."

"Gee, thanks!" Penelope downs her third glass of champagne. Suddenly, she pulls a pill vial out of her clutch. "Darn it I forgot to take a couple of these little babies...Hey, Champagne is okay to mix with my pain meds, right?"

Sienna's answer is to nod slyly as she pours even more bubbly into Penelope's glass.

The wrap-up can't happen soon enough. From the looks on the faces of the other women, I'm not the only one who feels that way.

The husbands join us in the mansion's luxurious living room before Dominic makes his entrance, sauntering down the mansion's grand staircase. "Things are heating up between the Housewives! Only three nights to go! You, the audience, still have time to vote for your favorite Hilldale Housewife."

The cameras weave around the contestants as Dominic pronounces, "Will you vote for beauty"—a camera zooms in on Sienna—"brains"—Another camera pans in on Cassandra—"or bravery?" A third moves in on Patty. Shocked, she steels herself to smile while James fumes at her side.

Dominic continues: "Are you turned on by sex"—Suddenly, I'm on camera—"or drama?" Penelope bats her eyes so fiercely at the camera that one of her false eyelashes flutters onto her cheek. As Peter reaches for it, she bats his hand away.

"Your favorite Housewife is counting on you, so vote now!"

He smiles until Brin commands, "Cut!"

James marches up to Dominic. "What the hell did you mean by that?"

Dominic, surprised, puts down the ever-present hand mirror he keeps in his pocket. "I beg your pardon, old chap?"

"Don't you 'old chap' me!" James is seething now. "You called her brave! Why? What makes her so brave?"

"Brave?" Taken aback, Dominic points at the teleprompter. "It's just a word—there, on the monitor. Frankly, old boy, I assume it's purely for alliteration: 'beauty, brains, bravery...' You get the picture now, don't you?"

"Oh, I get it alright," James growls. He looks around, then shouts, "Someone here is making my life into a joke! Well, it's not a joke! She's the joke!" He points to Patty, who cowers in fear. She holds her hands over her face. She's been here before. She knows what to expect.

"A meltdown? Yes! Yes! We've got to get this on camera!" Brin's ecstatic cry pierces her crew's ears through their buds. "Camera One—stay on sweet crazy James," Brin growls through the crews' earbuds. "Camera Two, get in tight on Fatty Patty! We want to see those tears! Camera Three, get some reaction shots!"

When Camera Three turns my way, I give it the finger.

Quickly, it swings toward Penelope, who clasps her hand over her open mouth like a silent film heroine who has just walked in on her husband kissing her sister.

"Just look at her! Look at my so-called wife!" James screams. "That asshole doctor said he could make her beautiful! Bullshit! She's still the same fat cow she's always been! She's still the biggest mistake of my life!"

Anger replaces the fear in Patty's eyes. She takes a step toward her husband. "I am not 'your biggest mistake!' And neither are our sweet, beautiful children! Quit blaming us for—"

Before she can get out another word, James backhands her across the face.

Everyone gasps.

Not me. I run to Patty.

And not Jack. With lightning speed, he's at James' side.

One punch from Jack takes James down.

Two men from the show's security detail scurry over.

"Cut!" Brin shouts. "Okay, crew, we've got tomorrow's opening! Jacked Jack is a ratings knockout! Television doesn't get much better than this, people!"

I hold Patty in my arms. She's sobbing uncontrollably. Mona is soon at my side. She too cradles Patty, murmuring, "It's okay. It'll be alright."

I scan the room for Lucy. When I catch her eye, I shout, "Get over here!"

At first, she hesitates—until she realizes I mean business.

I meet her halfway across the room. "What did I tell you? Call the cops—now."

She shakes her head. "I can't. I just can't"

"Sure you can." I pluck her cell phone from her tool belt.

"No. You don't understand. Brin won't want—"

"I don't care what Brin does or doesn't want! Patty can't go home with him! Her life is in danger! Her children's lives are in danger!"

"He'll cool off. You'll see." Her eyes skitter from side to side. Even she doesn't believe her own bullshit.

"How do you think he'll react when he sees this tomorrow, on television? Did you know he's got a basement filled with guns? Is that what you want to capture for your audience—a *massacre*? Look, I know you like to laugh at us behind our backs and treat us as your puppets, but don't you care even one iota that you're putting these people's lives in danger—not to mention those of your crew?" I shake her by the shoulder. "Just how sick are you people?"

"He'll...be okay," she insists.

I turn to find Patty standing behind me—with Brin.

Noting my disbelief, Patty adds, "He just needs time to cool down, is all. He'll be fine just as soon as he hears we're now in first place." Her voice is devoid of any emotion.

No, she doesn't believe this either.

"He beats you," I remind her. "Patty, I've seen the bruises! We all have."

"They're just…rough love taps."

"No. They aren't. Patty, you're black and blue—"

"From my surgery," she insists.

"No, from his beatings! You now have witnesses! You can get him put in jail. You can get a restraining order—"

"And then I get nothing!" She shakes with frustration. "You don't understand—we are his lifeline. Without us, he will break for good!"

"At least, come home with me and Jack, for one night," I beg her. "We'll run by your house and get the kids, too—"

Patty frowns. "Why? Are you looking for a three-way?"

"What? Why would you say—"

"Oh, don't act so innocent!" Angrily, she takes a step away from me. "He told me about your little visit. How you insisted on giving him your thong as a 'souvenir.'"

"What's that?" Brin's eyes narrow in on me like two heat-seeking missiles. "I never saw the footage of that!"

I grab Patty's hand. "I…I did nothing of the sort!"

"Franklin mentioned that Ariel saw you coming out of our house." Patty frowns when her words get the reaction she hopes she won't see:

I blush.

Her tears fall as she looks down at the marble floor. "Get away from me," she whispers.

"Nothing happened, Patty! I'm telling you the truth!"

She tosses off my hand.

"Whoa, whoa, Delicious Donna, get ahold of yourself! Give the poor woman some space, okay?"

I step nose-to-nose with Brin. "You've got to call the cops."

"No, I don't. She's a consenting adult. All submissive wives are." Her smile is as cold as her words. "And if you don't calm down, I'll have Security escort you out."

"Don't bother."

By the time I've reached our car, Jack is there to open the door.

He climbs into the back seat with me.

He puts his arm around me.

He holds me as I cry.

When I get ahold of myself, he moves to the driver's seat.

I stay in the back, curled up until we reach our house.

He waits as long as it takes for me to compose my face into some semblance of Happy Donna.

No need for the children to see their mother heartbroken over something she can't control.

WE ARE AWAKENED BY THE SOUND OF SIRENS.

Jack groans, but somehow rises to his feet and stumbles to the window.

"Police cars," he exclaims. "A lot of them. Could be SWAT."

"Are they headed toward Lion's Lair?" I ask.

"No, the new part of town—the Heights."

I jump out of bed and run toward the door.

He's on my heels. He knows what I'm thinking:

James.

IT IS JAMES.

He is lying under a blanket.

All it took was one shot to the head.

While Jack talks to one of the first responders, I take a seat on the curb.

A few minutes later, he walks over to me. "They're saying it was self-inflicted," he explains. "He did it in the kitchen. Patty had already taken her pain meds and fallen asleep. The two older kids woke her up when they heard the shot. She called the police, hysterical. The younger kids are practically in shock too. Still, all of the children validate their mother's story."

"Was there a note?" I ask.

"Just one word: 'Sorry.'"

I nod. "Will there be any further investigation?"

"Because it's suicide, the coroner will do an autopsy, but the evidence seems to align with what they claim occurred, so the house has been cleared as a crime scene." He pauses and adds, "Apparently this isn't the first time the police have been called to the Garret residence. Hilldale's men in blue have seen bruises on both Patty and Jenna. When asked, both mother and daughter refused to file a complaint against James. Personally, I think the cops are relieved he offed himself."

"Now that the first responders are leaving, I think I'll offer to stay," I insist.

Jack nods, helps me up, and holds my hand as we walk to the door.

JENNA GREETS US AT THE DOOR. SHE IS EVEN PALER THAN NORMAL. Jason stands behind her. He eyes us warily.

"May we come in?" Jack asks.

Jenna steps aside. Jason thinks twice before doing the same.

"We're truly sorry for your loss," I say.

Jenna glances at Jason. His response is no more than a shrug.

"Is your mother available? We'd like to offer her our condolences," I explain.

"Mom is stunned. She was still woozy from her pain pills. In fact, she took another pill and went back to sleep." I try not to shudder as Jenna points down the vast hall. "The other kids went to bed. They're…upset."

I nod sympathetically. "I can imagine."

Jason waits to see what Jack does.

Jack lowers himself onto the couch.

Jason, unsure of himself, does the same.

"I'm sorry your dad was such an asshole."

Jason tears up. "Me too." Furiously, he wipes away his tears.

"It's okay to cry," Jack assures him. "You're not crying for who he was now, but for the father he could have been."

Hearing Jack's words, the boy sobs harder. Jason drops his head in shame, but he can't stop the tears.

Jenna, dry-eyed, looks away.

I motion in the direction of the kitchen.

"Did the responders say it was okay to use the kitchen?"

Jenna nods.

"I'd like to get a glass of water. Would you mind if I—" Instead of waiting for an answer, I start walking toward the kitchen.

Jenna is too shocked to do anything but follow.

I stop halfway down the hall. "First, let's check in with your mom. Where is her bedroom?"

Jenna points listlessly at the door.

I peek in. Patty snores gently.

I walk to her bedstand. Beside a glass of water is a vial of sleeping pills: Ambien. I pick it up to read the directions on the prescription and then I put it back down.

Jenna is standing on the threshold. Her eyes follow my moves, but she says nothing.

I smile reassuringly at her. "I'll have that glass of water now."

Except for the blood spattered on the table and wall, and pooled on the floor, the kitchen is neat as a pin.

Jenna walks to a cabinet, takes out a glass, and hands it to me.

I'm already standing at the sink. Before I reach for the faucet, I look down. The sink holds only four items: an empty beer stein, a plate with the remnants of a steak and mashed potato, a fork, and a knife.

I fill my glass but leave the water running.

I then take my time drinking the water.

Jenna is silent, but her anxiety shows itself by the way in which her chest rises and falls.

She's been through enough hell for one lifetime, so I do her a favor. I empty the beer stein in the sink. Then I take the knife and scrape the plate of the steak scraps and the leftover mashed potatoes over the drain. When I'm done, I flip the disposal switch.

If there was any pill residue left, it is now down the drain.

I reach for a dishcloth. After I dry the plate, I hand it to Jenna.

As she reaches into the cabinet with it, she asks, "How did you know?"

"You cook the meals. From what I read on the directions of your mother's prescription, it's a pill short." Actually, I don't know. I'm guessing.

Jenna confirms it with a nod.

"Also, the one word in his suicide note was written in the same hand as the one you sent Mary." I turn to her.

Tears glisten in her eyes.

"I presume the police took the gun?"

Jenna nods. "It was…it was his favorite."

"Against the temple?"

She nods again. "He'd already nodded off. I don't think he felt the barrel against his head."

Maybe not. If so, would he have welcomed it? My guess is yes.

"Did Jason wear gloves?"

Again, she nods.

"Did he press your father's thumb and fingers against the grip and trigger?"

"Yes. He knows about gun residue—" Suddenly she stares up at the webcam left by the show's producers.

She slaps her hand over her mouth and falls to the floor.

I take out my cell phone and call Arnie.

"You rang, my mistress of madness?" Despite his playful tone, his voice is husky with sleep.

"The Garrett footage for the last twenty-four hours: vaporize it—*now*."

"Um…all copies?"

"Yep, archived in any clouds, and control room."

"On it." A long moment later, he adds, "Done."

I close my cell and crouch beside Jenna.

"You're safe. The issue is gone—forever. Now, move forward."

She nods as she scrambles to her feet. Hugging me tight, she whispers, "Thank you."

I expect they'll put the house on the market immediately. I wonder how long it will take for them to get a buyer? Peter won't like having to disclose that a suicide occurred there, but seriously, the home has bigger issues—like explaining why there's a military grade shooting range where the playroom should be.

18

Say Yes to the Dress

—A direct quote from Randy Fenoli, show host

There are a few unspoken rules about choosing a bridesmaid dress:

- *Rule #1: Don't look better than the bride. (I know, I know —
  with your ephemeral beauty and bodacious bod, it certainly
  presents a conundrum! Solution: potato sack! Assuredly, the
  bride will appreciate your sincere effort!)*
- *Rule #2: Stick to the bride's designated cut and color. (Agreed,
  yellow is no one's color. And if you have too much pride for,
  and much prejudice against, the Empire-waist gowns worn in
  the 1810s, begin the task of talking some sense into the bride
  concerning her lack of sensibility toward style and taste
  immediately.)*
- *Rule #3: You can always say "No!" to the dress that she's
  picked out for you. But before you do, weigh your refusal
  against all the times she's been there for you and comforted
  you over your petty dramas. I've no doubt you'll come to the
  very reasonable conclusion that the only right answer is a
  stoic (and much appreciated) "yes."*

(Tip: talk her into an open bar. When you're blitzed, even the ugliest bridesmaid's dress looks like a 10!)

JUST BEFORE SUNRISE, MY PHONE BUZZES WITH A TEXT FROM BRIN:

Good morning, Housewives! Your task today is loads of fun: bridesmaid dress shopping! The limo will pick you up at one o'clock. You'll convene at the Housewives' mansion at six o'clock for hair and make-up. For the live portion of the show, you'll model your gowns for your men—and your audience! Happy hunting!

Jack opens one eye with a groan. "What hellish act has she planned for you today?"

"Dress shopping at one, and then back at the ranch by six o'clock for a modeling competition during the live show." I bat my eyes.

He puts a pillow over his head—but not for long. Peeking out from under it, he asks, "So, she didn't mention James' untimely demise?"

"No. I guess she hasn't gotten word of it yet." I stretch. "Yikes! I don't want to be in the room when that happens—"

Jack and my phones buzz simultaneously.

Jack stares down at his. "Uh-oh. Ryan." He taps the line open. "Yes...yes, sir...Of course sir." He glances up at me. "She's reaching for the phone now."

"I brace myself with a deep breath before clicking on and purring, "What's cookin', good lookin'?"

Ryan is either stunned or seething in silence. When he recovers, he growls, "Arnie just informed me that you asked him to delete twenty-four hours' worth of video footage from the Garrett archive."

"Sorry, Donna," Arnie's mournful apology is barely a whisper. "I just presumed that Ryan already knew."

"No need for apologies, Arnie," I chirp in my kindergarten teacher voice. "Ryan, yes, well let me explain—"

"No! Let me explain!" My boss sounds as if he's hyperventilating. "The COMINT team picked up a text conversation late last night from the Garretts' ISP—"

"What time, exactly?" Jack interjects.

"Just after three in the morning," Arnie replies. "Why do you ask?"

"James was already deceased," Jack explains. "It couldn't have been either of them. Patty had taken a couple of sleeping pills. She was out cold."

"Hey, wait a minute," Arnie pipes up. "Something's not right about these intercepts."

"Come again?" Ryan asks.

Arnie sighs. "My guess is that the terrorist is playing it safe. He's bouncing his ISP signal between all the contestants' homes in case someone is on his tail."

Jack sighs. "So, what you're saying is that we're being spoofed? All this time we've been on a wild goose chase?"

"At least we know that one of our contestants is dirty," Ryan points out.

"And James' death lets us narrow the field," I point out.

"So does the Powells' resignation from the show," Jack adds.

"That leaves Roger and Sienna, Cassandra and Gerald, or Penelope and Peter," I reply.

"Penelope's phone was vetted, but not Peter's," Ryan reminds me.

"I'll get to it today," I promise him.

Another phone beeps, this time on Arnie's side. "Brin just texted Emma," he explains. "She just learned of James' death!"

"How? Who would have thought to call her?" Ryan asks.

I sigh. "Who do you think? Who knows everyone's business, and has got the biggest mouth in town?"

Jack thinks for a moment. "Your Aunt Phyllis?"

I frown at him.

Jack slaps his hand against his forehead. "Penelope. Damn it!"

"Brin called everyone in for a staff meeting immediately," Arnie explains. "Emma is leaving to go there now."

"Tell her to wear her Acme eyes and ears," Ryan reminds him.

A baby can be heard crying in the background. Arnie sighs. "I'll be right back."

We can hear him drop the phone on his bed. While he cuddles and coos at little Nicky, Ryan asks, "You never told me why you had Arnie destroy the Garrett video footage."

"I only did it because it revealed a very personal matter for the family which is in no way relevant to our mission."

Ryan grunts indignantly. "I would have liked to have had the opportunity to make that call myself. But if you can assure me that there was no obstruction of justice, I'm satisfied."

My silence speaks volumes.

Ryan sighs mightily. *"Oh, Donna."*

Finally, I say, "You're right. I overstepped Acme protocol. Then again, I did it on my personal time, and I certainly didn't act on our agency's behalf."

"No, you just used an agency asset and resources."

"Is that your way of saying that I'm forgiven?"

"Depends." Ryan retorts. "If you think that by dropping off a pie I'll let you off, you're mistaken—unless it's cherry."

I laugh. "Duly noted. One cherry pie, coming up."

"Which of you imbeciles dumped the Garrett footage?" Brin's screech has Jack and me wincing, even from four blocks away. I can only imagine how all that hot air feels up close. I feel for Emma and the rest of Brin's staff.

"Don't you get it? We may have caught him blowing his head off—and that would be ratings gold! ...No, make that ratings platinum!" The sound of her voice ebbs and flows, indicating the fact that she's pacing through the room. "Lucy, you were handling the Garretts. Didn't you realize the footage was missing?"

"No! I saw it upload into the secure cloud last night, while I worked on the post-production of the footage we got of his meltdown on the set. I just didn't have time to review it." Lucy's tone is frantic.

Brin snaps her fingers. "Wait a minute...Patty said Ariel saw Donna coming out of the Garrett house. Cuddly Mrs. Craig must also be our Housewife whore! Double-check the footage from the day before Ariel resigned...when was it again?"

"Day Three," Lucy replies. "When the Wives had their operations. I'll lay in the footage now..." A long minute goes by, then: "Oh, my God! The Garrett footage for that day is gone too!"

"What?" Brin growls ominously. "Why hadn't you reviewed it before now?"

"Because...because...I had all the pre- and post-op production to edit for that night's show! Besides, I didn't think anything could be happening at the Garrett home. It was the one day James didn't have Fatty Patty to slap around—"

"The operative phrase here is that you didn't think!" Brin shouts. "The only way we'd know there was something wrong with the cameras or the upload is if you'd been doing your job and checking it every day! That's it—you're fired!"

"Brin, please...Don't do this to me!" Lucy pleas. "This is my life...this is what I do!" Her sobs are louder now.

"Well, you don't do it for me any longer. Get the fuck out!"

"Wait!" It's Emma's voice. Jack and I turn to each other, eyes opened wide.

"It was me. I did it," Emma claims boldly.

"What?" Brin can't believe her ears. "How?"

"Last night, I was going to review the Bing footage to see if there was anything in there worth editing. I thought the viewers might be getting bored with Penelope's S&M exploits. Maybe we'd catch Cheever doing something like, oh I don't know—planning a bank robbery or something! But, by mistake, I keyed in the wrong archive code. When I realized I was in the Garrett archive instead, I got flustered and pushed the wrong button, I guess." Emma lets loose with a nervous giggle. "My bad!"

"I'll say it is," Brin growls. "Everyone, get the hell out of here—now!"

We hear the sound of feet shuffling—

"Except for you, New Girl!"

Gulp.

Silence.

When I next hear Brin, it sounds as if she's hissing in my ear: "You did it on purpose."

"What? ...I—I don't know what you're talking about!"

"You're sabotaging the show!" Brin declares.

"You're delusional," Emma retorts uneasily.

"Oh, yeah? Let's see if Addison thinks so!"

It takes a long minute for Brin to get him on the phone. "Addison? Brin...Yeah, well, this is what it looks like at dawn—all bright and sparkly. Surprise! Look, we have a bit of a situation. It concerns your latest lap dancer...Yeah, New Girl. First the good news: James the Abuser put a bullet in his head—at the kitchen table! ...Yeah, I know, tonight's ratings will be even bigger than last night's! But here's the thing: Seems that New Girl somehow vaporized the footage of him shooting his brains out, so I told her she's out on her ass."

For a while, there is silence. At least, we can't hear anything, but apparently, Brin is getting an earful because she starts stuttering: "But...But...That's bullshit! ...No, I...Yes. I hear you, Addison!"

Brin throws something against the wall. My guess is that it's her phone. Emma isn't howling, so at least it didn't hit her.

"New Girl, you must give incredible head. Otherwise, you'd be out on your ass," Brin growls.

"You heard Addison," Emma replies coolly. "You can't touch me."

"Sure I can," Brin assures her. "Because Addison needs this show to survive." Brin's declaration drips with venom. "Okay, New Girl, time to make amends. You've got three hours to cobble together the first hour of tonight's show. If it doesn't at the very least maintain our ratings, you're out of here; Addison be damned."

"Okay, sure." Does Brin hear the waver in Emma's voice? "Consider it done."

DURING BREAKFAST, AUNT PHYLLIS OFFERS TO DO SCHOOL DROP-OFF. I take her up on it, since I've got a very short window in which to find Peter Bing and scan his cell phone.

Jack has been summoned to meet with Brin again. Apparently, there's a bidding war between the networks for our show. We can do no wrong.

"We need Emma in play, but it sounds like Brin is going to make Emma's life a living hell," I point out. "Maybe you can use your influence with her to get her to ease off."

"Sure, I'll see what I can do," Jack promises, "but the last thing I want is to have her think we're in cahoots."

He's got a good point.

We part ways with a kiss.

PETER IS NOWHERE TO BE FOUND.

I leave a message on his cell phone, claiming that we may be upgrading to a new abode and would like him to show us a larger house in Hilldale.

Two hours later, no response.

I stop by Peter's office. His assistant says he's been out all morning. I tell her I'll wait anyway.

While she runs to get me a coffee: a caramel macchiato, sweetened with coconut sugar and lightened with almond milk. (You see, I've learned something from Brin: how to keep someone out of your hair.) I search his office, but he must have his laptop computer with him, and his phone because they're not here.

I'm out the door before the assistant comes back.

Where the hell is Peter?

I ask Arnie to hack the GPS system in Peter's car.

"It's parked in Hollywood—on the Warner Brothers lot, of all places," Arnie exclaims.

Indeed interesting, but of no help to me, since the Housewives limousine will be pulling up to my house any moment to whisk me away in search of a dress that I'll probably only wear once to a wedding I couldn't care less if it happens at all.

As much as I can't stand Roger or Sienna, a terrorist is the worst kind of wedding crasher.

Sienna has decided that all of her bridesmaids will be decked out in peach crinolines. "It goes with my theme," she insists. "'Southern Comfort.'"

"Does that mean our bridesmaids' gifts will be a jug of moonshine?" Penelope sniffs.

"For you, I thought a certificate to rehab would be more apropos," Sienna replies.

"'Comfort' for whom?" Cassandra asks. "We can't even sit down in these wretched things!"

She's right. Every time we try, the voluminous skirts of our dresses flip around us like the rings of a target.

"And how are we going to go to the bathroom in them? Admit it, Sienna! You're just trying to make us all look as fat and ugly as Patty, now that she's out of the picture."

"Poor, poor Patty," Sienna bemoans from her dressing room. "She's lived a hellish life. Who knew he beat her?"

"We all did, you dolt." Cassandra scowls down at her dress and mutters, "Well, at least she's avoided one indignity."

Penelope scrutinizes herself in one of Hilldale Bridal Boutique's full-length mirrors. "The only advantage to this skirt is that it makes our waists look even tinier, and our boobs look even bigger." For once in her life, she's right. Already her décolleté has suffered six nip slips. The audience of bystanders staring into the shop window is certainly getting an eyeful.

Lucy doesn't mind. Anything to pop the ratings, right?

I try to keep my tone casual as I ask Penelope, "Will Peter be back in time for tonight's little fashion show?"

She looks up sharply. Warily she retorts, "Why wouldn't he? And why should you care?"

"Don't get your panties in a wad!" I reply. "It was an innocent question."

"They're not. In fact, I'm not wearing any!" To prove her point, she raises the front of her hoop skirt.

The audience outside the shop hoots and claps.

When Penelope bows in response, her hoop skirt then flips up in the back, and we Housewives get a cheeky peek.

"Argh!" Cassandra moans. "Franklin should have offered her a butt lift too."

Miffed that Penelope has stolen her spotlight from the admiring crowd outside, Sienna calls out, "Okay, ready or not, here comes the bride!"

The dress she has chosen does not disappoint. The simple strapless silk dress hugs every curve.

The crowd applauds.

Sienna's smile doesn't waver as she murmurs, "What a waste of a dress."

I wonder what she means by that?

BECAUSE HILLDALE'S STREETS ARE NOW FILLED WITH RABID FANS OF the show, we are anticipated to arrive at the *Housewives'* mansion an hour later than expected.

To save time, Lucy insists that we stay in our dresses. If you think three women in hoop skirts and crinolines easily fit into a stretch limo, you are sorely mistaken. The skirts flip up.

We can't see above them.

Maybe it's for the best. Personally, I'm glad I was oblivious to Penelope's inadvertent mooning of anyone walking down the street as our limo crawled along beside them.

Her anonymity was taken away when one bystander took a photo of her butt tat of a heart entwined with two P's.

By the time we make it to the mansion, it is already trending on Twitter.

It puts Brin in a much better mood. "Six million likes, and counting!" she hooted. "And Pickled Penelope moves to the head of the pack!"

WHEN THE FIRST PRE-RECORDED HOUR OF THE SHOW UNFOLDS, everyone on the Acme mission team braces for the worst. If Emma doesn't pull off her assignment as per Brin's terms, then after tonight we'll be shorthanded at the worst possible time: with two nights left for the terrorist to initiate his jihad.

Her teaser opening is everything it should be: salacious (Penelope) touching (Cassandra fighting for the rights of her disabled son, Sami) and romantic (Jack and I, in a playful embrace).

The next segment plays off these stories beautifully. The audience is titillated, inspired, and touched.

However, the last three segments of the hour are dedicated to the Garretts. Intercutting the family's personal interviews with the tension caught through the in-home webcam, Emma's story arc builds dramatically to its tragic conclusion.

Whereas most of Patty and her children's declarations express their fear of and concern for James, other statements give insights to the better man he used to be—at least, as they choose to remember him.

As if answering a question asked off-camera as to what may have made him so angry and threatening, Patty sighs. "What he did for a living wasn't easy. It turned the man I married into a monster." As her tears fall to her cheeks, she adds, "You don't desert someone you love because they hurt so much. You just try to relieve their pain."

By the end of the hour, there isn't a dry eye in the control room. I imagine the same goes for the majority of viewers at home.

When the show fades to commercial break, the control room staff gives Emma a standing ovation.

Instead of clapping with everyone else, Brin shouts, "You pulled it off, New Girl! Best memorial service video ever! Okay, crew, battle stations for the live part of our show, which I'm calling 'Whores in Hoop skirts.' Wardrobe, do we have a peach bow tie for our hunky host? No? Well then, make one—and quick! Pull a Scarlett O'Hara and cut it from one of the bridesmaids' dresses—Penelope's. I don't know why she needs the dress anyway. As long as a camera points in her direction, she'd much prefer to walk around nude…"

～

WHILE THE PRODUCTION CREW SETS UP, I SEARCH FOR PETER. FINALLY, I see him, standing in the hall. Good, he's by himself.

I saunter over. "I've been looking for you all day," I coo sweetly.

His eyes widen in anticipation. "Really? What can I do for you?"

"You see, I think it's time for a bigger—"

He grins impishly. "So you've heard the rumors. Well, you've come to the right place, because they're true."

"Like your slogan says, around Hilldale, when it comes to quote-unquote bigger and better, you're known as the king." I put a finger on my lips. "But for now let's make this our little secret. You know, keep it out of the rumor mill—something nearly impossible, what with the show and all the publicity surrounding it." I nod toward the other end of the hall. "Can we talk somewhere in private?"

I don't have to ask him twice. The next thing I know, he's shoved me through the library's wide double doors and pulled up my hoop skirt.

If he hadn't gotten lost in all those layers of crinoline, he might have felt my hand in his jacket pocket, pulling out his cell phone. With one hand, I pull the scanner from my cleavage and insert it into the phone. With the other, I smack away his roving hands.

I'm still fighting him off when, finally, I hear the scanner's faint beep.

At the same time, Peter has fought his way through my petticoats. When he puts his hand on my thigh, I grab it by the wrist and twist it until he's on his knees.

He yelps when he feels my knee on his back.

Through my earbud, Ryan says, "Donna, COMINT has verified that Roger Pembroke's novels contain ciphers that coincide with covert operations conducted by foreign enemies occurring within a week of his book's launch dates. The CIA is sending a SWAT team to the house right now."

Thank goodness, this nightmare is finally over!

Just at that moment, Penelope opens the library's door. I'm sure it looks like I'm praying. She must think I'm asking the Good Lord for a bigger vote count because she just rolls her eyes. "Have you seen Peter?"

I look up at her innocently. "Um, nope! In here all by my little lonesome." To warn Peter to keep his mouth shut, I press my knee into his back.

He yelps again.

Penelope scans the room suspiciously. "What was that?"

I sigh. "New shoes. They hurt like hell."

"Where did you find a pair to match this ugly peach color?" Before I can stop her, she lifts up my skirt—

To find me straddling her husband.

"Peter?" Penelope's eyes open wide before narrowing into a glare. "So, this is who you've been slipping away to see—the show's slut?"

"Don't you mean the show's MILF?" Yeah, okay I'm proud of that.

"You heard what I said! Let me guess: he's your latest victim! Well, I'm not going to let you embroil my husband in your sick little love games!"

"Seriously, does this look like a love game to you? ...Don't answer that. I forget who I'm talking to." To prove my point, I let Peter get up.

As he scurries away, Penelope fumes, "First, you try to steal my brand, then you try to steal my husband?"

I can't help but laugh. "Since when is 'show slut' a brand?"

"So you admit it! Ha! Well, you can't use it! I've already trademarked it!" Penelope crows as she waves her arms wildly—

At a camera in the ceiling.

Oh.

Shit.

Suddenly, the double doors fly open. Sienna stands there, arms crossed. Two cameramen swarm into the room. "Hey, this is supposed to be my hour! I'm choosing my Matron of Honor, remember?"

Penelope frowns. "But…you promised me that I was to be your Matron of Honor."

"Not anymore," Sienna retorts. "In fact, I think your behavior on the show is an abomination. I don't want you anywhere near my wedding." She looks directly at the camera and declares grandly, "Twelve episodes, coming this spring on this network—"

"Ha! That's what you think!" Penelope turns triumphantly to the camera. "Roger and I have been having an affair!"

"Is that so?" Sienna turns to Roger. "This is the woman who left her thong in my bed?" She laughs uproariously. "Ha! And all this time, I thought it was Donna."

Roger rolls his eyes. "Darling, I told you that you were hallucinating about it. I wouldn't let that woman near our bedroom—"

I throw up my hands. "Me? Seriously? Don't you people get it? *I'm with Jack*! I don't want Roger, or any of these men for that matter—" Just then, Roger's words hit me: "Wait! You find the neighborhood slut more attractive than me?"

Penelope shoves me. "I told you—I've trademarked that phrase!" She draws quotation marks in the air with both index fingers: "T-M!"

Sienna retorts, "You're right. These men are pathetic, especially Roger. And, frankly, so is this show." With head held high, she glides down the hall. "Tah-tah, darlings! I'm out of here!"

"But…you can't go!" Roger panics. "You vet all my manuscripts! You're my muse!"

She stops to purr, "You don't need a muse, darling. You need a typist! At least, you needed one until your American publisher canceled your contract. If you want to salvage your career, learn how to turn on a computer."

Shamed, he hangs his head.

So, it's Sienna who has been planting the ciphers!

And with the traffic outside the mansion, the SWAT team won't get here in time.

Sienna is now running down the hall.

I'm running too—

Out the back door.

I reach her just as she opens the gate to the back alley.

She seems surprised to see me.

"This is for this ugly dress," I say, as I take my punch.

She's out like a light.

It takes the SWAT team another fifteen minutes to get there.

By then, Brin is doing cartwheels. "Best. Show. Ever!" Brin shouts joyously! "Lucy, let's line up a future bride in every season. Afterward, we'll pitch the network a spinoff: *Battling Bridesmaids*! I love the smell of ratings gold in primetime!"

Oh, it smells, alright.

Jack and I head home. By the fourth time he begs to peek under my hoop skirt, I'm too tired to say no.

"At least, wait until we get home," I warn him.

He honors my request.

Then he honors a few more.

Okay, yeah, I honor a few of his as well—

Including his suggestion that I hang it in my slut gear closet.

Kinky comes in all shapes and sizes.

19

Leave It to Cheever

"Boy, everyone around here is wise to me. I might just have to
move to a new town and start over."
—Eddie Haskell, *Leave It to Beaver*

Here's how you know when someone is a wise guy:

- *Tip #1: You've caught him lying one too many times.*
- *Tip #2: His life is all fiction and no fact.*
- *Tip #3: He embodies the adage, "Promises are made to be broken."*
- *Tip #4: He creeps out your friends.*
- *Tip #5: He avoids both your family and his.*

Here's why you don't need a wise guy in your life:

- *Reason #1: You don't live in a fairy tale—and certainly not one of his making.*
- *Reason #2: His troubles should be yours as well.*
- *Reason #3: The only bag you'll ever want to be left carrying is one with makeup samples.*

- *Reason #4: You don't look good in orange, let alone wide black and white horizontal stripes.*
- *Reason #5: You respect your friends and their opinions—and you love your family. They'll respect you all the more when you're with the right guy.*

~

"CONGRATULATIONS." RYAN'S CALL COMES IN AT FIVE IN THE morning.

I'm still too groggy to comprehend what he's saying. "So, when did ISIS turn her?"

"It didn't," Ryan explains. "She's an operative with the GRU—"

"Russia's foreign intelligence agency?" Jack sits straight up. "That means she must have been under deep cover for quite some time."

"She was recruited as a teen when she was still modeling," Ryan replies. "The profession gave her carte blanche and all the international travel gave her a perfect cover."

"Roger's books are published in many languages, all over the world. Being Roger's so-called 'muse' allowed her to plant clues in them for the GRU," Jack adds.

"Syndication of *Hot Housewives of Hilldale* would have done the same," I reason. "Since reality shows aren't scripted she could communicate with verbal codes instead of ones buried in Roger's lousy prose."

"There's one thing I don't get," Jack says. "The text messages weren't from the GRU; they were from ISIS. Since when is Russia supporting Middle Eastern terrorism?"

"Great question," Ryan agrees. "The CIA has a theory on that. Considering Al Qaeda's ties with Chechnya, Russia has already felt the sting of domestic terrorism. It realizes ISIS is better funded, and that it is ramping up its recruiting efforts abroad—including

Russia. Because Putin would prefer it be someone else's problem, why not nurture ISIS's growth in Western democracies by helping it gain a greater presence here, and in Canada, and the UK? That way, the West is forced to divert its military resources to ISIS while Putin plays footsie with Syria's Assad, and other Middle Eastern dictators."

"Has Sienna admitted to espionage?" I ask.

"There has been no formal admission from the suspect," Ryan admits, "But the CIA is interrogating her now, so I assume one is imminent."

Ouch. That won't be fun. Been there, done that.

"So then, why was Sienna so willing to walk away from Roger—and the TV show?" Jack asks.

"When Roger's publishing contract wasn't renewed, he was no longer any use to her or the GRU. And according to Emma, because of the show, Sienna's talent agent feels that his client's Q Score—the entertainment industry's popularity rating—is now high enough to entice a producer to create a spin-off around her. In fact, she'd already lined up a meeting with Addison."

"Ha! I'll bet Addison will be disappointed that Sienna is headed for maximum security," Jack says.

I laugh. "While there, she'll still have a few webcams watching her every move."

"I wonder how Roger is taking it?" Jack asks.

"Interestingly enough, quite well—now that he's back in 'the Game.'" Ryan replies.

Jack's eyebrow peaks. "By 'Game,' do you mean covert ops?"

"Yes," Ryan admits. "The CIA asked him to approach Sienna's handler—who just so happens to work in the international rights department of Roger's literary agency. He explained to the handler that he knew of Sienna's cover all along and that he'd continue planting ciphers for them, for the right price."

"Do you think they bought his line?"

"Apparently so. In fact, the GRU operatives have already lined up another U.S. publisher for him. He may be bigger in other countries, but there are still many GRU operatives based here too. It's a perfect set-up. Roger keeps writing and dropping clues. The CIA can see who uses them, and then blackmail them into playing double-agent."

"Genius," I murmur. "And now we can finally say bye-bye to Brin and her hench hag, Lucy."

Jack laughs. "Wow! That was Brin-worthy!"

"My guess is that they won't take it very well. With Sienna's arrest, they're down to two contestants. Neither are audience favorites. According to Emma, to shore up ratings and beef up the competition, she's reached out to Patty and Ariel again."

"Makes sense," Jack replies. "They both left the show at the peak of their ratings."

I shudder. "Why would they jump back into that hell hole?"

"As far as Patty is concerned, she could use the money," Ryan points out. "And Lucy promised Franklin to quadruple the show's donations to his charity."

"You're right. Ariel would never do it for herself, but she'd jump through hoops for Franklin. And so would Cassandra. I'm sure she'll be ecstatic when she finds out."

"We're hanging up," Jack declares. "We've got a resignation call to make."

I laugh. "Ha! I wonder if Brin will try to keep us on board with a financial sweetener too?"

"Oh, yeah…about that." Ryan sighs contritely. "Somehow I neglected to remind you that contractors working with United States agencies are forbidden to accept fees or gifts from outside sources."

Jack and I stare at each other—

And then we're laughing so hard that we fall off the bed.

"Goodbye, Ryan," We shout in unison. Our cells click off at the same moment.

"Why, that sly old dog!" Jack sputters. "He dangled that worm—"

"And we ate it up, with relish," I remind him. "Speaking of dangling worms, I'll let *you* call Brin about our resignation from *Hot Housewives of Hilldale*. At the same time, you can tell her that we're also passing on the chance to have a show of our own."

Jack picks himself up from the floor. "I'm on it." In no time at all, he dials her direct line. "I'll talk to her downstairs so that I don't wake the kids."

Good move, since, from the sound of things, Brin isn't taking Jack's call very well. Even from our upstairs bedroom, I can hear her screeching at him.

When Jack finally hangs up on her, he comes back into the bedroom.

I pat the bed to beckon him over. "I'm sorry you had to go through that."

"Hell, it was worth it, just to hear her beg, plead, quadruple her offer, and then throw it in my face that she didn't need me because she already had Peter." He chuckles. "I wished her luck with that!"

"You mean to tell me that she's creating a spinoff for Peter?" Ah! So, that's why he wasn't in his office the other day.

"Something like that. It's called, *Diary of a Divorce*."

"Peter is finally kicking Penelope to the curb—and on live television?"

Jack leans back onto the bed. "It certainly looks that way."

I sit straight up. "Wait…you mean to tell me that her meetings with you were to convince you to kick me to the curb—on national television?"

"International television. Don't forget the syndication rights."

I don't pick up a pillow. Instead, I grab the lamp off my night table.

He ducks in anticipation of my excellent aim. "Honey, come on —I never actually considered it! But it was sure fun stringing her along." He frowns. "Gee, I've just thought of something."

My arm goes back. "Quit stalling. Take your punishment like a man."

"No—wait! I'm serious." His eyes widen. "Let's hope Ryan doesn't have us reconsider her offer. What if he realizes that international syndication will allow us the same opportunity to pass cryptic messages to Acme operatives all over the world?"

I leap up and cover his mouth with my hand. "Bite your tongue!"

He kisses my palm. "I prefer you do it to me."

Instead, I kiss him.

He reciprocates.

Ah, it's great to sleep in—

Even if there's no sleeping involved.

LIFE IS NORMAL AGAIN.

News travels at a digital speed in the ever-changing world of celebrity journalism. Within twenty-four hours the paparazzi decamped from the sidewalk in front of our house. Apparently, we are no longer somebodies.

That's okay. Anonymity suits the Craigs like designer couture.

Babs and Wendy are more disappointed about her defection from the show than Mary is herself. On the upside, her concern for Jenna's ability to handle the spotlight instills in her the grace to accept the shy girl's friendship. With Arnie's help, they've opened text accounts on secure servers. Mary won't jump back into the spotlight, but texts Jenna tips for maneuvering the shark-infested waters of high school mean girls.

Ironically, the Craigs are too addicted to *Hot Housewives of Hilldale* to turn it off this late in its one-week run. Despite Jack's threats, Aunt Phyllis plops herself down in the media room and flicks on the show, warning us: "Get lost for a couple of hours. It's the most fun

I've had in years! Besides, Howard Stern is waiting for my recap." And on my quest to monitor my children's homework progress, I catch Mary, Evan, and Jeff watching it on their cell phones.

What's the use? "Okay! Alright! You can watch with Aunt Phyllis."

Their stampede down the stairs leaves me hugging the wall.

I find Jack in the kitchen, making popcorn for everyone. He shrugs. "If you can't beat 'em, join 'em, right?"

And so we do.

TONIGHT'S SHOW OPENS WITH A TIGHT SHOT ON DOMINIC AS HE proclaims, "Welcome back to the sixth night of *Hot Housewives of Hilldale!* After yesterday's suicide, shopping spree, and the capture of a spymistress', no doubt the question on everyone's lips is, 'What will those wacky women do next?'"

He beams at the camera, which then pulls back to show Patty Garret on his left, and Ariel and Franklin Powell on his right. The women look uncomfortable. However, as always, Franklin is unflappable.

But when Dominic puts one arm around Ariel and another around Franklin, the Powells grimace. "We're happy to welcome back Ariel and Franklin Powell, a family who is always an audience favorite! We'll catch up with their typical good deeds more tomorrow night."

Then, taking Patty's hands in his, Dominic looks soulfully into her eyes and intones, "Patty, may I speak for all of us, both here at the *Housewives* mansion and for the greater world as a whole when I say, 'I feel your pain.'"

When she sobs, he pulls his kerchief from his tux and dabs her cheeks for her.

Penelope tosses back her champagne. "How many votes do

you think she earned with that?" she hisses to Peter, knowing full well that the audio boom will pick up her question.

Peter glares at his wife. "I hope you'll be half as heartbroken should I die before you."

"With what you purchased as an insurance policy, oh, I'll be crying alright," she mutters.

The show's next segment focuses on how Patty is dealing with her younger children's trauma over their father's death. Her tenderness is touching, as is her ability to focus on the goodness in her husband as opposed to the evil.

When not attending to their grief-stricken mother, Jason and Jenna keep the household running with military precision without threats, punishment, or retaliation. Jody and Jordan naturally follow their lead. Having expressed their grief for, and hatred of, their father publicly, they are now freed from his toxic self-loathing.

They have the fierce love of their mother and each other to move forward with their lives. Hopefully, this very public platform will inspire others to do so, too.

The final segment of the prerecorded hour showcases the trials and tribulations of the Farnhams.

Cassandra's meetings with Hilldale High's administration and its teachers weren't video-recorded because of school policy, but her seething anger is evident in every caustic remark. "I'm well aware that Adam can be…a handful. But considering all he's been through, you'd think they'd try harder to help him fit in! Not all children were born in a war zone. They come out of it with one thought: survival. If they want him to look beyond himself, they shouldn't shut him out. They have to do what they can to challenge him to look beyond himself. Gerald, Sami and I do it every day. It is…our cross to bear."

"They are good parents," Evan declares. "Unfortunately, he's a rotten son."

"Why do you feel that way?" I ask.

"Because he likes to take the easy way out," Evan explains. "Lies, intimidation…and now that he's famous, he's using that too."

Mary nods adamantly. "I tell every girl who asks that he's worse than a player. Worse than a man-ho. He's…evil!"

My sympathy for Cassandra just increased tenfold.

When the segment cuts to her at home with Sami, we see a calmer, happier woman. Dominic's voice-over declares, "As for the bullies who taunted Sami, all is forgiven."

"Hardly," Jeff snorts.

"What do you mean by that?" I ask.

Jeff purses his mouth—a telltale sign that he'd rather not say anything that may get him in trouble.

"Jeffrey Harrison Craig, I'm waiting for an answer," I warn him.

Jeff weighs his options. They aren't pretty. Finally, he mutters, "The bullies are still pissed, but we've got them under control."

"Oh yeah, how?" Jack asks.

Jeff shrugs. "One of the creep's girlfriends asked Sami for his autograph. He said he'd take a selfie with her instead. He did it with his cell and then texted it to her. That gave him access to her phone—and her boyfriend's. Apparently, the asshole is two-timing her. Sami threatened to tell her unless the creep and his posse backed off." He pumps the air with a fist. "One for the geeks! *Boo-yah!*"

I slap my forehead. "Please, no 'booyah-ing'!"

Jack is still frowning. "You boys know that what you did isn't legal, right? If you get caught, it could mean jail time. I suggest you not do it again."

"Even if it's for a good cause?"

Jack shakes his head. "There are better ways to help a good cause."

"What if someone's life is in danger?" Jeff insists.

I'm getting the feeling that this is no game. "Whose?" I ask.

His lips tighten. "No one. Nothing. Forget I ever said anything." He turns back to the television.

Jack taps my arm. From the look in his eyes, he's concerned too.

As we roll into the last segment of the show, I can see now why Penelope may be winning this thing: all the world loves a clown.

Considering the other contestants' drama, her tragicomic antics are a welcomed relief.

For the Housewives' last task, to be aired tomorrow, Day Seven, they are asked to coordinate a potluck dinner party.

As Dominic puts it, "Your 'last supper' as a *Hot Housewife of Hilldale* will take place here, in the *Housewives'* mansion, which holds so many wonderful memories for you!"

Wonderful? Um, I don't think so…

"You will be judged by your theme, your process, and on how well others receive your dish."

"We're going to be seeing a lot of fingers going down a lot of throats," Jack murmurs.

Aunt Phyllis chuckles. "Maybe the producers should have kept Tiffy Swift as a contestant."

"And as always, the audience will vote with its texts," Dominic declares. "Choose your dishes, ladies." He hands them a cut-glass bowl holding envelopes.

Cassandra draws first: the appetizer.

Patty draws next: the dessert.

Penelope pulls the main course, and Ariel must provide either a salad or soup.

"I think I'll make flan," Patty pipes up.

"I hope she doesn't eat the whole thing before we get there," Penelope mutters cruelly to Peter.

"Why are you always such a bitch?" he retorts, disgusted. "Can't you just lighten up?"

"'Lighten up?' Ha! You've just made a joke—at her expense!" Penelope's never-empty champagne flute is in her hand.

"What do you think: is Peter upset with her, or is he setting her up in anticipation of his own show?" I whisper to Jack.

"She personifies the word 'bitch,' so it's a hard call," he replies.

"I guess Peter hasn't yet told her about Brin's offer," I reason. "When he does, how do you think she'll take it?"

"Sadly, with aplomb." Jack shrugs. "Penelope lives for adulation and the spotlight."

I nod. "She's come a long way from the Penelope I first met."

Jack shakes his head. "I don't think so. If given an opportunity to play to a larger audience—even if the role is that of a bitch—she'll take it. Remember, hate is a form of love too."

Where have I heard that before?

Oh, yes. Franklin said the same thing to Jack, on the golf course.

In his line of work, the good doctor sees self-loathing every day.

No matter how many incisions he makes, he'll never get to the underlying cause of it. Sadly, his patients don't realize this.

To them, he'll always be a saint.

SUNDAY STARTS WITH A FEW PRAYERS:

That those I love stay happy and healthy;

That the day is serene, and that all corners of the world are blessed with a day of peace;

That no calls come in from Acme that have Jack and I scurrying to save the world;

That I end my day with the same big smile, I offer up now—

To the man already gazing at me in adoration.

"Morning, Sunshine," he murmurs. "Hey, I was thinking of having a cook-out today. How do you vote on that?"

I raise my hand. "If you grill the meat, I'll make the fixin's."

"You're on." He puts his hand behind his head as it falls back onto his pillow. "Hey, what do you think of inviting Arnie and Emma too?"

"Love it!"

"And I think Abu retired from his Uber job when he got his cameraman's union card. He may be around, too."

I laugh. "Hail, hail, the gang's all here—by what, sixish? Include Ryan on your call list. I promised him a cherry pie. It'll go well with steaks on the grill."

"Should we ask the kids who they'd want to have over?"

I nod. "I'll get a head count."

But first I collect my kiss before heading down the hall.

Trisha is sound asleep, but Jeff is already up and on his computer.

I look over his shoulder. "What are you working on?"

Startled, he closes the top with a click. "Um…nothing! Fantasy stats."

Yeah, right. "We're grilling out for dinner. Have anyone you'd like to invite?"

Jeff rolls his eyes. "Cheever will be here later today."

"Ack! Why?"

Jeff shrugs. "He's got nowhere else to go."

Odd. "The show has its big finale tonight. Won't he be there with his parents?"

"He's been banned from his house—and from the set."

"Whatever for?" I ask.

"His mom stayed up all night making individual lamb pot pies for tonight's dinner party. He took a bite out of each one."

For once, I feel sorry for Penelope. "Okay, he can hang here, but make me one promise: if he wants food placed in front of him on a table as opposed to tossed at him while he's caged, he must be on his best behavior."

Jeff thinks for a moment before nodding. "Now that his mom is a star, he doesn't get fed much. So I can safely vouch for him."

I give him the thumbs up before moving down the hall.

Mary is up too, checking her text messages. She looks up at me and smiles. "What's up?"

"We're cooking out tonight—steaks and burgers. Six o'clock. Invite a friend, if you want."

"Oh." Her smile falters. "I've been asked to babysit this afternoon, starting at four."

"Congratulations! I guess you'll add it to your car fund. Who's the lucky kid?"

"That cute little toddler, Conner—you know, Dr. and Mrs. Powell's boy."

I laugh. "Ah, yes. The finale of the show is tonight. Another reason to celebrate."

"Mrs. Powell feels the same way." Mary frowns. "She doesn't want to go, but Dr. Powell insisted on it. He says they owe it to the show for being so generous to his foundation." She laughs. "And they're spreading the wealth! They offered me three times my rate if I stay the whole night."

I give my second thumbs-up of the morning. Today is looking great indeed.

My last stop is Evan's room, over the garage. "Hey, steaks and burgers tonight! You'll be back from lifeguarding by six, right?"

"Um…" He blushes. "I'll be out on a date. In fact, I'm taking off at five."

"Oh…sure, no problem." I keep the smile on my face as I shut the door.

Still, I can't help wondering if it's with Jenna.

Does Mary know? If not, I won't be the one to tell her. They're old enough to sort it out. I'm just going to keep my head down and make my pie.

In fact, I'll make two of them: one for guests; and as promised, one for Ryan to take home. Don't want to disappoint the boss.

LIFE IS GOOD.

While Jack shifts the steaks on the grill rack to make room for a couple of burgers, Jeff and Cheever toss some sort of squishy ball back and forth. Whenever it drops out of one of their gloves, they fall to the floor, giggling.

Oh, dear, I better check their soda cans in case Cheever thinks he can pull one over on us. I swear, there's a stretch in the hoosegow in that kid's future.

At least they've been out of our hair most of the day. In that regard, I follow one policy: don't ask, don't tell.

Ryan is the first guest at our cookout. He brings vanilla ice cream that he cranked himself.

"This should go great with the pie," he explains.

"You shouldn't have gone to all the trouble," I tell him.

He shrugs. "It gave me something to do today other than put together client summary reports."

"Hey, I hear you." I give him a kiss on the cheek. "This was very thoughtful of you."

"I always appreciate a home-cooked meal," Ryan assures me. "I get tired of eating out of cans."

I steel myself from tearing up. Ryan has seen his fill of tragedy. It's why his dedication to Acme is so strong;

And why I, and the rest of my mission team, revere him.

Arnie and Emma are close on his heels. Arnie uses one hand to hold onto their toddler son, Nicky. A six-pack of micro-brewed beer is in the other. He hands one of the beers to Ryan and then heads over to the grill to give Jack one too.

Emma sets a huge salad bowl on the picnic table. "From the garden," she says proudly.

"Yummy, thanks!" I exclaim, as I stroke Nicky's cheek.

"Mahwee?" He looks around the backyard for the girl of his dreams: my eldest.

I laugh. "Sorry, little guy. She took a babysitting gig tonight. You'll have to settle for your second crush." I put his little hand into Trisha's palm.

When he giggles, she rewards him with a kiss. It's the start of a game: he runs just far enough away so that she can catch him and kiss him again.

"Whom is Mary babysitting for?" Emma asks.

"Believe it or not, the Powells. They're on the show's big finale tonight."

"Should we take bets as to who will win?" Arnie asks.

"They're all losers, as far as I'm concerned," Abu declares as he opens the back gate. "To put themselves through all that grief? And what for?"

"Well, in Franklin's case, it's a way to raise money for his charity," Jack replies.

"Yeah, you know, I put it into Charity Navigator. Its ranking might as well have been nonexistent."

"That's not a good sign," I murmur.

"It wouldn't have mattered to Brin as long as he came through with the surgery," Emma declares. She looks around. "Where's Evan?"

"Evan is on a date," I'm doing a piss-poor job of hiding my smile.

Cheever snickers.

Not a good sign. Time to ask—and then, possibly, to yell: "Did I say something funny, Cheever?"

He shrugs and then tosses his silly little ball to Jeff.

By the time Jeff throws it back, I'm close enough to Cheever to catch it one-handed—

But it is slippery enough to fall out of my hand. It plops onto the terrace floor.

The boys are laughing so hard that they fall onto the grass.

I lean over to pick it up. "What's so funny? And what the heck is this thing?"

They break out into another spasm of giggles.

I pull Cheever up by the neck of his shirt. "Maybe I should drop you off at your house…just in time for your mother's little dinner party."

That sobers him up. "It's…a boob."

Jack spews his beer. "Come again?"

"You know—a titty! A knocker. A tah-tah—"

I slap my hand over his mouth. "We get the picture." Angrily, I turn to Jeff. "Where the hell did it come from?"

Jeff blushes a deep red. "Dr. Powell's home office. The window was open, so we climbed in to spy on Mary…and Evan."

"Evan is over there—with her?" I'm so angry that I toss the breast.

Jack catches it with one hand.

"Hey, that's mine! Give it back!" Cheever shouts.

"No, I'm going to give it to its rightful owner: Dr. Powell," Jack informs him.

"I'll just bet," Cheever growls. "Admit it! You like how it feels." He puts up both palms and squeezes them open and shut as he makes kissy sounds.

"Hardly," Jack retorts. "There's nothing like the real deal." He nods toward me.

"You're only saying that because your wife happens to be standing right beside you," Cheever jeers. "If I'd taken two of these, you'd shove her onto some operating table in heartbeat—"

I twist Cheever's arm behind his back.

"Aw, hell! There's a rip in this thing…and it's…" Jack's face is now ashen.

"What?" I say crossly. With my free hand, I reach for my cell. How dare Mary—

Cupping it carefully in both hands, he walks it over to Ryan.

Ryan stares down at it. He picks it up to take a closer look. "Emma, get the kids in the house."

Without question, she picks up Nicky and grabs Trisha's hand. Jeff, stunned, follows her. He knows better than to ask questions.

Cheever stares at all of us, slack-jawed. I shove him toward Emma. "You heard him—move! Now!"

After Emma shuts the door behind them, I walk over to Ryan. "Is that what I think it is? I ask.

"An IED? Yes," Jack says. He grabs his beer and pours it directly onto the exposed metal pieces. "We better get over to the show—*now*."

Jack stares at me. The realization hits us at the same time:

Franklin Powell is the terrorist.

$$\frac{\qquad\qquad\qquad\qquad\qquad\qquad}{}$$

20

Deadwood

"The world ends when you're dead. Until then, you got more punishment in store. Stand it like a man... and give some back."
—Al Swearengen

Have you ever wondered what it's like to die?

Unfortunately, there are very few around to give you the deets. So here is some wisdom from those who were nearly dearly departed and lived to tell their tale:

First, the lack of a physical presence means that many of the sensations you're accustomed to will no longer distract you. (Huzzah! Gone are all the aches and pains! Oh, pooh! So are all those euphoric orgasms.)

Next: Yes, you emotionally feel, but you can't physically touch.

Yes, you are there—but somehow, strangely, you aren't.

Yes, some will feel you near them—but they can't acknowledge your presence.

Yes, they can mourn you—but ask yourself: wouldn't you rather they move on and find happiness again?

And finally: Despite lacking the senses we have learned to rely on for a lifetime, other sensations come to fill this void. You'll recognize them as love, joy, remorse, sadness, and anger. Ironically, they matter less now because you can no longer share them with the living beings whom you have known and loved for a lifetime.

Do the next best thing: while you're alive, thank them for the joy that they have contributed to nearly every day of your existence.

ABU STILL HAS HIS LINCOLN TOWN CAR. BUT BEFORE JACK AND I PILE into it with him, Jack grabs the bomb detector from the trunk of my car. "In the off chance that not all three patients—Penelope, Cassandra, and Patty—are body cavity bombs, we can pinpoint the right victims," Jack says.

"Good thinking," I reply.

"The BCBs will probably be activated by a cell call, which enables an electrical charge," Ryan explains. "If Franklin reaches for his phone, I'll subdue him."

"I don't have the cell phone jammer here. It's at Acme," Arnie opines. "I'll alert the Orange County bomb squad to get over here ASAP. They're sure to have one."

"Abu, drive as close as you can get to the mansion so that you can stand by to drive them to the hospital," Ryan commands.

"On it, chief," Abu declares.

"Donna, as quickly as possible, hustle the women out of range of the detonator," Ryan continues.

"Will do, boss," I assure him.

Thank goodness we still have access to the webcams set up by the production staff so that Ryan, Arnie, and Emma can provide eyes and ears.

"The show is already in the second segment," Emma informs us. "They're about to start on the main course."

"I'm right behind Jack and Donna in case you need back up," Ryan declares.

"The more, the merrier," Jack assures him.

I wonder how Brin will take to us crashing the show?

Not that it matters. If we don't succeed, Brin will get the highest ratings she ever had.

Unfortunately, she may not live to appreciate the moment.

ABU WAVES AT THE SECURITY DETAIL AT THE FRONT GATE OF THE mansion. Because they recognize him, they don't even bother looking at their manifest. Instead, they wave us right through.

The Town Car screeches to a stop directly in front of the mansion's grand entry. Jack and I pop out of the vehicle and run up the steps.

We rush into the dining room. Penelope, Peter, Cassandra, Gerald, and Patty are seated at the table—

And the bomb detector's arrow is jumping around the screen like crazy.

But Franklin isn't there.

Penelope is talking to the camera. "Now, to get the flakiest crust possible, start with—" Spotting me, she stops mid-sentence and frowns. "What the hell are you doing here? Missing the limelight already?"

Jack jerks Peter up out of his chair. "Where is he—Franklin?"

"Well, what do you know! Delicious Donna and Doctor McDreamy must have been an item!" Brin crows joyously "Damn, that girl is a player! Camera One, dump Pickled Penelope and follow Jacked Jack! Camera Two, stay with Donna!"

Peter, in shock, stutters incoherently.

Concerned, Cassandra rises from her chair. "Franklin was called away to an emergency surgery. He's on his way to his office."

I look around. No Ariel. "Is Ariel with him?" I ask.

Cassandra shakes her head.

The others crane their necks, looking for her. Finally, Patty points outside. "She said she promised to check in with the babysitter at seven-thirty."

I follow her gaze: Ariel is standing by the pool.

"Donna—take the women out of here!" Jack shouts as he runs toward the pool.

I shove Cassandra and Patty toward the front door. "There's a Town Car out front, waiting for you! Get in it—now! Your lives depend on it!"

The women see the look in my eyes. They don't wait for me to ask twice.

Gerald leaps up as well and runs after them.

Penelope takes my wrist. "Donna Stone Craig, you're always ruining my chance to shine! Well, not this time!"

She grabs a candelabrum from the table and swings it in my direction.

I duck just in time.

Unfortunately, Peter does not. As he falls backward, he pulls the tablecloth with him.

Plates, silverware, and glasses clatter to the floor.

I slip on something—apple jelly, I think. I force myself to my knees so that I can look out toward the patio—

Just as Jack tackles Ariel, taking her with him into the pool.

"Get your wife to the Town Car outside now!" I shout at Peter.

He knows better than to argue. He is a bottom, after all.

As I run to Jack and Ariel, Abu's voice comes in through my earbud. "I've explained the situation to the women. We're headed for Hilldale Medical. Doctors are standing by for their emergency surgeries."

Ironically, I can't get Brin's shrill voice out of my ear. "The only thing better on that man than a wet T-shirt is no shirt at all," Brin declares. "Hey, New Girl! Go with him to—"

"She quit. Remember?" Lucy says wearily.

All of a sudden the house goes dark.

Make that the whole block.

Arnie declares, "I pulled the plug. Acme has officially canceled *Hot Housewives of Hilldale.*"

About damn time.

Brin is screaming now—about the disappearance of her cast; about the angry texts coming in from the viewing audience; about the livid studio execs whose concerns over her doing the show live are now validated; and above all, for Lucy to turn on the backup generator.

We also hear Dominic bemoan the imminent loss of, as he puts it, "my previously assured Emmy nomination."

Boo hoo.

By now, I've reached Jack and Ariel. Ryan isn't far behind me.

Wet and disheveled, Ariel shivers as she sobs, "But...why? Why would he plant bombs in those women?"

Jack kneels beside her. "This may be hard for you to believe, but he's a terrorist." He holds up her wet cell phone. "And calling from this cell would have set off the bombs."

Ariel stares at the phone.

"You were out here for a while, but nothing happened. Why didn't you dial the phone?" Jack asked.

"I tried. But it's Franklin's cell, not mine," she explains. "I couldn't use it because I don't know his passcode. I must have picked it up by mistake before we left the house."

Thank goodness.

"We all could have all been murdered!" Suddenly, she's sobbing even harder.

I reach down to put my arm on her shoulder. "Ariel, everything is okay now. No one got hurt."

Not yet, but the bomb detector's arrow is jumping again.

Ariel sees the shocked look on my face when I remember:

He enhanced her breasts too.

"Our boss, Ryan, will take you to the hospital," Jack tells her gently. "But Ariel, before you leave, we need your help. By now, Franklin knows we're looking for him. He won't be at his Beverly Hills office. Where would he have gone instead?"

"I don't know! Maybe…" Her back stiffens. "He has a storage unit in Long Beach, near the Queen Mary, on Hanjin Road. A few months ago, I saw the rental invoice for it in Franklin's desk drawer. He told me it was for old office equipment and old family mementos…his brother's stuff." She shakes her head as if waking from a dream.

"It was one of our leads," Jack exclaims. "The meth house that we raided! It'll be locked and empty now."

Ariel's eyes glitter with anger. "Franklin would never make meth!"

"But he'd put bombs in women's breasts?" I point out.

Her face crumples at the realization that she doesn't know her husband at all.

The bawling starts again.

Ryan waves us on. "I'll be taking Mrs. Powell to the hospital. Afterward, she'll be held for further questioning. I'm sure she knows more than she realizes."

With what Franklin has done to her, she'll be ready to talk.

By the time Jack and I reach the front door, Abu is back from the hospital. "Where to?" he asks.

"Long Beach. The meth warehouse. Different bin."

And we're off.

WE PARK A QUARTER MILE FROM THE WAREHOUSE. THE MOON'S GLOW can't permeate the fog-shrouded sky.

The cement wall isn't all that high: just six feet. We move up and over it in silence.

The warehouse is made up of several rows of long buildings—running a quarter-mile perpendicularly, from the highway to the waterfront. The ones closest to the water have their own docks.

The former meth lab is located in one of the many rear units in a back warehouse. The unit's roll-up door sports police tape and a humongous lock, courtesy of the DEA.

We anticipate that Franklin will be armed. Since we had to load out in a hurry, we are only carrying our service pistols. Still, he may not be alone. Damn it, what I'd give to have my MP5 about now! A rifle is always better in a gunfight.

"Let's spread out," Jack whispers. "There are six rows. I'll take the two furthest away—we'll call them six and five—and work my way toward the water. Donna, you search the first and second rows. Start at the water's edge. Abu, you cover rows three and four."

We slip off quietly in different directions.

When I reach the first row, I scan for lights, try each lock, and listen for noises that sound different from the waves lapping up against the piers.

After checking the last unit, I head over to the second row—

But I don't make it very far because whatever is in the sack that smacks me on the side of my head puts me out like a light.

THE ONLY REASON I WAKE UP IS THAT THERE'S A LIGHT SHINING IN my eye.

I can't see who's holding it, but I have a very good guess. "So, you're Franklin's brother," I declare. "Phillip, isn't it?"

He freezes. His silence seems to fill the warehouse. Finally, he has to ask: "How did you know?"

"The photo in Franklin's home office—it's signed in your real name. You'd sent it to him—your identical twin."

"Good catch." Phillip laughs as he slaps on his surgical gloves. "Actually, I sent it to Ariel. Franklin would have tossed it in the trash. She framed it, and put it in his office. She knew it would get under his skin."

I look around to adjust my eyes to the light. "But you kept it because you're still very proud of your work you did in the field."

"I'm proud of my work now too." Then why does his voice sound so defensive?

Not that I should point this out while strapped to a gurney.

I've got to stall until Jack and Abu find me.

Time to show I feel his pain.

I lift my head and look around. "You operate here too?"

He shrugs. "Sometimes."

"Let me guess: you use it to alter the features of other ISIS sleeper cells."

"Move to the head of the class, Mrs. Craig. Brains if not beauty."

"I do okay with all the original body parts." I shrug. "Was it easy for you—killing your brother? Not to mention having to break the Hippocratic Oath and all. You know: 'Do no harm.'"

Phillip laughs. "Honestly, it was much easier than I thought. It always is, when the cause is just." He shrugs. "It helped that Franklin hadn't cared enough to come looking for me after my capture by ISIS. For him, life went on as usual."

He wheels a small cart in my direction. It's filled with medical instruments: a couple of scalpels, a few forceps, and all sorts of long scary needles, some attached to syringes.

"And now you have that life—*his* life," I point out. "Along with his fancy money-machine of a Beverly Hills plastic surgery practice. And let's not forget his loving, beautiful wife, and adorable little son—"

"No!" His perfect smile fades. "Connor is all mine! Franklin was too busy fucking his famous clients to give Ariel the one thing she wanted—a child. He convinced her that her body would never have recovered." He rolls his eyes at the thought. "And besides, a kid would have been a complication in a divorce."

Connor is now two, which means Phillip has been under deep cover for three years at least.

"You think he would have left her?"

Phillip nods. "Yes, eventually. The only person he cared about was himself."

He walks to a cabinet to get another scalpel. The ones he left on the cart are just out of reach. While he has his back to me, I inch closer...closer...

But the best I can do is finger one of the long needled syringes.

"I take it Ariel never found out you took your twin's place in her life after you came back from the dead and murdered him?" I ask nonchalantly.

Phillip shrugs. "She never could tell us apart. When we were in high school, we took turns fucking her. I'm sure she flipped a coin to decide which one of us to marry."

"She knew exactly what she was doing. She chose the smarter brother," I reply.

Phillip stops what he's doing—filling a syringe with some clear liquid—to contemplate this contention. Finally, he nods. "In hindsight, you're right. Franklin was smart enough to swap our Medical College Admissions Tests when he figured out that a weekend spent stoned as opposed to studying wouldn't get him into med school. And he was smart enough to convince me to sign up with the Army as a way to pay for my med school, so that it got me out of town for a few years. And he was smart enough to open a practice in Beverly Hills as opposed to work in a part of the world that very few people know or give a shit about; one that most people would prefer to have wiped off the face of the Earth."

"But you cared about your captors. Even when they starved and tortured you, you didn't hate them."

He shrugs. "It's hard to hate people who have so little, and yet believe so fiercely in something—especially when that something is to stop the rest of the world from decimating your land and stigmatizing your way of life."

"The insurgents saw that you cared about them," I say. "You proved it by saving their lives when they came back from battle. And you proved it when you took their religion. They became your brothers."

"Yeah, well, that's what happens when you're left for dead by your family and your country. In those two years after my capture, no one came looking for me—just like no one is coming for you."

He lays towels at the foot of the gurney.

Stall...Stall...

"How did you convince your new brothers to send you back to the land of the living—the land of the rich and beautiful?"

He smirks, "Believe me, if I could, I'd be back there instead. But our leaders are right. The Infidels have to taste their own blood for our cause to matter to them. As an American and a physician, I was the perfect choice for the mission—the only choice: imploding a few vain inconsequential women. And *Hot Housewives of Hilldale* was the perfect showcase." He chuckles. "No one mourns celebrity deaths like us Americans."

"One of the women was a lost love. The other was your adoring wife."

"Cassandra believes in causes—and she loved me greatly. Had she died for mine, she would have accepted it gladly."

"You flatter yourself. She believes in helping those whose lives are shattered by you. As for Ariel?"

He smirks. "She'd served her purpose. As Franklin's wife, she gave me the perfect cover. Had she died, the sympathy for me would have served as a great catalyst for donations to the foundation. Such irony!"

Oh, hell—he realizes my eyes have shifted toward the door.

He sighs and shakes his head. "Donna, I already told you. No one can save you now."

"You're wrong," I declare. "They're probably outside there now."

He laughs. "I doubt it. While you were out cold, one of the IEDs I planted beside this warehouse went off." He raises his hands together and then shoves them apart as if emulating an explosion. "It's a shame. Jack was a nice guy."

I fight back my tears. I can't let shock and memories cloud my mind now.

I must focus on getting off this table—

So that I can kill this son of a bitch.

As if reading my mind, he replies, "You're smarter than you look, Donna. Now, here's the good news. When I'm done here, you'll be a knockout! Unfortunately, you'll also be unrecognizable —and a mute. Believe me; I'm doing you a favor! Where you're going, men don't like chatty women."

He flicks the needle on the syringe. Satisfied with its flow, he moves in closer.

Too close, but perfectly positioned for me to stab the pilfered syringe into his groin.

When a man has a needle in his nuts, his scream could wake the dead.

Apparently, the Dead drive eighteen-wheelers.

The one that comes crashing through the metal door of my torture chamber doesn't stop until it has crushed Phillip against the far wall.

Jack hops out. He ignores Phillip's final gasps. Instead, he runs to me and unstraps me from the gurney.

I hug him. "He said a bomb went off—and that you were killed!"

"The bomb scanner picked it up first. When you disappeared, we thought setting it off would bring him out of his hiding place, but it didn't. Finally, we noticed a ray of light through a window that wasn't completely blacked out."

A moment later the place is swarming with an NSA SWAT team. Abu comes in amongst them.

"Let's get out of here," I mutter.

I don't have to ask twice.

We're halfway home when Jack sighs. "Damn it! By now, our steaks must be burnt to a crisp."

21

The Good Wife

"I want a happy life, and I want to control my own fate."
—Alicia Florrick, *The Good Wife*

The traits of a good wife are simply this:

She stands by her man. (Unless it's in the pouring rain, and she's wearing expensive heels. He will understand, since he knows how much it will cost to replace them.)

She shows her appreciation with random acts of love. Hint: Lingerie optional. As far as he's concerned, naked is always your best look. (Sorry, honey, he's just wired that way.)

She sings his praises in public. (Doing so in private is also appreciated, by the way.)

And, finally, she saves her disappointments for their private moments. (Jeering at him after locking him in a closet is perfectly acceptable since no one else will hear you.)

WHEN WE GET HOME, OUR FAMILY IS WAITING UP FOR US.

I don't deny them what we all want: a group hug.

But when we finally disentangle our arms, if not our emotions, I turn to Mary and Evan: "We need to talk."

Their nods acknowledge their shame.

"Time to make some hot cocoa," Aunt Phyllis says briskly. Trisha and Jeff take that as their cue to leave.

Jack tries to sneak out too, but I grab him by the shirt to hold him back.

He groans.

Trisha's mournful wave goodbye to Evan is her way of asking: Will I ever see you again?

Good question.

I wait until she shuts the door behind them before making my only request of my oldest daughter: "The truth."

Mary and Evan's gazes move to each other. They know what I'm asking.

Mary takes a deep breath. "Evan and I have feelings for each other."

Ah.

I sink to the sofa. I never thought I'd learn that my daughter lost her virginity while sitting on the most formal piece of furniture in my house: the living room settee.

I look down at the settee: Oh, my God—what if she lost it here?

Quickly, I stand up again and mutter, "Go on."

"Mom, I won't lie." Mary hesitates. "Yes, we—"

"You love each other. We know," Jack interjects. "You'd have to be blind not to see it in the love and respect—and yes, the concerns you have about each other—"

"Jack, this isn't a trial. And you aren't their attorney." I take a deep breath. "That being said, I second what Jack said. And, frankly, where you stand currently in your relationship is none of my business."

"*What?*" Mary and Evan exclaim together.

"Don't misunderstand me," I warn them. "I have not given you my approval—or carte blanche—to do anything. I'm just saying I'm happy that your mutual attraction has a firm foundation in your shared admiration and respect. The physical act of making love is the icing on the cake—"

"Amen to that," Jack murmurs.

His aside earns him a glare: "But it is not 'the cake,'" I continue. "If what you share continues to feel right—years from now, I mean; like after college—"

"Wait…you're saying you want us to wait until after college to —" Mary shakes her head, frustrated.

"You mean…you haven't…already?" I feel my mouth widening into my deranged clown grin again.

Mary crosses her arms. Frowning, she declares, "Mom! Really? After our conversation, you still think—"

Yikes. Time to backpedal: "But Evan was with you while you were babysitting—and he said he had a date!"

"It was a date…sort of. But not with me. With Connor. He'd promised Mrs. Powell he'd give him private swimming lessons. She was all right with him swinging by while I babysat. We took Connor to the pool together."

"Oh…kay." I have to poke Jack; he's laughing so hard.

Mary kisses me. "Yes, okay! Thank you!"

Hmmm. "For…what?"

She pulls Evan in for a hug.

He kisses her—on the lips.

Then he kisses me—not on the lips, thank goodness.

They are out the door before I find my voice. I stare at Jack. "What just happened here?"

He smiles. "I think you just gave your approval for them to do the dirty deed."

"No! *No*—that isn't what I said!"

He hushes me with a hug. And a kiss. And another.

Ah, young love.

We part when we hear a knock on the door. We set a bad enough example as is.

It's Jeff. He's upset. "Mom…we should talk."

"I'll say." I point to one of the wingback chairs.

"I'll let you two talk." Jack kisses my forehead then takes his leave.

Jeff starts by clearing his throat. "I know we shouldn't have snuck over to the Powells' home to spy on Mary and Evan. I guess they told you they weren't even there."

"Yep." I pause. The one rule about a suspect interrogation is to give them plenty of dead air. Usually, they say enough to hang themselves.

Jeff looks down at his feet. "Mom, I know what Cheever and I did was wrong. And stupid—and potentially dangerous. Please forgive me." He looks up, beseechingly. "Please?"

That's all I need to hear.

I pull him into my arms. His relief rolls out of him in a long sigh. "Thanks." He ducks his head shyly. "Oh, and I've got a favor to ask. May I have an advance on my allowance?"

I laugh. "Why? Are you losing your shirt in fantasy football?"

He shakes his head. "No. But I did lose a bet—to Sami. I told him I thought his brother was the terrorist you were chasing. He insisted it was Dr. Powell, so I owe him ten bucks."

"You know what we do is not for public consumption! Why would you have told Sami we were chasing terrorists?" I frown. "And why would you have guessed Adam?"

"Remember the night Adam got everyone drunk? I told you I saw something odd about one of the kids. A week later, I remembered what it was: Adam has a tattoo on his arm. It's an Al Qaeda insignia."

Oh, no.

"I didn't tell him exactly what Dad and you do, but when I

mentioned to Sami that I'd have to tell you because it was important, he got upset. He said Adam is angry because everyone already thinks he's a badass, so he plays the part. It's already cost his family a lot."

I can't even imagine.

"Why did he think Powell was the bad guy?" I ask.

"Because…well, he happened to be sitting next to his mother's cell phone when she received a text from Dr. Powell." He blushes. "He read it, and he didn't like it. So he hacked the doctor's computer."

"I see."

"It was before Dad warned us to stop unless we wanted to end up in jail," he insists.

"I understand." I try hard to smile. "Get some sleep. There's still school tomorrow."

I get a second hug from my son.

When I lean into him, I realize he's now as tall as me.

They grow up too fast.

RYAN INFORMS ME THAT PENELOPE, ARIEL, CASSANDRA, AND PATTY are being held at Hilldale Hospital for at least three days so that they can recuperate fully.

I'm bringing each of my former competitors—my neighbors—a bouquet of roses.

I stop at Patty's room first. She already has guests. Her children surround her hospital bed. They are laughing and smiling. Jenna cradles her youngest brother, Joey, in her arms. Juliette and Jody's arms are entwined. Jason and Jordan's arms are around each other's shoulders.

"Oh! I don't mean to interrupt," I insist.

"No, please, come in," Patty's tone is sincere. She holds something in her hands: a photo album. It is turned to a page holding an old picture.

The setting is a barren hilltop. James holds Patty in his arms. She is skinny except for a huge baby bump. He looks down on her with a broad smile. Their youngest daughter—Juliette, a toddler— is wearing only a diaper. Jenna can't be more than ten. Like her younger siblings—Jason, Jordan, and Jody—she is all smiles as she looks up adoringly at her parents.

"We're remembering good times." Patty points to the picture. "This was taken at Death Valley when Jimmy was first assigned to Creech Air Force Base. It was his assignment for his third tour of duty." She sighs. "If he'd only stopped after the second."

Her wistfulness wipes the smiles from her children's faces. Realizing this, she shakes her head. "It's okay. We all know it. We know he never really came back from Creech. We know he did something that changed him. He died there." She stares at the photo.

Jody pats her mother's arm. Jason kisses her forehead. Jenna wipes away a tear.

They are finding their redemption in the fondest memories they have of their father.

"I heard that Brin offered you a spinoff," I say matter-of-factly.

Patty nods "She did, but the family took a vote. Unanimously, we elected to pass on the offer." She shrugs. "If we're frugal, we can get by on James's military pension. When the time comes, I can use his GI benefits to send the children to college. I'm also getting my teaching certification. And we'll be selling James's gun collection." She shrugs. "I never felt comfortable with so many guns in the house."

I smile. "You only need one, right?"

"By the way, we're selling the house and moving out of Hilldale. Don't tell the Bings, but we'll be using another realtor." She shudders.

"Perfectly understandable," I murmur. "I wish you all the best."

Jenna walks me out the door. "Please thank Evan and Mary for me."

I shake her hand. "I hope you stay in touch."

"You don't think Mary will mind?" Jenna asks hopefully.

"I think she'd welcome it."

"Thank you…for everything." Her hug is tight and quick.

ARIEL'S ROOM IS TWO DOORS FURTHER DOWN THE HALL. SHE LOOKS away when I enter.

She already knows.

When she's ready to face me, she holds her chin proudly. She doesn't wait for me to ask: "I never knew."

"Yes, he actually believed that," I assure her.

She frowns. "But you don't."

"What I believe doesn't matter, does it?"

"You're right. It doesn't," Ariel declares. She takes the flowers from me. "Thank you. I guess I had you all wrong."

I'm not cruel enough to point out that this seems to be a pattern with her: first Franklin, then Phillip–not to mention everyone else's skewed opinions as to who is whom, or who's doing what to whom in Hilldale.

She'll soon find out how quickly others' opinions will change about her too. Having married a known terrorist casts doubts on those who should have seen the signs.

In Ariel's case, was it denial, or was Phillip just that good at leaving her in the dark?

At this point, it doesn't matter. As his wife, she'll always carry part of the blame.

Carl taught me that.

She doesn't watch me go. Instead, she turns her head back toward the wall.

~

I'm relieved to find Cassandra alone. Gerald must be at work and the boys at school.

I'm sure that, like me, she'll want to keep what I have to ask her in confidence.

I'm not at all surprised at Cassandra's bluntness: "Is he dead?"

I nod.

Her mouth purses, but that doesn't stop the tears from falling.

As I lay down the bouquet beside her, I say, "Sami helped us discover who he was."

Hearing this, she practically jumps out of bed. "My son? But...how?"

"He happened to be standing by your cell phone when one of Phillip Powell's emails to you lit up on the screen," I explain. "Sami was curious as to who enthralled you enough to threaten your marriage, so he hacked into Phillip's computer. What he saw scared him: he recognized some of the ISIS rhetoric and leaders' names from personal experience; and because Jeff had divulged to him that my security agency was searching for a possible terrorist cell. He wanted to alert us without giving you away."

Cassandra blushes at the thought of her son's concern.

"He wondered how we'd missed the man he now knew only as 'Franklin,' and tried to put us on the right track by leaving us digital breadcrumbs. One led us to Powell's secret surgical bay in a Long Beach warehouse, but we ended up raiding a well-guarded meth lab instead. Unfortunately, Sami transposed the numbers in the address. We thought our elusive target did it to hoax us. Phillip was already masking his ISP address so that we couldn't trace the texts being sent to him by his ISIS handlers."

"Yes, well, when Sami doesn't take his time, he types careless-ly." She wipes away a tear. "Still, I'm proud of him for trying."

"You should be. If we'd raided the right place, we would have had Phillip. As it turns out, we never got around to scanning Dr. Powell's cell phone." I lower my eyes. "I blame myself for that. Like everyone else—that is, everyone but Sami—I wanted to believe he was above reproach because of his noble calling with Plastic Surgeons Without Borders. Little did we know it was a front to ship money and ammo to ISIS. We weren't even aware that Franklin had an identical twin—Phillip—until last night." I sit beside her on the bed. "Cassandra, how did he coax you into an affair?"

Cassandra sighs. "I'd known Phillip in a past life—five years ago, when I was a relief effort coordinator in Fallujah, Iraq. He was working for a UN medical team that was saving the lives of bombing victims—Sami's included." She shrugs. "We became lovers. At the time, Adam was almost twelve. The year before, I'd adopted him from a relief center in Chechnya. He adored Phillip! Then, when I thought Phillip had died in a bombing attack, to honor his memory I adopted Sami too. But I was too heartbroken to stay in Iraq. The boys and I moved to Dubai, where I met Gerald." She grimaces. "He wasn't Phillip, but he was good with the children."

"You must have been shocked to see Phillip again here in Hilldale."

Cassandra nods. "On the night of the show's first episode, when he was introduced by his brother's name, I believed he was who he claimed—until he reached for his water glass. You see, the one feature distinguishing Phillip from his identical twin brother was a battle scar on his right wrist. After the first episode, when I shook his hand goodbye, I pressed down on it. He knew I was hurt that he'd pretended not to know me, and also confused as to why he now went under his brother's name. That night he sent me a text—the one you mentioned Sami had seen—asking to meet with him at his house the next morning while Ariel was out."

"How did he explain the identity switch?"

"He told me a U.S. Army patrol found him unconscious in a pile of rubble and shipped him back to the States to recuperate. When he heard his brother had died searching for him in Iraq, he was too upset to go back to the Middle East. Now stateside, he began using his middle name—also his mother's maiden name, Franklin—as a tribute to his brother. He told me he allowed himself to fall in love and marry Ariel because he assumed I'd lost hope for him and had moved on. Donna, I never knew he absconded with Franklin's life, including his wife! When we were in Fallujah, he mentioned his brother only once—and not at all fondly. And trust me, he certainly never mentioned her!"

"What a guy," I mutter.

Cassandra bows her head. "The heart believes what it wants to. I now realize that Phillip allowed our affair to pick up again because he was afraid I'd become suspicious of his story—or perhaps even jealous of Ariel and tell her all about us."

And it could have derailed Phillip's plan right then and there. He couldn't let that happen.

Cassandra strokes one of the flowers gently. "I was angry about Phillip's on-air recommendation that I have a boob job. When Gerald tried to goad me into it on television, I was livid. I knew why my husband was doing so: we needed the votes that could bring us the money. We'd finally get out of debt." She sighs. "Phillip texted me later that night to tell me he could never see me again if I couldn't understand how important his charity work was, and what the foundation meant to him. I finally said yes to the operation because I couldn't stand the thought of losing him again." A tear hovers on her cheek. "Little did I know that I'd agreed to a death sentence at the hand of the one person I thought would always love me; whom would never harm me."

"He was no longer your Phillip. He'd become…a monster."

She looks down at her bandaged chest. "Despite what he did to me, I now choose to remember him as he was."

More proof that redemption is inevitably stronger than hate.

"One last question: what is the real reason you and Gerald took the children out of Dubai?"

"Adam took Phillip's loss very hard. He became sullen and defiant. It was like losing his biological father all over again. One of the ways he lashed out was to get an Al Qaeda tattoo. One of his teachers in Dubai saw it. Adam was thrown out of school and threatened with prison for being an insurgent. To top it off, Gerald was asked to leave his teaching position at the university. The Arab Emirates take any threat of terrorism very seriously. Recently, Gerald divulged to me that he took out a loan in order to bribe the authorities to keep Adam out of prison. We'll be paying off that debt for some time to come."

Well, that explains the Middle-Eastern loan shark in Gerald's office.

"By the way, we're moving from Hilldale," Cassandra says. "It's too cruel and too petty—too removed from the real world! Let me put it this way: it's just not our kind of town."

I nod. "In other words, it's too normal."

Cassandra laughs as hard as me.

A moment later, her smile fades. "Isn't it ironic? Even when Adam was in the *Housewives'* mansion with Phillip, he never recognized him as the man he once so revered."

"Phillip wasn't that man anymore," I counter.

"I guess you're right." She pauses. "I wonder how Sami would feel to learn that the terrorist he chased down was also the man who saved his life?"

"Do you plan to tell him?"

She shakes her head. "Like you just said, Phillip wasn't that man anymore."

When I hold out my hand to bid her goodbye, she pulls me in for a kiss on the cheek as well.

LAST AND CERTAINLY LEAST, I GO TO PENELOPE'S ROOM. WHEN I enter, I see she already has company: Brin, Addison, and a few men in well-cut black suits.

When Penelope realizes it's not a nurse but me, she scowls. "Oh, no! Not you again! Nurse! Guards—"

I hold out the flowers. "Penelope, calm down. I'm here to drop off this."

She looks suspiciously at my offering. "There's not a bomb in there, right?"

Brin and the Men in Black chuckle nervously.

Not Addison. He knows me too well.

"Okay. Thanks. Now leave. My talent agent and these network people need me to sign off on my new spin-off."

I roll my eyes. "Oh, really? What's the title?"

Penelope shrugs. "I don't know. I'm sure they'll think of something. The great news is that Peter has consented to play along. Finally, he's doing what I want for us!"

I think Peter is doing exactly what he wants for himself. Penelope will find this out soon enough.

I'm halfway out the door when I hear the footsteps I've come to dread: Brin's.

"Hey, wait up, Delicious Donna! I've got a question for you."

I sigh, but I turn to face her anyway. "Brin, the answer to any question you want to ask me is 'no.'"

"Even if two million dollars is attached to it?"

"Again: NO."

"But what you and Jack do—I mean, *really* do—is ratings gold!"

I wonder how much Addison has told her. "What is it, exactly, that you think we do?"

She can't seem to find the words. Finally, she exclaims, "You love each other, unconditionally. That's really all television viewers want to see: a happily ever after."

For once, Brin is right.

"By the way, on the last night, who had the biggest vote count?" I ask.

"Oh…didn't Jack tell you? The Craigs—by a landslide!"

Boo-yah!

"The check is being couriered over as we speak," she promises.

Well then, I'd better get home, pronto.

I COME HOME TO AN EMPTY HOUSE. BUT WHEN I GLANCE OUT THE kitchen window, I see a familiar dip in the hammock: my husband is doing his favorite thing: relishing a day off to enjoy the warm breeze on a sunny September afternoon.

Like me, he loves to be normal.

He stops crooning *Night and Day* when I come into view and he scoots over so that I can climb in beside him.

"How are the Housewives?" Jack asks.

"Still a bit dazed. For at least three of them, the thought of being a human bomb has put many things in perspective."

"Let me guess: Penelope is still oblivious about how close she was to dying."

"Go to the head of the class." I shake my head in awe.

"By the way," Jack says casually, "I have some exciting news."

Ah, here it comes. "Yes?"

"Guess who won the vote count for most popular family on *Hot Housewives of Hilldale*?"

I pretend to ponder the quesstion seriously, but he knows my tell all too well: my deranged clown grin.

We are now laughing deliriously.

Pulling the certified check from his pocket, he sputters, "Was Ryan serious that we can't keep this?"

"He'd bust a gut if he even knew we had it." I snap my fingers.

"The least Acme should do is donate it to the Farnhams. Sami's tips were valuable, and I know the family could use it."

"I guess you're right," Jack admits grudgingly. "If we were any other normal family…"

But we're not. We both know this.

We are Donna and Jack Craig.

And you better not cross us.

—THE END—

The Housewife Assassin's Deadly Dossier

(Book 15 - Series Prequel)

In this full-length prequel to the series, Acme Industries' black-ops agent, Jack Craig, is tasked with investigating the mysterious death of his organization's most prolific hit man, Carl Stone--only to fall in love the the dead man's wife, Donna: a woman he must never contact, but who may hold the key to her husband's disappearance. When Acme approaches Donna to join the organization as an assassin, Jack takes on an undercover mission that will change both their lives forever.

Other Books by Josie Brown

The True Hollywood Lies Series

Hollywood Hunk

Hollywood Whore

The Totlandia Series

The Onesies - Book 1 (Fall)

The Onesies - Book 2 (Winter)

The Onesies - Book 3 (Spring)

The Onesies - Book 4 (Summer)

The Twosies - Book 5 (Fall)

The Twosies – Book 6 (Winter)

The Twosies - Book 7 (Spring)

The Twosies - Book 8 (Summer)

More Josie Brown Novels

The Candidate

Secret Lives of Husbands and Wives

The Baby Planner

How to Reach Josie

To write Josie, go to:
mailfromjosie@gmail.com

To find out more about Josie, or to get on her eLetter list for book
launch announcements, go to her website:
www.JosieBrown.com

You can also find her at:

www.AuthorProvocateur.com

twitter.com/JosieBrownCA

facebook.com/josiebrownauthor

pinterest.com/josiebrownca

instagram.com/josiebrownnovels